Raves for James Patterson

"A legendary novelist." —*CNN*

"One of America's most influential authors."
—*New York Times*

"The man who can't miss." —*Time*

"The page-turningest author in the game."
—*San Francisco Chronicle*

"One of the greatest storytellers of all time."
—*New York Times* bestselling author
Patricia Cornwell

"Patterson is in a class by himself." —*Vanity Fair*

"Patterson boils a scene down to the single, telling detail, the element that defines a character or moves a plot along. It's what fires off the movie projector in the reader's mind."
—*New York Times* bestselling author
Michael Connelly

2 SISTERS MURDER INVESTIGATIONS

For a preview of upcoming books and information about the author, visit JamesPatterson.com or find him on Facebook, X, or Instagram.

2 SISTERS MURDER INVESTIGATIONS

JAMES PATTERSON
AND CANDICE FOX

LITTLE, BROWN AND COMPANY
New York Boston London

Little, Brown and Company
Hachette Book Group
1290 Avenue of the Americas, New York, NY 10104
littlebrown.com

First Edition: April 2025

Book interior design by Marie Mundaca

ISBN 9781538758472 (pb) / 9781538774366 (large print)
LCCN 2024949126

10 9 8 7 6 5 4 3 2 1

CW

Printed in the United States of America

2 SISTERS MURDER INVESTIGATIONS

CHAPTER 1

THERE'D BEEN NO DOUBT in my mind that Baby wasn't going to last the whole stakeout. I just hadn't thought she'd quit it by crawling out the passenger-side window and onto the roof of my car.

I'd sat calmly in the white 1958 Chevy Impala for two hours, watching the dark apartment windows through my binoculars, listening to the humid Los Angeles night's sounds enveloping the parking lot. Crickets, distant sirens, Latin music. My sixteen-year-old sister, Baby, had twisted and turned in her seat, variously twirling her hair, napping, scrolling social media, drumming the dashboard, and trying to engage me in rounds of Kiss, Marry, Kill with celebrities I'd never heard of. Two stakeout highlights—one man leaving the apartment building briefly to smoke a cigarette, another driving off and returning with a bag of items from a nearby pet store—did little to disrupt Baby's bored agony or my quiet focus.

Then, without warning, my sister was clawing her way out the car window with the speed and dexterity of a praying mantis escaping a bug jar.

I exited the car in a considerably less nimble fashion, using my weight to rock and shunt myself out the narrow door. Yes, we shared DNA, but if Baby was like a praying mantis, I was like the star of *Kung Fu Panda*.

"Hey!" Baby sat on the Chevy's roof and yelled up at the building, cupping her hands around her mouth. "Listen up, you stupid pricks! We know you're in there! We know you've got L'Shondra! Hold on to your balls because we're a-comin' in!"

I grabbed one of Baby's sparkly black boots, yanked her sideways, and caught her in my arms like a doll before she could hit the ground. If there's one thing my kid sister hates, it's when I manhandle her. Unpredictability is one of Baby's teenage superpowers, but one of mine is being able to throw other human beings around like bed pillows.

"Rhonda, what the hell are you doing?" she wailed at me.

"What am *I* doing? What are *you* doing? You just blew our cover!"

"So what? We've been sitting here doing nothing!"

"We're gathering intel!"

"We know the guys in that apartment have our girl! How much more *intel* do you need?"

A couple in the street beyond the edge of the parking lot had overheard Baby and were now pressed together, trying to figure us out. I caught the word *police*.

Baby wriggled out of my arms. "I'm tired of sitting on my ass watching these guys and doing squat to save L'Shondra. You gave me lead on this case," she said. "I've decided. We're gonna charge the doors, grab our girl, and go get tacos to celebrate. We'll be home by midnight and done with this *sickeningly* dull case."

She popped open the trunk and went rummaging around behind the seats.

"Giving you lead on this was a big mistake." I sighed. "This was your first chance to show me you have the patience and maturity to make major decisions at the agency. You failed, Baby."

"I failed?" She straightened, laughing. "Rhonda, I've never failed at anything in my life."

"Could have fooled me."

"Why do I need to show you anything? I don't have to prove myself to you. You know, there're a whole bunch of decisions that seem to automatically fall to you," she said. "We decided to start this detective agency together. We've both been private detectives for the same amount of time. Now suddenly you're in charge and you're picking the cases. You're grading me. You're 'giving' me lead."

"Baby, I *am* in charge," I said. "Dad's dead. I'm your legal guardian. I'm more than twice your age. And I'm a lawyer. Okay? I know criminals. I know investigations. I know cops.

I know the kind of cases we can and should take so we can establish our street cred. Legally speaking, you're still a child."

"Oh, give me a break."

"*You* give *me* a break!"

A man stepped up to us. He seemed to materialize from behind our vehicle, where the trunk abutted the wet palms. The hammer of his huge revolver clanked down heavily as he pointed it at Baby's face.

"Don't move," he said. "Either of you."

CHAPTER 2

A BOLT OF ADRENALINE hit my chest, freezing all thought. For a second there was nothing but the gun and my kid sister in the line of fire, the purest manifestation of all my worst nightmares. It didn't matter who the guy was. What mattered was his finger on the trigger, the ability of that single digit to destroy my entire world.

"Phones," he said. "Slowly."

We extracted our phones from our pockets and handed them to him. I glanced around, sweat already beading on my brow. The curious couple was gone. The gunman tossed our phones into the palms.

"Move," he said, gesturing toward the apartment building with the gun.

We walked. I gave Baby a *Don't do anything stupid* glare. She shook her head, disgusted.

"Listen," I said, glancing back at our captor. I clocked the tired expression on his stubbled face. "We don't even know where you want us to go."

"Third floor," the guy said. "It's the apartment you've been out here watching. The one you were just shouting at."

"We weren't—"

"Don't play dumb with me, all right? I don't get a lot of sleep in my line of work. My patience is at an all-time low."

The man grabbed a handful of my shirt and shoved me onward. We started up dimly lit stairs, and my stomach sank. There were good signs about the situation, but not many. The guy hadn't patted either of us down, which meant he was probably unaccustomed to, maybe unprepared for, actual violence. The gun he carried was big and chunky and awkward in his hand. It looked unused, something meant only to scare us. But my fluttering confidence took a nosedive when we reached the third floor. There was another, much shorter man at the door to the apartment. He also had a gun and looked tired but he seemed meaner than his partner. I heard dogs barking inside. One had the wet, hysterical, savage bark of a big animal losing its mind.

Baby and I were shoved into the apartment. It was dark, lit only by colored LED lights in dozens of reptile and fish tanks lining one wall. I saw lizards and spiders and snakes in there, huge coiled pythons sagging over branches, and hairy tarantulas scaling rocks. Beneath the aggravated, panic-driven barking of the dogs was a different rumble of noise—parrots squawking in another room, fish-tank pumps humming and bubbling, cats whining.

A dozen dogs of different breeds rushed over and swirled around us, some snuffling and pawing at our legs, others standing back and yapping, muzzles up in challenge.

Among them, I spotted our girl: L'Shondra, a sleek and googly-eyed Italian greyhound who stood trembling at the back of the pack.

The dog that was on the border of insanity was a hellish hound who looked like it could have swallowed L'Shondra whole. The dog was chained to a U-bolt mounted to the wall; its scarred, boxy black head was held low, and its clipped ears shone pink in the weird light. All the other dogs stayed well outside the range of its chain.

The dog's yellow eyes were fixed on Baby. I felt her cold hand slip into mine. Not for the first time since I'd met my sister less than a year ago, I was overcome by the intense, soul-squeezing maternal instinct to protect her, and I knew someone was about to get hurt.

I just didn't realize how bad.

CHAPTER 3

THE TWO ARMED MEN huddled near us.

"What were you thinking?" the small one asked the tall one. "Are you a goddamn idiot?"

"I wasn't thinking anything. I can't concentrate with all this noise."

"What are we supposed to do now? They've seen everything. They've seen our faces!"

"They'd already seen our faces, man. I think they've been out there for hours. Probably saw me leave for cigarettes. Saw you bringing up the birdseed."

I forced a long, slow breath, tried not to think about the guns and the surprise and desperation that these two men were clearly feeling, or about how guns and surprise and desperation made terrible bedfellows. It was time to argue. I told myself this room was no different than the hundreds of courtrooms I had commanded in my life.

"Hey," I called and pointed to L'Shondra. "We're here about that one dog. Just give her back and we'll clear out. There's no need to make things worse than they already are, okay? You've already committed California Penal Code two forty-five A and two oh seven PC here tonight, guys. Assault with a deadly weapon and kidnapping. That's twenty years. Don't do anything that's going to make it life for the sake of a few thousand bucks."

The gunmen stared at me. I felt like I was getting through to the big guy, at least. He looked calm, ready to listen, his gun almost forgotten by his side. A tiny wave of relief rose in me. It crashed when the smaller man raised his weapon and shot his partner in the head.

CHAPTER 4

WETNESS ON MY FACE. The sound of the gunshot blasted through every living being in the room, even the tiniest ones. The dogs around us sank down in unison, cowering. The birds in the other room began to scream and thrash in their cages. My kid sister clung to me.

The taller gunman slumped on the hardwood floor. His partner, frighteningly calm, stared down at his lifeless friend.

"It's not just a few thousand bucks," he said. "There's half a million in this room alone."

I stifled a furious growl of regret. In my haste to focus on positive signs about the big man who'd abducted us, signs that pointed to our chances of surviving, I hadn't paid much attention to the signs that his little partner was a cold-blooded psychopath: The icy, empty eyes. The scratched and beat-up gun. The expert way he handled it, like an artist with a brush.

"Listen," I said. "Please, just listen."

"No, you listen," the gunman said. He pointed to his dead partner. "You see that? That's the kind of mood I'm in. Eric and I have been working on this gig for three months. What happened to him just now is what happens when people push me and push me and push me."

"Okay," I said. "We get it. Nobody's trying to push you."

"Bringing you up here?" He shook his head. "He's been doing dangerous stuff like that for days. It's like he wanted us to get caught."

A moment of opportunity. The gunman glanced around the apartment, trying to decide, I supposed, how he was going to hold us. Whether he would even bother. Baby used the precious seconds to shrink away from me. I wanted to grab at her and tuck her behind me, but I knew she was being smart. We shouldn't stick together, make ourselves one target. It was two of us against one armed man, and we had to split his focus. I understood Baby's strategic thinking. I edged sideways to put myself against the tanks. The gunman lifted his weapon and aimed at me.

"No, no, no," he warned. "Step away from the tanks."

It was exactly what I'd hoped he'd say. It confirmed my assessment of the man: He was a dealer in lives. Every creature in the place had a dollar sign attached to it—except me and Baby.

"Let's talk. Let's talk, okay? You just lost your partner," I said. I put my hands up, rapped a knuckle against the glass behind me. "There's no need to put everything else you have at risk."

"Step *away*," the man repeated. "From the *tanks*."

"How's your aim?" I asked. "Can you drop me like you did your partner without getting one of these guys? Huh? *He's* pretty." I pointed to a big green lizard in a tank beside my head. "What's he worth?"

Movement caught my eye. Baby was running with my idea. She picked up a woolly black puppy that had been cowering at her feet. The gunman swung around, pointed the gun at her, then immediately lowered it so the barrel pointed at her legs, away from the dog.

"Ooh." Baby's eyes widened. She was smiling, but her cheeks were hard and tight. "Did you see that, Rhonda? I think I might have one of the big-ticket items here."

"Okay, don't be stupid," the man said. "That's a twenty-thousand-dollar dog you're holding. Put it down or I'll shoot you in the foot."

"You do that and I'll throw the puppy to Cerberus over there," Baby said. She edged closer to the big dog on the chain. "You hungry, boy? Yeah. You want an expensive snack?"

I let my eyes drift down to the tanks beside me. I saw a coiled-up snake. It was acid yellow and black, striped, too pretty to be harmless. The monster dog was almost choking itself trying to get at Baby and the puppy, its growls becoming strangled snorts, claws ripping at the carpet. The gunman was inching closer to them, corralling Baby into the beast's bite range.

"Put it down." The man tightened his grip on the gun. "Put the dog down!"

"You put the gun down!" Baby yelled.

"Hey!" I called. The gunman pivoted toward me. I pushed off the top of the tank next to me, grabbed the striped snake, and hurled it at him. The man dropped his gun, and in the microseconds during which he twisted, his instincts warring between catching the snake and cowering from it, Baby seized the chain connecting the dog to the wall and unhooked it.

They say you should never run from an attacking dog. When you act like prey, it sets off its killer instincts, the wolf inside. The man chose to flee from the snake; he turned, and in that single vulnerable motion, he lit a fire in the big dog's brain. Baby dropped the puppy and grabbed the fallen weapon as the beast rushed at the gunman. The air was filled with human screams. I saw my sister aiming the gun and struggling to decide if she should take the animal's life to save the life of the man who was trying to kill us. The girl full of bravado was gone, and a scared kid with a deadly weapon and an impossible choice was standing in her place.

I took the gun from her hands and shoved her out of the apartment.

CHAPTER 5

BABY PACED THE PARKING lot, her head down, swiping furiously at her phone, which she'd rescued from behind the palm trees. Nervous energy and excess adrenaline. I leaned against my Chevy, thinking back over the statements I'd just given to a pair of detectives. The LAPD and Animal Control were swarming the apartment. It was after midnight. Now and then, Baby returned to me and shoved her phone in my face.

"The puppy was a Tibetan mastiff. Look. The guy was right. Twenty grand apiece."

"Uh-huh." I sighed.

"The snake was a banded krait."

"Okay."

"It's the sixth-deadliest snake in the world."

"Baby—"

"Its venom causes paralysis. Liquefies your lungs. Makes your eyeballs bleed."

"Baby, you're not helping," I said.

A patrol officer in an immaculately pressed dark blue uniform approached me for another exhaustive run-through of the murder in the animal apartment. She noted everything down on a small pad while I marveled at how shiny her badge was. Her name tag said RAMIREZ. In the distance, the gunman who had been mauled by the monster dog was being wheeled out on a gurney, his body swathed in bandages. Ramirez told me that after mauling the gunman, the dog had gone and sat quietly in a bedroom without harming any of the animals in the apartment. I admired the dog's restraint. The big dog seemed to innately know who was good and who was bad in the world, which was something I wasn't sure I'd mastered myself.

"When can we get back in that apartment?" I asked Ramirez when she began to wrap up.

"Oh, you two are done here," she replied. She looked us up and down. "Animal Control's in there trying to find the snake you let loose. We'll call you if there are any further questions."

"That's bullshit." Baby pointed at the apartment building. "All those animals up there are stolen. We found them. They're ours to reunite with their owners."

"No, they're not."

"It's our bust!" Baby exploded. "There'll be tens of thousands of dollars in reward money!"

"Well, boo-hoo, Ace Ventura." Ramirez sneered at Baby. "I'm not in the business of handing over evidence so that wannabe bounty hunters can make some cash."

"Look," I said. "You're a newbie, right? I mean, you must be *real* new. That badge is so bright, I'm getting a headache from the glare. Plus, even though two detectives have already interviewed us, you've been sent over to do it again. They're not worried they didn't get the story down. They just think you need practice taking statements."

Ramirez's jaw tightened. I put my hands up, letting it go.

Baby jumped in. "All Rhonda's saying is, maybe you don't realize the opportunity you have here." She jerked a thumb at me, then herself. "My sister and I, we're also just starting out. For the next six months, our business is going to be making connections, doing intel. Learning about various bail jumpers and drug-addled kleptomaniacs. Maybe we can all help each other here."

"She's right. You'll want to prove yourself." I riffed off Baby's energy. "The first year on the job is hell. They'll hand you impossible cases, cleanup work, bullshit security gigs. But imagine if you had PIs on speed dial, investigators who could tell you where some parole-dodging loser was hiding."

"Or where there was an apartment full of stolen animals," Baby added. "Or which gangster's wife was cheating on him and with who."

"I get it," Ramirez said. "I get it."

Baby and I waited. The rookie looked back at the officers taping off the stairs to the apartment building. Then she sized us up.

"How's your hand-eye coordination?" she asked.

CHAPTER 6

BABY AND I WAITED in the darkness of the alley, side by side. In my peripheral vision, I could see the flickering blue lights of the police cars at the front of the apartment building, but the two of us were transfixed by a small lit window on the third floor.

"Fifteen hundred bucks." I heard the smile in my sister's voice. "Not a completely wasted night."

"Don't count your dog before you catch it."

"I got this. I was on the JV basketball team."

"You're pretty confident for someone who made the mess we just had to clean up," I said.

"What are you talking about?"

"I'm talking about how the whole point of us staking out

that apartment was so we could figure out how those assholes operated," I said. "Learn their habits. Enter the place while they were out, when it would be *safe* to do so. Now one of them is in an ambulance and the other one's in a body bag, and we almost were too."

"They're animal thieves!" I could feel Baby watching me. She'd completely forgotten the window above us. "They steal people's pets! How was I supposed to know that one of them was going to—"

"You *don't* know," I said. "That's the whole point, Baby. You *wait* and you *watch* and you *listen* until you *know*."

The third-floor window slid open. I braced myself.

"You mean I should do whatever you say, even when it's my damn case," Baby snapped.

Hands holding a skinny gray dog emerged from the window. L'Shondra shook violently as she eyed the distance to the ground.

"Can we talk about this later?" I said to Baby.

Ramirez let go. The dog fell. I caught L'Shondra in my arms in a tangle of bony limbs, and both the animal and I yelped in terror and relief.

When I turned around triumphantly, my sister was gone.

CHAPTER 7

WHEN THE MAN EVERYONE in America suspected of killing his wife walked into the 2 Sisters Detective Agency, I was up on a ladder, painting over cigar-smoke rings on the ceiling.

The office was slowly transforming in the wake of Earl Bird's death six months ago. Baby and I had decided to take over our father's business, Early Bird Private Investigation, after an earlier case had forced us together only hours after we'd met for the first time. Despite having different mothers, no previous knowledge of each other's existence, and a twenty-plus-year age gap, we'd somehow managed to track down a hit man, a group of murderous youths, and a drug-running gang. The experience had left our brand-new relationship tattered in some places but sewn tightly in others.

My kid sister and I were deeply, deeply different. Aside from troubled histories with our shared father, we had almost zero in common. When I was thirteen, Dad ditched me and my mom; when Baby was a toddler, her mom left her with Earl and never returned. I look an awful lot like our father, if he'd had extensive tattoos and pink hair; Baby acts like Dad, but she's tall, Black, and gorgeous—she clearly got her looks from her mother's side of the family. But Baby (aka Barbara) and I had had heartfelt conversations as we'd tackled the horror show of Earl's messy office together, and we'd busted up laughing over emails from bizarre potential clients. I'd felt the purest sense of motherhood or sisterhood or whatever it was while staring down the barrel of a gun with Baby by my side. We were, somehow, a team.

The detective agency office, in the part of Los Angeles known as Koreatown, was still in the process of being de-Earled. My father had stuffed every inch of the room with newspapers, weapons, racing-ticket stubs, crime scene photographs, packages of expired fortune cookies, and badly taxidermied animals. It had taken us three months to clear enough space for Baby and me to coexist here at all and another three for us to do it comfortably. What I hadn't thrown in the dumpster behind the crab shack downstairs, I'd stacked in clear plastic tubs against one wall.

Today, there was paperwork to file, calls to make, and cases to assess, but I needed a mindless task. I'd caught maybe an hour or two of sleep at most after I'd returned L'Shondra to her tearful owners in Anaheim and collected our reward money. By the time I got back to Dad's spectacular house in Manhattan Beach where Baby and I now lived (a place he'd almost certainly acquired through shady means that I wasn't going to think about), the sun was nearly rising. I'd slipped Baby's half—seven hundred and fifty dollars—under her bedroom door, wondering what I'd say if she threw open the door. But she didn't, and there'd been not a peep from the angry teen this morning either.

Guilt and anger were warring in my brain. I decided to focus on our long to-do list instead of waiting around for Baby to wake up, so I'd driven over to the office early. An hour or so later, from atop the ladder, I'd seen the figure of a man hovering in front of the frosted glass of the agency door. I'd looked through the big bay windows behind my desk and spotted two LAPD squad cars in the parking lot.

Curious.

But when my visitor walked in and I saw who it was, the police presence made more sense.

The man came into the office clutching a cardboard box to his chest and glanced up at me in the same vulnerable, evasive way I'd seen him do on TV.

"Uh, hi," he said.

"Uh, hi, yourself," I said. I put my paintbrush down. "You're Troy Hansen."

"People keep saying that," Troy said, looking everywhere but at me. " 'You're Troy Hansen.' Like I'm a famous actor."

"Well, you're famous for something."

"Hmm," he said, frowning.

I'd recognized Troy Hansen immediately. News channels had been running hourly updates on Troy—or, more specifically, on Troy's missing wife, Daisy, who hadn't been seen for almost a week.

Daisy was the type of missing person who usually captured the nation's attention: White. Middle class. Blond. Tanned. Athletic. Perfect teeth. The internet was aflame with analyses of her husband's awkward body language, the lack of warmth in his tone, the timeline of his movements on the night Daisy had disappeared.

Even though I'd actively tried to avoid the tawdry trial-by-media, I'd still managed to absorb most of the details of the case. I'd seen the same video of Troy—floppy-haired, pale, scratching the back of his neck while avoiding eye contact with a reporter on his porch—so many times, I was sure I would remember it in my nursing-home days. I knew that Troy had not reported that his wife was missing until almost two days after she'd disappeared. I knew there'd been evidence of a struggle in the family home. Broken glass had been found. Blood too. I knew that Daisy hadn't used her phone, her social media accounts, or her credit cards since she'd disappeared.

"I'm looking for Earl Bird," Troy told me, putting his box on one of the chairs in front of my desk. I got down from the ladder, and he handed me a small, faded business card. I recognized it from the thousands I had tossed out while cleaning the office.

"Aha." I handed Troy back the card. "Look, I'm Rhonda Bird. Earl was my father. He passed away last year."

"Oh. Damn. So are you closing this place down?"

"No, my sister and I run the business now. But we don't go about things the same way Earl did. So if somebody gave you this card with a recommendation— "

"No, no, it was pinned to a board over at central booking. They took me there for questioning. I, uh . . . I liked the slogan: 'No judgments.' "

"Right," I said. "I suppose you're getting a few early judgments on what happened to your wife."

"You can say that again."

Troy Hansen was in hot water that was steadily climbing to the boiling point. What had happened seemed obvious to me and the rest of the world: Troy and Daisy had had an argument, and Troy had killed her. I assumed that Daisy's body would soon be found in some remote area, probably by someone walking his dog. It was an old story and one I didn't particularly want to watch again.

Troy's appearance at my office was a twist in that tale. I didn't know yet if it was a good twist or a bad twist. "So, what are you doing here, Troy?" I asked.

"I guess . . . " He shrugged. "I'm here for the same reason anybody comes to see a PI. I need help, and I can't go to the police."

"Well, I'm not gonna lie. I'm well aware that you're involved in a major, major case," I said, choosing my words carefully. "But I've got to say, if you really are innocent of . . .

whatever it is, you should be sticking close to the police. By hiring a PI, you're only going to annoy the hell out of them. You should hire a lawyer instead."

"I'm actually not here about Daisy," Troy said.

For a moment, I was so stunned I couldn't speak. What on earth would Troy Hansen be here about if not his missing wife?

"At least, I don't think I am," he continued. "I mean, it . . . it can't be hers."

"What are you talking about?"

Troy lifted the cardboard box from the chair and put it on the desk, then gestured at it with a nervous swipe of his hand.

I hesitated, then gingerly lifted the top flaps of the box. Inside was an assortment of neatly arranged zip-lock bags.

I lifted out one of the bags. When I saw what it held, my knees went so weak, I had to flop down into a chair.

CHAPTER 8

I KNEW WHAT THIS WAS.

This was a trophy box.

The first time I'd ever seen one was back in Colorado more than a decade ago, when I'd been a relatively new public defender. I'd been assigned to represent Darcy Statesman, a forty-three-year-old married father of two accused of committing a home invasion and rape. The case had been a welcome interruption to my typical parade of drug-possessing idiots and their cousins, the DUI losers. My first meeting with Darcy Statesman had convinced me that he was innocent, that the police had gotten it all wrong, that he was a loving father ensnared in a devastating miscarriage of justice that only I could rectify.

The discovery of Darcy's trophy box changed all that. That box, which the prosecution submitted into evidence, was polished mahogany with gold hinges, about the size of a shoebox. Inside were sixteen pairs of women's panties, each tied with a delicate pink ribbon at the left hip. On the ribbons were the names and addresses of women from as far away as Japan—including the name and address of the most recent victim, the case he'd just told me he'd had nothing to do with.

I'd dropped the case. Darcy was eventually charged with sixteen rapes and convicted of fourteen.

As I eyed Troy Hansen's cardboard box, I felt a hot wave of nausea wash over me, the same as I'd felt looking over Darcy Statesman's trophy box, and I experienced a similar world-shaking realization: There was a universe where people did things that were unspeakably bad. Inhuman. And somehow a piece of that world had fallen into mine.

The zip-lock bag I'd pulled out held an old wooden hairbrush with a hand-painted image of a bunny on its oval-shaped back. It also contained a newspaper cutting with the headline "Search Continues for Local Teen Missing in Mountains" above a photo of a lanky Hispanic teenage girl with tumbling brown curls sitting on a park bench in the lotus position.

I got up unsteadily, slipped the bag back into the box. The box itself was dusty, bits of dirt collected at the bottom. I rummaged in the desk drawers and found a pair of latex gloves—you never know when you might need them—put them on, and pulled out another, larger zip-lock bag. It appeared to contain a tightly rolled T-shirt or jersey of some kind. I could see printed white lettering on navy-blue fabric. There was a newspaper clipping in here too, and I moved the bag around until I could read the headline: "Parents Desperate for News of Troubled Son."

Troy Hansen sat silently in the chair in front of my desk as I flipped through a few of the bags in the box, not wanting to disturb them too much. I glimpsed other items. A wool hat. A small painting kit. Each bag seemed to have a newspaper clipping. The contents were carefully organized, indicating the same thoughtful intention and sinister orderliness that Darcy Statesman had used in his collection of sick trophies.

"What in the world is this?" I asked Troy as I sat down behind my desk. "Why do you have this box?"

"I was searching the house last night," he said, finally looking me in the eye. "Trying to find something that would help me figure out where Daisy is, maybe some clue to where she went. I checked out the crawl space that's under the house, and I noticed some disturbed earth. That's where I found the box. It was buried down there. Not deep. There was only maybe an inch of dirt on top."

"Are you kidding me?" I said. "You're saying you found this box with all of this...stuff...in it *buried* under your house?"

"Yes."

I waited for him to say more. I had a ton of questions for Troy. How long had he and Daisy lived in their house? When did he last access the crawl space? What exactly had happened on the night Daisy went missing? But I'd always found that the best way to get suspects talking was to give them the space to wander verbally on their own and let them take me on the journey.

Yet Troy was unlike any man I'd ever had sitting in the chair before me. He wasn't taking me anywhere.

Troy alternated between avoiding eye contact and giving an unnerving amount of it, staring at me with the unnaturally still, eerily calm gaze of a doll. As the seconds ticked by, a parade of thoughts marched through my mind. I thought of the gun I kept strapped to the underside of my desk. Of the phone in my back pocket. Of the squad cars in the parking lot. Of what I would do if this man tried to hurt me the way he had, perhaps, hurt his wife and the people whose precious items were contained in that cardboard box.

I found myself wondering if I was sitting across the desk from a monster. Troy's strange and depthless eyes did nothing to alleviate my concerns.

"Troy, this makes no sense," I finally said, lifting my hands helplessly. "No sense at all."

"I know."

"You have to give me some answers here."

"I don't have any," he said.

"Your wife is missing," I said, my frustration rising. "From everything I've heard, it looks like there was a struggle in your home. Your behavior since has been... it's been odd. Undeniably odd." My exasperation made me blunt. "You come across terribly on camera, Troy. And in person, you're not much better."

"I know," he said again. "I'm not hugely social or... practiced with people. I'm not close to my parents, and I don't have a lot of friends. I have one buddy, a guy from work, and I have Daisy. I never wanted or needed much else."

"But you see how it looks, Troy. Like you're an unsocialized loner with a missing wife who pops up in my office carting what seems to be a creepy collection of artifacts from other missing people."

Troy sighed and put a hand up. "I know how it looks. It looks like I... like I killed Daisy, and while the world is howling for me to be charged for that crime, I decided to come clean about all the other killing I've done. Or... I don't know... maybe it looks like I'm trying to pin these crimes on her."

"Is that what you're doing?" I gestured to the box and laughed humorlessly at the sheer absurdity of this whole conversation. "Are you trying to say that this is *Daisy's* box?"

"No," Troy said. "I'm not saying anything about the box at all. I don't know for sure what the stuff in this box is. I don't know who it belongs to or how it got under my house. But I see those newspaper articles about all the people who are missing, just like Daisy. I didn't want to open the bags, and I can't easily look into any of this or even google the names to find out more because the police have all my stuff. My phone, my computers."

I held my head in my hands.

"Try to imagine that what I'm saying is true," he said. "I didn't kill Daisy. I don't know where she is. Just try, will you?" Troy pleaded. For the first time, I saw a flicker of an emotion in his eyes: desperation. "Imagine that I came home to find my wife gone and that I really, genuinely, have no idea what's happened to her. I don't even know if she's alive or dead. And if that's not horrible enough, imagine that everyone in the world is pointing a finger at me. Imagine that all week, the police have been following me and watching me and questioning me for hours on end. Imagine me getting so tired and scared that I decided to search every square inch of my house for clues about what the hell happened to my wife. Now imagine how I felt when I found *this*."

He pointed at the box on my desk.

I did as he asked. While Troy stared at his feet, I sat and imagined, or tried to imagine, the predicament he'd described.

"You haven't told the police about the box?" I asked.

"Would you?" he responded.

CHAPTER 9

I HAD TO THINK hard. Troy's story about finding the box under his house and having no idea why it was there sounded far-fetched to me—to the cops, it would be simply unacceptable. I knew that the police who were hounding Troy were unshakable in their resolve to pin this crime on him. The husband is always the first suspect and remains that way unless he's definitively cleared. There would be no creative thinking. No wavering. As soon as the police learned about the contents of this box, they would arrest Troy. The internet would melt down. Troy would be torpedoing his own case if he reported this now.

"So you're saying that you want to hire my agency to find out where this box came from," I said. "And why it was buried under your house."

"Right." Troy nodded.

"And you want us to do that without informing the police of its existence."

"Please."

I laughed. Sometimes it's all you can do. "Troy, that's not a good idea. I've got to think about my business. My investigator's license. Not to mention the families of those missing people in the newspaper clippings. If this is what I think it is and you don't go to the police with that box right now, we could both be charged with withholding evidence and interfering in a police investigation."

"I understand." He put his hands up. "But, Rhonda, I'm telling you the truth. I didn't kill my wife, and I have nothing to do with whatever happened to those people. That's why I'm here. Because I know what will happen if I bring this to the police, but I don't want to ignore it. I'm hoping you can at least look into this for… I don't know. A day? Would you give it a day?"

"And if I say no?"

"I'll eventually hand the box in, I suppose." He leaned back in his chair. "Let the police take a crack at it. But if their behavior so far has shown me anything, it's that they've already made up their minds that I'm the bad guy here. They'll probably approach those other cases with the same tunnel vision."

I took off the latex gloves and tapped the edge of my desk, my mind racing, loyalties colliding. I stood up and went to the window to look down at the squad cars. There was an officer standing between them, leaning on the roof of one car, talking on a cell phone in the sunshine. His partner was in the cruiser. The other cruiser was empty. My guess was that the two officers from the second cruiser were stationed in front of the crab shack or in the hall outside. A four-man team was a lot for a single surveillance target, and those were just the guys I could see. Given all the publicity on Daisy's case, it wouldn't surprise me if the cops were putting covert tails on Troy, possibly even planting listening devices in his car and house. They'd want to put pressure on the man. Make him squirm. See if he did anything stupid.

"Every cop in the state is on me," Troy said as though he could hear my thoughts. "But if I'm a . . . a killer . . . nobody's in any danger from me right now."

"Hmm," I said.

"So will you do it?" he asked. "Will you help me?"

"I don't know," I said. "I need more time to make a decision."

"Okay," he said. Troy stood and waited uncertainly in front of the door, his hands clasped. "I, uh . . . I told the cops at my house when they saw me leaving with the box that it was full of paperwork and that I was coming here about a private matter. I suppose they'll want to question you as soon as I'm gone."

"I'll fend them off until I've made a decision," I said. I opened a desk drawer and pulled out a spare burner phone I kept there. "Take this. I'll call you in an hour and tell you what I'm going to do."

CHAPTER 10

BABY FUMBLED FOR HER phone on the nightstand in the pure blackness of her bedroom, knocking a bottle of water, a packet of gummy bears, and a box of tissues to the floor. "Hello?"

"You'll never believe who just showed up here," Rhonda said, her voice tight with excitement.

By the time her sister was finished recapping her encounter with Troy Hansen, Baby was fully awake. She stood squinting at the beach view outside her window; the blazing sunlight reflecting off the ocean and the bizarreness of the tale had rocketed her into consciousness.

Baby inhaled deeply. This was *big*. Stories about Daisy Hansen, Troy's missing wife, were all over her socials and

FYP, and the hashtag **#troykilleddaisy** was everywhere. "No. Freakin'. *Way*," Baby said.

"Yes freakin' way." Rhonda sounded like she was getting in her car. Baby heard the thunk of the Impala's door closing, the whiz of the seat belt, and the grunt of the engine coming to life. "I was just interrogated outside the crab shack by some of the cops who've been tailing Troy. They wanted to know what he was doing at our office, of course. And they wanted to see what was in the box he brought over."

"What did you do?"

"I played my lawyer card. They have no legal right to know what Troy or I discussed or what's in the box."

"You cited penal codes?"

"It works, Baby."

"So are we going to take this case?"

"Are you crazy? Of course we are," Rhonda said.

Baby felt a flame of exhilaration ignite in her chest. It was quickly snuffed out when Rhonda continued. "But, Baby, I'm lead on this. If last night showed us anything, it's that even the most benign cases can turn malignant in an instant. This could be a murder we're dealing with. Or, if it turns out that the contents of the box and Daisy's disappearance are linked, a series of murders. So if I tell you to— "

"C'mon, Rhonda." Baby slumped to the carpet, leaned her head on the windowsill. "Can you press pause on the lecturing for, like, half a minute?"

"Do you know why I lecture you all the time, Baby?"

Rhonda said, getting heated. "It's because I actually care about you."

"Ugh, don't go all lovey-dovey on me."

"Listen, if we slip up or if we get too confident or if we—"

"You mean if *I* slip up," Baby said. "If *I* get too confident. If *I* blow our cover and *I* get us made into a serial killer's skin-suits. That's what you're thinking, isn't it?"

After a moment, Rhonda said, "I don't think that."

"You sure?"

"Baby..." Rhonda sighed. "Fine. You're right. I'm sorry."

"What was that? I think my phone cut out."

"I said I was sorry!"

"Uh-huh. Yeah. Listen, have you left the parking lot yet? Because maybe two crab rolls would make up for this. *Maybe*. It's worth a shot."

"Don't get too smart with me," Rhonda said. But Baby heard the engine cut off. "I just need to know that *you* know that I'm lead on the Troy Hansen case. That's all."

"Say less, boss." Baby yawned.

Once her sister hung up, Baby scrolled through her notifications. She had a message waiting for her on Craigslist. She opened it, read through it, and smiled. Rhonda might be lead on the cases at the agency, but she wasn't lead in Baby's life.

Never had been. Never would be.

CHAPTER 11

I STOPPED BY THE house with the crab rolls for Baby. I was hungry too, so I'd gone ahead and bought us six.

After we ate, I hustled her into the Impala for the hour-plus drive from our house in Manhattan Beach to Glendale, where Troy Hansen lived. I figured we should visit our new client at the scene of the crime. So to speak.

Baby was applying lip gloss and admiring herself in the passenger-seat sun visor's mirror as we approached the Hansen residence on Bonita Drive. I slowed when I spotted a dozen or so media vans crowding the intersection ahead. Bonita Drive itself was blocked and guarded by police. Troy had mentioned that they would allow only residents and known guests through.

"This is insane." Baby flipped the mirror back up and looked at the huddles of press standing in the sunshine, comparing notes. "Tough luck if you live on Troy Hansen's street. You've gotta go through a police checkpoint every time you go anywhere."

"True, but still, I'd be grateful for the protection from gawkers and the press," I said. "Without the blockade, both the media and amateur web sleuths would be free to knock on anyone's door looking for sound bites."

I pointed to where a woman was filming herself on her iPhone across the road from the TV reporters. As we drove past, Baby and I heard her voice through our open car windows.

"...with theories about what time Troy *actually* arrived home the night Daisy disappeared. Like and follow for part two, guys."

We identified ourselves to the police and were let through. Two drones appeared and hovered maybe thirty feet above us as we walked up to the Hansens' uncovered front porch. We rang the bell and Troy opened the door wearing flip-flops, sweats, and a muscle shirt. There was a scrubbing brush in his hand. I heard the buzz of the drones behind us as they tried to get closer and I all but threw myself at Troy in a likely futile attempt to block their view of him holding cleaning supplies.

The police blockade would help keep the press away, but nothing stopped rumors entirely, and those rumors hit the internet fast.

"What the hell, Troy?" I said as Baby and I hurried inside. I slammed the door shut behind us and pointed to the scrubbing brush. The air smelled of bleach. "What are you doing?"

He pushed back his floppy hair and glanced at Baby as though she could help. "The police said I could clean whatever I wanted as long as I didn't touch the kitchen."

"Troy." I pinched the bridge of my nose. "Don't clean anything, okay? Don't throw anything away or try to sell anything either. While you're at it, don't start inquiring with your life insurance provider. Don't get on a dating app. Don't hook up the porn channel. These are all textbook examples of guilty-husband activities."

Troy stared at the carpet. I waved a hand at Baby. "This is my kid sister, Baby. She's my partner at the agency."

"Don't start doing any gardening either." Baby took up where I'd left off. "Those drones film you in the yard with a shovel, and the whole internet will fry. Satellites will burst into flames in the stratosphere and tumble to the earth."

"I have to do something." Troy went to the couch in an immaculate living room. "I'm going nuts. If I go out there, people start filming me or yelling at me. If I stay in here, all I have is the television, and it's either murder documentaries, murder dramas, or coverage of Daisy and me."

"So let's give you something to do," I said. "You're going to walk me through what happened the night Daisy went missing."

Troy's pale, hairy toes twitched on the rubber surface of his flip-flops. The drones buzzed outside, a tap dripped somewhere, and the house stood otherwise still and empty and smelling of cleaning products. I noticed a bowl of decorative wicker balls sitting on the huge coffee table. Magazines were fanned out near them; they looked pristine and unread.

Eventually, Troy spoke. "I came home. Daisy's car wasn't here," he said. He gestured over his shoulder toward the kitchen without looking at it. "I saw the blood right away."

CHAPTER 12

AS TROY AND RHONDA spoke in the living room, Baby wandered into the kitchen, unable to stay away any longer. The infamous Hansen kitchen, center of social media speculation, was there before her, marked with the telltale signs of an exhaustive forensic effort.

Baby had seen a couple of crime scenes in her time, had been dragged along by her father when she was a little kid. She recognized the photographic exhibit tags, the lines made with erasable markers, the strips of painter's tape. There was the acidy smell of luminol and the smudge of a pencil on the otherwise spotless white marble counters. The shiny appliances were in a weird group at one end of the counter. Several of the cabinets were standing open, and others had had their doors completely removed.

There was no visible blood, but Baby could tell where it had been by the clustering of forensic detritus. Something had happened in front of the sink.

Rhonda's voice traveled to Baby from the living room. "So you saw the blood right away. Tell me the story."

"What, all of it?" Troy asked.

"Yeah, all of it. I don't want to get your version mixed up with what I've heard and make assumptions."

Baby heard Troy blow out a lungful of air. She went to the kitchen doorway and watched him tell his story.

"I got home at six. That's usually when I get home from work," he began. "Depends on the traffic and whether or not I've stopped at central to chat with my buddy George." Baby saw him glance at an end table that held several pictures, one of which was Troy standing next to a bearded Black man. The rest were tastefully framed photos of Troy and Daisy. "But generally I get back at six. I walked in, put my bag on the kitchen counter, and straightaway, I saw blood and glass on the floor."

Baby turned away and used the hem of her shirt to cover her hand as she opened the fridge. She saw a stack of Tupperware containers labeled with the days of the week in pretty cursive writing. Must be Daisy's lunches. Organization freak. The Thursday through Sunday meals were still there.

"What do you do for a living, Troy?" Rhonda asked.

"I repair and service utility poles. I'm responsible for the phone lines," he said. "A landline connection goes down, I go out there, find the pole, figure out what's gone wrong. Then I hook it back up and write a report."

"Who is your employer?"

"The Public Utilities Commission."

"Pretty dull job?"

"Maybe to some people. I like it. Lots of driving around alone, running my own show. And it's different. One day I'm in the city, next day I'm in the desert."

"But the hours are pretty regular?"

"Well, I don't get overtime unless it's urgent, so I don't take any nonurgent calls that would mean I'd have to work past five," Troy said. "So if somebody says, 'Hey, some kids threw a pair of shoes over the wire out at Pomona and now the phones are out,' and I look at my watch and it's three twenty-eight p.m. and the call's not from a hospital or a fire station, I push it to the next day."

"Okay. So that night, you come home. You're right on time, as usual. You come into the kitchen, and you see broken glass. You see blood," Baby heard Rhonda say. "How much blood was there?"

"Maybe a tablespoon or two?"

"That's an oddly specific way of describing it," Rhonda said.

"Well, the cops have asked me that same exact question a hundred ways." Troy sighed. "I've had some time to think about it."

"Where did the glass come from?"

"It was one of our water glasses," Troy said. "I recognized it from the hexagonal bottom. The police have it now."

"Was it cracked? Was it in half? Was it shattered everywhere?"

"Shattered everywhere."

"Any water or other liquids on the floor?"

"None that I saw."

Baby went to the cupboard beside the fridge. The doors were propped open. More Tupperware. She looked at the next one. Four wineglasses, three water glasses, all spotless.

"Why did you clean up the glass and the blood?" Rhonda asked.

"Because that's what you do with blood and broken glass," Troy said. "You clean it up."

"Come on."

"Look, at that point, I didn't know anything was wrong." Baby heard Troy heave a huge sigh. "Daisy works from home—she's a nutritionist and has a lot of followers on social media, so she has to do her Instagram postings and so forth—but she's usually at the gym when I get back from work. So when I got home and saw the mess, I just thought, *Looks like Daisy dropped a glass and cut herself. She must be here somewhere.* I walked around the house looking for her and calling her name, but she wasn't here. And her car wasn't here either."

"What kind of car does she drive?"

"A Honda Civic. A little red one."

"Okay. So then what did you think?"

"Nothing."

"Nothing?"

"There wasn't anything to think," Troy said. "Daisy somehow broke a glass and cut herself. And then, apparently, she went out without cleaning it up. That's all I knew."

"You weren't concerned, even though she was obviously hurt? You didn't wonder why she hadn't cleaned the mess up herself?"

"Well, sure, it seemed a little inconsiderate to leave it like that, but it didn't seem serious, as far as I could tell. You never hear about people dying from water-glass injuries. I just figured she'd gotten distracted and she was probably at the gym like usual."

A pause in the conversation in the other room. Baby kept listening while staring out at the Hansens' beautiful backyard. She wanted to rush back into the living room and blast Troy for all his weirdness and nonsensical answers. But Rhonda's warnings lay over her like a blanket. Rhonda was lead. Baby needed to take a back seat, let her sister do the talking.

"So after you came home at six," Rhonda said, "you stayed in. You didn't go out looking for Daisy. You didn't try to contact her."

"No."

"What *did* you do?"

"I watched TV and then went to bed."

"It didn't concern you when Daisy didn't come home that night?"

Another awkward pause.

"I get it. I get it," Troy said. "People keep asking me, 'Why didn't you text Daisy? Why didn't you search the neighborhood? Why didn't you call the police? Why didn't you preserve the crime scene?' I didn't know it was a crime scene! I just came home and saw something weird, that's all. It's not like I opened the fridge and found her severed head in there."

Baby stopped a surprised laugh just as it hit her throat, swallowed it. She leaned against the kitchen doorway and looked across the hall to the living room where Rhonda was sitting on the couch. Baby caught her sister's eye and raised her eyebrows, but Rhonda didn't respond.

"Troy," Rhonda said. "You shouldn't be saying things like that. Not to me, not to anybody. I sure hope you haven't been talking so casually about your wife's possible death with the police."

"I can barely remember what I've said," Troy said. "The first interrogation was eight hours straight. No food, no water."

Baby left the kitchen and checked out the bathroom. The mirror was spotless, and a bucket of hot soapy water stood steaming in the middle of the floor in front of the toilet. There was soap in the grout in the shower. She spotted more signs of police activity: The drain covers in the sink, shower, and floor were all missing. She opened the mirrored cabinet and found empty spaces where she assumed there had once been bottles of pills that had been taken into evidence.

"When did you first try to make contact with Daisy after you came home and found the blood?" Rhonda was asking as Baby returned to the living room.

"The next morning." Troy watched Baby, only his eyes

moving. "I texted her that I was going to work and to have a nice day. I expected her to call me at lunch."

"Troy." Rhonda was sitting on the edge of her seat, her hands tightly clasped. Baby could sense the frustration coming off her in waves. "You must understand how strange this all is. Your behavior."

"I'm a strange guy, I guess." Troy fiddled with his fingernails. "I've been told that before. The police keep telling me a normal person would have assumed Daisy was in some kind of danger when he saw the blood and she didn't come home."

"Exactly!" Rhonda opened her hands.

"I just *didn't* assume that." Troy shrugged.

"Why not?"

"Daisy is a smart, capable, independent woman. I didn't immediately assume she needed rescuing from some kind of perilous situation. And the odds that somebody came in here, into our house, hurt her, kidnapped her, and brought her to . . . to some unknown location?" He threw his hands up. "They're infinitesimal. Daisy and I, we're not drug dealers. We're not international spies. What possible reason could anybody have for doing that?"

Rhonda didn't answer.

"I assumed that something much more likely had happened," Troy said. "I figured she'd gone to a friend's house after the gym or maybe went to a doctor to get stitches for the glass injury or whatever."

"And you weren't curious as to which one of those had happened?" Rhonda asked.

"No."

Baby caught Rhonda's eye again and beckoned her over. Rhonda left Troy sitting on the couch staring at his hands, and the two sisters walked down the hall toward the guest bedroom.

"We've hit the big time," Baby said in a low voice.

"What makes you say that?" Rhonda asked.

"Because this guy murdered his damn wife," Baby said. "It's as plain as the nose on my face."

CHAPTER 13

RHONDA WAITED, HER ARMS folded over her Opeth T-shirt. The sunlight from the windows overlooking the manicured yard made her round cheeks glow.

"We're going to take down Troy Hansen," Baby said, trying to put her thoughts in order. Excitement was fluttering in her chest. "We're going to be the ones to get him. Not just for killing Daisy, who is clearly lying around here somewhere decomposing, but for killing all those other victims too. The movie rights are going to sell for millions." Baby grinned at Rhonda.

Her older sister looked unimpressed, verging on disgusted. "Where's your smoking gun?"

"We're standing in it. Look around you," Baby said. "This

place screams *Sleeping with the Enemy.* The labeled Tupperware. The soulless knickknacks. The hotel art. The whole house looks like a Zoom background."

"Baby," Rhonda said. "You need to play your own devil's advocate here, okay? Yes, the house looks like an IKEA showroom. So what? Maybe Daisy likes it that way. You wanna analyze the decor and use it to accuse Troy of murder, you can go right outside with all the other wannabe TikTok sleuths. The hedges look pretty tidy. Maybe Daisy's buried under them. You wanna go check?"

"Rhonda—"

"Look, Baby, I want a *partner* on this case. What I want from you is criminal investigation, Baby. Not thirty-year-old movie references. Not clichés and prejudices."

"He didn't even try to call or text her, Rhonda!"

"I know this may be hard for you to believe," Rhonda said slowly, "but once upon a time, people didn't call and text each other every six seconds. You could be dating someone and go a whole week without speaking to them. Husbands and wives didn't know each other's exact geographical location down to the square foot all the time."

"Okay." Baby backed away. "Now you're talking to me like I'm an idiot."

"I'm trying to get you to think laterally," Rhonda said. "We've got to exhaust all possibilities to determine that Troy didn't do this."

"Why?"

"Because no one else is going to," Rhonda said.

"Oh, don't give me that 'Innocent until proven guilty' bullshit, Rhonda."

"It's not bullshit, Baby. It's the basis for our entire justice system."

"Well, you go ahead and exhaust yourself. Report back to me when you've finished wasting your time," Baby snapped.

Before Baby could turn away, Rhonda grabbed her arm. "If you're gonna storm off, can you at least do me a favor?" She slipped a small, cold metal disk into Baby's hand. A GPS tracker. "Tag Troy's car, and don't let the cops see you do it."

Baby stepped out onto the Hansens' porch and watched the shadows of the drones cross over her without looking up at them. She kept her head bowed, went to Troy Hansen's blue truck, and leaned against it, then took out her phone and pretended to read a text. Rhonda's dismissal of her excitement over the Troy Hansen case had made the muscles of her neck tighten with fury. For months, she and her sister had been chasing insurance fraudsters, cheating boyfriends, and missing pets. Now they were deep inside a *real* mystery, and all Rhonda wanted to do was plod around searching for alternatives to the plain reality that Troy had killed his wife—and probably several other people.

Baby sighed, then opened and scrolled through TikTok. The third video that came up on her For You Page was of a young man with a buzz cut, and Baby felt a pang of surprise as she realized that he was standing in front of footage of herself and Rhonda arriving at the Hansen house less than an hour ago. She unmuted it.

"All right, guys, this just in. My man at the DMV ran the plates of the car that just pulled into the Hansen driveway, and it seems a Ms. Rhonda Bird is at the house today. She runs a private detective agency in Koreatown. Seems to unofficially employ her younger half sister, Barbara, who we can see on the left there. Barbara is also known as popular fashion and travel influencer Baby Bird, but she's gone quiet, probably training to become full partner in the agency once she's old enough to get her license. But, look, this is a crazy, *crazy* development in the case, everyone. Have these women been hired by Daisy's parents? Or by Troy himself? What do the cops think? Comment your theories and I'll be back when I have more."

The video ended. Baby scrolled through a few more videos, Duets, and blind reactions to the one she'd just watched. Then she went over to Craigslist and checked her messages again. There was a new one waiting.

I'll be here. Come any time!

Baby squeezed the GPS tag Rhonda had given her, looked at the Hansen house. She could see Rhonda and Troy through the windows. Baby was literally on the outside of the investigation looking in.

"Fuck it," Baby said. She bent slightly like she was scratching her hip, tucked the tag under the wheel hub of Troy's car, and listened for the click as the magnet locked on. Then she walked down the driveway and into the street toward the police checkpoint as she called an Uber. She put her home address in as a quick stop on her two-part journey.

Where she was going, she'd need to bring a gun.

CHAPTER 14

AFTER BABY LEFT, I stayed and talked to Troy a little longer, but he didn't reveal much more. Baby's sudden absence felt like the elephant in the room.

When I passed the police checkpoint, I felt dozens of eyes watching. I wasn't terribly surprised when I was pulled over barely two streets away from Bonita Drive. Squad car with flashing lights, sirens. I recognized the officer in the vehicle and put my forehead on the steering wheel. He took his time striding over to my car and leaned his huge forearm on the window frame when he got there.

"Dave." I gave him a smile that was so fake, it actually hurt my cheeks. I hadn't seen David Summerly since I'd stopped answering his calls after our last date.

"Rhonda."

"You're assigned to the Daisy Hansen thing?"

"I'm *one* of the officers working the case." The tall, sandy-blond, square-jawed police officer glanced around the inside of my car. RIP to my beloved leopard-print '72 Buick Skylark, but this new-to-me '58 Chevy Impala was a classic. It had been three months or so since Summerly was in it. I'd driven us to a movie, then dropped him off at his apartment after midnight. "I'd just love to know what you were doing over there," he said.

"Troy Hansen may or may not have engaged me in a private matter." I took my sunglasses from the holder and slipped them on, driven by the instinct to hide. "I really don't want to get into it right now, okay? It's...you know. It's complicated."

"It's complicated?" Summerly raised his eyebrows. "Now, that sounds familiar. Isn't that one of the tired, vague old lines you fed me after you ghosted me?"

"I didn't ghost you. I drifted away."

"That's what ghosts do. They drift. They're kind of known for it."

I swallowed. "I'd really hate for you to make my work with Troy Hansen difficult just because our relationship didn't turn out the way you wanted it to."

"So you admit that you are working with him? What has he hired you to do?"

"No comment."

Summerly smiled and looked away. I remembered the dimples. I glanced out the front window. Sunny Glendale sprawled around us: Gardeners tending manicured lawns. Bored dogs barking in yards. I thought about the cardboard box sitting in the trunk of my car.

Though I hadn't technically agreed to take Troy's case, I was willing to hold on to the box for a day or so until I worked out the right thing to do. Before I left, Troy had led me to the crawl space under the floorboards, which was accessed through the linen cupboard, and I'd looked at the bare dirt under the house and seen nothing out of the ordinary beyond the disturbed earth. But now, with Summerly standing only feet away from my car, the box in my trunk seemed to be humming with evil energy.

"I know you like to root for the underdog, Rhonda," Summerly said. "From what you've told me about your cases back in Colorado, Troy Hansen is exactly the type of person you like to defend. Misunderstood. Victimized. Vulnerable. Alone."

I nodded, conceding that was true.

"Let me deromanticize this for you," Summerly said. "That seems to be your theme lately, right?"

I sighed.

"Troy Hansen is none of those things," Summerly said. "He's a killer, and in a day or two we'll have enough cause to arrest him. We know he's lying about when he arrived home from work the night Daisy went missing."

"How do you know that?"

"We have footage."

"What footage?"

"He's lying about the state of their marriage too," Summerly went on, ignoring my question. "The dynamic had changed recently. Big-time. If you heard more lies from Troy just now, you have a responsibility to pass them on to me."

I bit my tongue, pictured the box in the trunk.

"Think about your detective agency's reputation. If you throw your lot in with Troy, the internet wack jobs already crawling all over this are going to come for you too. That can't be good for business."

"Thanks so much for your concern." I gave him an icy smile. "I'm so lucky to have you looking out for me."

"Uh-huh."

"Maybe if you gave me access to Troy's and Daisy's data, I'd see reason a lot faster," I ventured.

"No comment," he said, enjoying it.

"At least tell me if you've found her car."

Summerly laughed humorlessly. "You're kidding me, right?"

"Hey, you're telling me I'm hanging out with a wolf in sheep's clothing, so prove it. You guys are the ones with all the Hansen household phones and computers. Maybe you know where her car is too. Don't just tell me that I'm wrong here, Dave. Show me. Help me see it for myself."

"I don't have to help you, Rhonda." Summerly stepped back from my car. "In fact, I don't have to talk to you at all."

He went. I forced myself not to check out his ass as he walked away.

"My number's the same if you change your mind!" I called after him.

CHAPTER 15

BABY SAW NOTHING REASSURING at 101 Waterway Street in Culver City. It had taken her almost two hours to get here, since she'd had to go from Glendale back home to Manhattan Beach before coming up here.

She sat frozen in the Uber, looking at the weathered Federation-style house with its peeling shutters and overgrown yard, the only house on the block not surrounded by cyclone fencing. There were no other cars on this street. A thin, raggedy cat lay in the gutter, sleeping or dead.

When the driver nudged her, Baby got out and walked to the house with her hand on the pistol in her purse. It was Rhonda's gun, which she'd secretly removed from the safe in her sister's bedroom, not for the first time. Her face burning with defiance, Baby knocked on the door and told herself that sometimes good things came in crummy packages.

An ancient white man answered. Her mouth dropped open when she saw the gray-haired white dude holding the door frame, peering at her with the same incredulity.

"Arthur?" she said.

"Steve?" the guy asked.

"Whoa, okay, wait up." Baby took her hand off her gun to hold her head. "You're not who you said you were. At all. This is not cool. You said you were twenty-eight. You said— "

"*You* said you were twenty-five." The old guy looked her up and down. "*And* a man!"

"Well, that's just the oldest rule in the book: Don't let strangers on the internet know you're a young woman. How dumb do you think I am?" Baby dropped a hip, challenged him with her eyes. He didn't flinch.

"I wanted a man's help," the old guy said. "Not a little girl's. How old are you really? Twelve?"

"Sixteen."

"Well, call your mama to come pick you up. Right now."

"Too bad! You got me. So let's do this." Baby flicked her hands at him, shooing him out of her way. He didn't budge. She stepped around him. The house was old, huge, the foyer dusty and bare. She turned and saw Arthur was holding a sawed-off shotgun down by his thigh. "What the hell? Are you this friendly to everyone who comes to your door?"

"You're one to talk. I saw you from across the way." Arthur jerked a shriveled, crooked thumb toward the street. "Either you got some hundred-dollar lipstick in there or you're packing heat too."

"Packing heat?" Baby had to laugh. "I like that. That's gangster." Her assessment of the old guy and his house was shifting, softening, as the seconds ticked by.

Arthur shut the door, marched past her into a spacious but cluttered kitchen, and dumped his shotgun on the counter. The floorboards creaked and popped for the entire journey.

"You said you wanted a man's help." Baby put her hands up. "I get it. I can see this isn't the nicest neighborhood. Looks like the apocalypse just hit outside. But let me try to sell you on my capabilities. I'm handy, okay? I can fix things. I can garden. I can cook. I can keep an eye on things around here."

Arthur wrinkled his nose, sucked air through his dentures. Baby's phone pinged in her handbag. She reached in and silenced it, annoyed. Rhonda chasing her again.

"Give me twenty-four hours," Baby said to Arthur. "How 'bout it? If you think I'm cramping your style after a one-day probationary period, you can tell me to beat it. But this place looks like it could use a woman's touch."

Something flickered in the old man's eyes. He didn't answer.

"Great." Baby grinned. She dumped her bag on the floor, went to the kitchen sink, and picked up a glass. "Let me get some water and we'll get started right now."

She put her hand on the faucet and felt an electric charge hit her body in an explosive wave.

CHAPTER 16

I STOPPED AT A café in Silver Lake to do some research on Daisy and Troy Hansen while I waited for Baby's latest tantrum to blow over. The café's aesthetic had attracted me—indoor plants, tattooed staff, and polished concrete. Regret hit when I saw that the menu was wall-to-wall rabbit food. I opened up the app that monitored the tracking device I'd had Baby place on Troy Hansen's truck, and checked where it was. Still in front of the house on Bonita Drive. Good. At least Troy was staying put. I opened my laptop in unison with three other people in the big sprawling room and looked up Daisy Hansen's socials.

Troy's wife did look like the type of woman who went to the gym right after work. In her Instagram profile picture,

Daisy posed with her toned arms behind her head, a big toothy grin on display. Her blond ponytail was thick and lustrous, and a twinkle in her eyes said *We're friends!* in a way that probably got people to take her advice on nutrition and forget the price tag. More prettily filtered shots in the feed: Daisy on her laptop in bed brandishing an oat-milk coffee in an ethically made mug, Daisy's feet on early-morning grass with two similar but unmatching sneakers on with the hashtag **#whoops**.

I scrolled. There were no photos or mentions of Troy.

A gentle fluttering sound drew me away from the screen. I turned and saw on the wall above me a big flip clock with black-and-white flaps that fell as time passed. I watched the *2* in *5:42* fold itself into a *3* and wondered where Baby was.

Dave Summerly had suggested that the Hansens' marriage had changed recently. I endured my depressing bowl of grains and grass and tried to catalog the number of ways a relationship dynamic could change so badly that it resulted in a disappearance. Had someone else come into the equation? Had there been a big fight in the Hansen household? Had someone been given an ultimatum? I tried to be more creative. Maybe money had come in—or gone out? Maybe Troy had an addiction? An illness? A love child? Maybe *Daisy* had one of those things?

In the comments section of Daisy's online world, most people—predictably—were screaming that Troy must be having an affair. But as I scrolled, I saw that it was Daisy who had begun exhibiting the classic signs. Starting about three months ago, she'd lost a noticeable amount of weight, changed her hair, and begun posting cryptically about learning and growing and being true to herself "no matter who it upsets." I wondered if Troy had never been shared on her feed or in her stories, or if he had, but she'd recently scrubbed all traces of him.

I searched public records for a divorce application by either of the Hansens and came up empty. I did learn that they owned their house and hadn't defaulted on any mortgage payments, and neither one had a criminal record. Daisy's Instagram nutritionist business was registered and solvent. I trawled a few popular dating sites for profiles that featured either Daisy or Troy, explicitly or in disguise. Nada.

My phone pinged. Hoping for Baby, I bristled when I saw the text from Dave Summerly: **Stop wasting your time with Troy Hansen.** I gave such a dramatic sigh, several other laptop jockeys looked over. I'd been told "Just stop!" many times in my career, almost always when I was chasing hopeless cases.

Then I noticed the video attached to Summerly's message.

A surveillance video of a sprawling, recycled-brick driveway lined with hedges. There was a slice of road and neat houses beyond it. The yellow time stamp at the bottom of the footage gave the date: the same Wednesday that Daisy had gone missing. I watched Daisy Hansen's little red Honda Civic, a car that presumably police had not yet recovered, cross the screen. The time was 5:37 p.m.

The video jumped to 7:40 p.m. I watched Troy Hansen's

work truck cross the screen in the same direction as the Honda. The video jumped again. Now the truck was heading in the other direction, presumably away from the Hansen house. At 10:39 p.m.

I put the phone down and held my head. The footage made two things painfully clear: Troy Hansen had lied to me about what time he'd returned home on the night of Daisy's disappearance, and he'd lied to me about not going out again that night.

Flap. Flap. Flap. I held my head for three minutes, counting them off against the flip clock's gentle automated sounds. Why would Troy lie about something so easily proven false?

I opened my eyes. I looked at the clock. Then I looked back at my phone, at the yellow numbers at the bottom of the video screen.

I texted Summerly back and asked him what brand of camera had captured the footage he'd sent. I waited. No answer. I texted again, asked him where the camera was located, told him I wanted to speak to the owner about the device. Still no answer.

I took a screenshot of the footage and opened a blank message to my security guy, Jamie. The kid was a local in Koreatown who had been sourcing spy gear for me and Baby ever since we'd started the agency. He had sold me the tracker that was on Troy Hansen's truck.

Maybe I'm deliriously optimistic, I texted Jamie. **But you can't tell the brand of a security camera just by looking at the footage, can you?**

Jamie wrote back right away. Tech people. They're always online.

Sure can, he said. **But not for free.**

I rolled my eyes. Jamie was a student, putting himself through school to earn some kind of technology degree. He was always hustling. The one time I'd asked Baby to pay him for his services, she'd been three days late with the check. Jamie hadn't forgotten that and never would.

Sending funds and footage now, I said.

Jamie got back to me in two minutes. **That's a Jettno,** he wrote. **Numbers are always yellow. Not the best res but they have a good battery life. If you're looking to buy—don't. I can get you better, cheaper cams.**

I'm not looking to buy, I texted. **I want to know HOW those cameras know what the time and date are. Do they just do it automatically, like your iPhone? Or could those numbers at the bottom of the screen be inaccurate?**

Jamie sent me a link to Google. I groaned. Tech humor.

Twenty-one minutes later, I finally found an online user manual for a Jettno home-security camera. It took another three minutes of googling to discover that the camera's time and date settings were set by the user and were not automatic. I sent a text to Dave Summerly explaining what I'd learned, and then asked:

Are you absolutely certain the date and time attached to this footage are correct?

After seven minutes—I watched them go by on the clock—he finally replied.

I'll check, Summerly wrote.

I could feel his frustration and embarrassment in those words. That made me give a mean little chuckle, which disturbed the people around me.

Now who's wasting time? I thought.

CHAPTER 17

"WHAT IN THE HOLY goddamn hell!" said Arthur.

Baby woke up on the kitchen floor several feet from where she'd been standing. Some inexplicable instinct told her she'd been out for only a second or two, but it was still an effort to claw her way back to reality and figure out where she was and what had happened.

Baby sat up and looked at her left palm, which felt like it was burning. A red streak was seared across the flesh. Her head throbbed.

"What, what, what—" Arthur went to her and hovered uncertainly at her side. "What the hell happened?"

"The sink." Baby shook her tingling hand and got to her feet. "Don't touch it. Don't touch anything."

"I don't understand." Arthur followed Baby to the sink. She examined the faucet without touching it, then bent down and opened the wooden doors under the sink. She noted the copper pipe that disappeared behind the cleaning products into the cabinet base. She shut the cabinet, straightened up, turned, grabbed her phone from her purse, and walked out the front door.

Arthur stayed at her heels as Baby walked through the waist-high weeds at the side of the house. She located the kitchen window, then looked down and spied the weather-worn lattice covering the crawl space beneath the house. She slid her phone in her back pocket, gripped the lattice, and tried to yank it back. The rusted nails groaned.

"Tell me what's going on," Arthur pleaded.

"Your kitchen sink is electrified," Baby said.

"It's *what*?"

"When I grabbed the faucet, the electric charge went into my hand." Baby bent and yanked hard at the lattice, threw her back into it. It came away from the side of the house. She set it in the long grass. "I saw a kid get shocked like that once at camp. The idiot stuck his finger in an electric outlet."

Baby crawled under the house, looked up, and followed the copper pipe that emerged from the kitchen floorboards and ran horizontally along the brickwork.

"What you're saying doesn't make sense." Arthur's voice reached her from the yard. "I used the kitchen sink last night. I—I set up the coffee maker."

"Have you used it today?"

"Uh . . . no?"

"So whatever happened to it must've happened between last night and now."

"We should call an electrician," Arthur said. "And we should get you to a hospital. Get your ass out of there."

"I'm fine. Fortunately, I barely touched that faucet." Baby crawled deeper into the dark, following the pipe to where it met the ancient water heater. "Electrician, yes. Hospital, no."

She pulled her phone from her pocket and turned on the flashlight. She could see what she assumed was the source of the problem: An old brick pillar beneath the house's entryway had crumbled, tipped, and smashed into a solid wood beam as it fell. The wooden beam played host to both the copper water pipe from the kitchen sink and a black electrical cable. Baby shuffled in the dirt until she was right up on the pipe and the cable and examined the meeting point. The corner of a brick, it seemed, had squashed the pipe and the cable together, denting but not bursting the pipe and cutting into the plastic casing of the cable, exposing the live wires.

Baby was no electrician, but she knew that electrical wires and metal pipes weren't friends. The collapse of the pillar had caused the two parties to meet. The only question was whether the pillar collapse that had added Arthur's faucet to the electrical circuit was a freak accident or something orchestrated.

She shuffled closer still. Her iPhone light picked up the edges of the plastic casing. They looked sharp. Like they had been cut, not smashed.

She froze, and a tingle passed through her that had nothing to do with electricity. She swept the flashlight over the dirt beneath her. She could see the imprints her boots and hands and knees had left. She also saw other marks coming from a different direction. Baby followed the other tracks to the back of the house.

By a piece of lattice at the back stairs, she saw a handprint in the dirt. The hand was much bigger than hers. Probably much larger than Arthur's too.

Arthur had tracked her. The old man crouched with difficulty outside the wooden lattice and peered in at her.

"Arthur," Baby said. "Don't go back inside the house, okay?"

"Why?"

"Because someone is trying to kill you."

CHAPTER 18

I WAS IN THE kitchen of our mansion on Manhattan Beach when Baby came home.

I had the trophy box sitting on the table. I'd slipped on a pair of latex gloves and carefully pulled out all its bagged contents, and now I had ten zip-locks lined up in front of me. Each bag contained an item and a newspaper clipping about a missing person, and each article featured a photograph: Jarrod. Maria. Dennis. Dorothy. Luis. Brooke. Luke. Charlie. Francis. Tia.

I looked over the collection and wrote down a few things in a spiral notebook. I glanced at some of the names.

Maria Sanchez, sixteen, last seen at the entrance to Franklin Canyon Park. Her item was a hand-painted hairbrush.

Dorothy Andrews-Smith, sixty-two, last seen at her home in Redondo Beach. Her item was a tiny oil-painting kit.

Dennis Maynar, forty-seven, last seen at his workplace in Bell Park. His item was a silver watch with a broken clasp.

Jarrod Maloof, seventeen, last seen at the Santa Monica Pier. His item was a high-school sports jersey, slightly frayed at the hem but clean, smelling of laundry detergent. He was the most recent victim. Reading between the lines of the articles I'd found online, I gathered that Jarrod, who came from a middle-class family in Torrance, had run away from home several months before he disappeared, and his family knew he'd been living on the beach, but no one had seen him in three months.

As I took notes, my heart sank. Nothing obvious connected the victims to each other. Not age. Not race. Not occupation.

Ten disconnected lives.

Missing from a beach.

From a hike.

From a supermarket parking lot.

That's when Baby came into the kitchen holding a to-go cup of coffee. Something about her movements seemed jittery, overloaded with energy. She also had an ice pack secured to her hand with a dish towel.

"Are you okay?" I pointed at the ice pack.

"Lid wasn't on tight. Coffee got me."

"Is it bad?"

She shrugged.

"Well, you're injured, but at least you're alive!" I said as she dumped her purse on a chair next to me. "What happened? Did you drop your phone into a tar pit? Did it get stolen by coyotes? I'm so eager to hear what grave misfortune has prevented you from answering my texts and calls for hours."

"You didn't pass the vibe check." She shrugged.

"The *what*?"

"I'm just here to grab some things, then I'm heading out again." Baby dropped the ice pack and the towel in the sink and set her coffee on the kitchen counter. "We can talk about it later."

"No, we can't, and no, you're not."

"I'll be out all night. One of my besties is having an emotional crisis. I need to debrief with her."

She reached for her purse. I grabbed the strap.

"You're not going anywhere," I said.

"Rhonda, we have been over this, okay?" Baby glared at me. "You do *not* get to tell me what I can and cannot do."

I knew it was a losing battle, so I changed tactics.

"Listen, Baby, I need you on the Troy Hansen case. You're my business partner, and you've committed to this job. Troy is our client. Okay? He's the one in crisis."

"You can handle the Troy Hansen thing on your own for a while," Baby huffed. "He'll keep."

"No, he won't. I know the cops are all over Troy about Daisy, and they want to learn what she did right before she disappeared. We have an angle here that nobody else knows about yet. If we can start working through the missing people in this box, maybe we can find a link between them and the Hansens."

Baby was texting the whole time I talked. I balled up my fists to stop myself from smacking the phone out of her hands. When a minute had passed and she still hadn't looked up from her screen, I banged on the table.

"Baby! Are you listening to me? I need you to pull your weight and come down to Santa Monica Pier with me. We're going to see if there's anything we can find out about what happened to Jarrod Maloof."

"Who's Jarrod Maloof?"

"He's a missing teenager whose name was in the trophy box," I said. "The most recent case. He disappeared about three months ago."

"I don't get why you can't just do this yourself." Baby glared at me. "You insisted on being lead. Can't I call in sick?"

"No, you can't! Not when there might be a serial killer on the loose! Jesus!"

She sighed.

"If you can't bring yourself to actually care about finding a bunch of missing—maybe murdered—people," I said, "or about helping a potentially innocent man escape the bear trap that's about to close on him, maybe you'll care about this."

I took out my phone, opened my voicemail, and hit play on the last message. I put the phone on speaker. A man with a dark, low voice came on the line.

"Yo, I'm calling to leave a message for Rhonda and Barbara Bird of the Two Sisters Detective Agency," he said. "I just wanna say y'all are fucked up, try'na help Troy Hansen get away with killin' his wife. Y'all better drop that case or watch your backs, bitches, for real."

Baby was unfazed by the message. She dropped a hip and crossed her long, lean arms while I played more messages, all in a similar vein:

"Hi. I just saw on Facebook that you guys are helping Troy Hansen, Daisy Hansen's husband. If that's true, I want you to know how disgusted I am that— "

"...why anyone would want to stop the police from doing their goddamn jobs! You must be absolute psychopaths yourselves, and— "

"...need to wake up! Because Troy Hansen is a wife killer! If you don't know that already, you can follow my channel and— "

Baby waved at the phone. I put it down.

"How many messages are there?" she asked.

"Dozens? Hundreds? They keep coming in," I said.

As though to illustrate my point, my phone began buzzing on the table. Caller ID said **Unknown number.**

"We're already in too deep, Baby," I said. "Our agency is at stake here. This is our *thing*. This is our *partnership*. When we decided to work together we . . . we really came together as sisters, you and me. You know? And all of that's threatened now. If we don't solve this before the police do, we're going to look like idiots. Like we have no instincts. Like we can't tell a client from a killer. The agency could fold over this, okay? And if it folds, what the hell are you and I going to do?"

The words tumbled out of my mouth. I braced for an angry reaction but kept going.

"Look, Baby. We can't walk away from this now. Backing out would make us look like we're the kind of investigators who bow to public pressure. We're not. We're truth finders."

Baby sighed.

"The world is angry at us because we're on Team Troy," I said. "Let's show them that we made the right decision."

"I never agreed to be on Team Troy," Baby grumbled. But she sent a lightning-fast text, pocketed her phone, and grabbed her coffee.

"All right, sis," she said. "Quick, to the Mystery Machine. Before I change my mind."

CHAPTER 19

SANTA MONICA ROLLS WITH the sun, showing its seedier underbelly only when the big red ball dips below the horizon. Once the parking lots are empty of tourist rental cars, the pier lights up and the roller coaster rattles by, trailing screams.

Baby and I sat on the sand, watching the sunset and snacking on overpriced food from vendors near the pier. Dave Summerly texted and reluctantly confessed that the date had indeed been incorrectly entered into Troy Hansen's neighbor's Jettno security camera. A shiver of both vindication and curiosity ran up my spine. I texted back immediately and asked if he had footage of the *actual* evening that Daisy disappeared. Did it line up with Troy's account of when his wife disappeared?

He didn't respond.

"I don't know why you ghosted that guy," Baby said.

"I didn't ghost him."

"Yeah, you did. He was perfect for you and you blew it."

"Thanks for the advice, Dr. Love," I said.

"I'm just saying, if you had a man in your life, you'd be less up in my business."

The sand was clearing, the crowds evolving. The eyes were growing meaner, more driven. We watched our first group of homeless youths pass by, cardboard signs in hand, unrestrained mongrel dogs trotting at their feet. We got up and started canvassing for information about Jarrod Maloof, knowing that if Jarrod had been living out here on the beach, the night folks were more likely to recognize his picture on my phone than the folks who hung out here during the day. Baby and I stopped drifters, grifters, beggars, peddlers, and the occasional surfer who seemed comfortable enough with the terrain to be a local.

A theme emerged as we got closer to Venice Beach. Several people did recognize Jarrod and remembered the teenager as hopped up, paranoid, spouting conspiracy theories and accusations that some camp dwellers had been spying and colluding with the police. Jarrod might have been part of the Muscle Beach crew, we were told.

"But watch yourself," people said. "They're all crazies down there."

The Muscle Beach camp was a slab of concrete behind a row of souvenir shops. It was strung with tarps and makeshift lean-tos, overcrowded, overrun with scrappy dogs. As we neared it, I saw a tall man with a mop of curly black hair step back from the raggedy-looking youth he'd been talking to and start yelling. Other camp dwellers, windswept and emaciated, watched from the fringes.

"You've got two choices, okay?" the curly-haired man barked. "You give it to me, or I get the cops down here to arrest your ass!" Curly was obviously not part of the camp. His clean clothes and clear eyes told me that.

The teenager being yelled at was wearing a backpack and scratching at the sweat-stained collar of his hoodie, a defiant grin on his face.

"Man, you don't wanna play it like that," the teen said. "Fastest way to get us all to scatter is by bringing the law down on us. You'll be back to square one."

"What's going on here?" I asked as Baby and I approached.

"I'm looking for my nephew Jarrod." Curly didn't look at me. He was locked on the teen with the backpack, his jaw tight. "He was a part of this camp, and he's missing."

I glanced at Baby. Her eyes were electric.

"We're trying to find Jarrod too," I said. "I'm Rhonda Bird." I offered my hand to Curly.

"Oliver Maloof." The man finally turned his eyes to me, but only for a second. I could see the resemblance to Jarrod. I'd shown the photograph to dozens of people, and Jarrod Maloof's lopsided grin was now burned into the backs of my eyelids. "You part of the church group looking for Jarrod?"

"No."

"Must be the Facebook people, then," said the teen in the hoodie, laughing. His mullet was so greasy, it shone in the streetlight. He sneered at me. "Or are you with the Red Cross? Police volunteers? True-crime podcasters? Hell, you could be one of a hundred goddamn people kicking over rocks looking for Jarrod. It's just been one nosy asshole after another stopping by here. Nobody can get any sleep! But thanks so much for coordinating. Now I can tell all of you to fuck off at once."

"So where is he?" I asked. "You want people to stop parading through your camp? Help us out."

"I don't know!" The teen threw his hands up. "Nobody knows. He split. Probably hopped a train. There was a crew from further down toward the pier who were heading to Florida. Probably joined them."

"Too many *probably*s for my liking," Baby said. "Come on. Think hard."

"Nobody knows where he went," the kid repeated. "I told this loser already. All I got is the bag, and that's goin' to the highest bidder."

"What bag?"

"Jarrod's bag." The teen gave me a brown-toothed smile. "I found it this morning. All this time we been thinkin' Jarrod must have taken it with him wherever the hell he went. But I found it when the recycling pickers came through. Lucky me, huh?" He shuffled, making the backpack he was wearing flap against his shoulders. I felt my eyes widen; my fingers itched with the desire to reach out and grab the bag.

"Give it to me," Oliver Maloof snapped.

"You know my price."

"I'm not paying for something that belongs to my family!" Maloof snarled. "Jarrod might be hurt somewhere! He might be—"

"How much do you want for it?" Baby asked. "Rhonda, give me your wallet. I only have Apple Pay."

"Don't give him any money," Maloof ordered.

"Don't do it!" someone from the camp echoed. There was a rumble of excitement around us, some warning us off, some egging us on.

"Baby, wait." I put my hand on hers but kept my eyes on the backpack. I could see the weight of the contents inside it pulling on the straps, making shapes in the fabric. Precious answers.

"I don't see what the big deal is. The backpack is right there. Don't we want to find him? A little cash seems a minor sacrifice."

I reluctantly pulled out my wallet, but I hadn't even slid the bills all the way out before the kid with the bag snatched them from my fingers.

"Thanks, bitch!" He laughed. Then he twisted away, stuffed the notes into the pocket of his hoodie, and came out with a thin, dark object. The stabbing happened so fast, I didn't get a good look at the shank before the teen plunged it into Oliver Maloof's side.

CHAPTER 20

FIVE JABS, LIGHTNING FAST. A prison-style shanking. Maximum damage, minimal time. The kid was turning to run almost before the shank in his fist left Oliver Maloof's body the last time. I had blood on my shoes; the alley seemed to tilt beneath my feet as I realized what had happened. Maloof went down hard and fast, probably more out of shock than a reaction to the pain or the new holes in his rib cage. Baby tried to catch him. As red flowers blossomed on his shirt, I twisted and ran after the kid with the backpack.

It was the wrong move. I'm not out of shape, but Baby is the runner, long-legged and lithe, the natural athlete. I'm a weight lifter—I sacrifice cardio for bulk. Still, something in my brain had decided that between the two of us, she should be the one to care for the victim while I pursued the attacker. I would face the danger while she picked up the pieces.

My heart, my lungs, my joints, were all immediately on fire. I felt disastrously shaky, a machine performing a task it wasn't designed for, a big low Cadillac plowing uphill through rocky bush terrain, engine roaring. I tried to convince myself that legs that could squat-press four hundred and fifty pounds were good for something. I kept after the kid, slowly gaining on him. I didn't have speed, but I had power. Heads turned as I chased him down the alley and into the street. As he rounded a corner, he maintained his pace, hands flat and arms pumping, head down and leaning into the turn. I smashed into a parked car and bounced off it, making the whole vehicle rock and the alarm go off as I changed direction like a carnival bumper car.

The kid ran along a strip of restaurants, dragged a valet cart into my path. Fifty sets of keys jangled and fanned out on the concrete. I charged through the whole mess—the keys, the papers, the cart, everything—battering it all out of the way, my calves screaming, sweat pouring down my back. The row of restaurants became a bridge, then a palm-lined street, then a cramped path back down to the beach. We both hit the sand, my breath shunting out of me like hot exhaust, the backpack bouncing on the kid's back, mere yards beyond my grasp.

When I realized where he was heading, my heart lurched into my throat. The surfers gathered around a bonfire at the edge of the dunes looked like they were participating in some ancient ceremony; flames danced on the pockmarked sand amid haunting silhouettes. The kid glanced back at me, a smug grin on his face. I knew what he was thinking. There were two ways to get me off his tail: give me the bag or destroy it. He unhooked a strap as he ran, heading right for the big fire.

I gave it all I had, seeing the photo of Jarrod Maloof in my mind, that fresh-faced teen in the football jersey. Imagining his backpack, maybe the key to finding him, consumed by the flames up ahead.

A hundred feet. Fifty. Twenty. I put on a final burst of speed.

I crashed into the teen three feet short of the fire. Surfers scattered and shouted all around us as I rolled and pinned him to the sand. I raked the backpack off him, feeling like the bonfire heat was boiling the sweat on my face. I gripped Jarrod's backpack so tightly in my fist that my knuckles cracked. With my other hand, I knocked the shank away, then held on to the kid as if my life depended on it.

"Somebody . . . call . . . the . . . police," I said, gasping, to the surfers. Catching my breath seemed impossible. My lungs were squashed against the inside of my ribs, spasming with pain. "And someone . . . get . . . me . . . water."

Two male surfers grabbed the kicking, howling, struggling teenager who'd stabbed Oliver Maloof. A girl with long, blond beachy hair handed me a bottle of water. I took two sips, almost threw up on the sand, and promised myself that I would never, ever run again.

CHAPTER 21

I LIMPED BACK TO the Muscle Beach camp, lugging the backpack and favoring my strained tendons and angry joints. A sea of red and blue lights greeted me. Baby was talking animatedly to a trio of homeless men but came over when she saw me. I told her I'd handed the teen over to the cops who'd responded to the campfire scene.

"How's the uncle?"

"The EMTs seemed to think it wasn't that bad," Baby said. "The dude's stabbed people before, I'm guessing. Knew how to put him down without killing him. Got him in the belly fat. Missed the liver."

Together, we watched the street cops question camp dwellers about the incident. My sister's face was sharp and angular in the light, her eyes narrowed with thought. I felt a quiet rush of pride. One night, this kid was clobbering gunmen with a tire iron to save her own hide, and the next, she was front row for random stabbings on LA's mean streets. Almost any other sixteen-year-old would have been a weeping mess by now, but not Baby, which was undeniably cool.

Then I questioned the pride I felt, turned it over. It was our father who had hardened Baby like this. Made her strong, resilient, streetwise. But Earl had done that by completely obliterating healthy boundaries. He'd taken her along on stakeouts even when she was a little girl. Brought criminals into their house. Paid for her school lunches with shakedown money. Was my making Baby a partner in the PI agency just a continuation of all that? Shouldn't my job as her big sister and legal guardian be to stop the danger at our doorstep, not chase after it?

I didn't have time to pursue those thoughts. Baby broke out of her own reverie and grabbed the backpack from my shoulder.

"Let's do this thing," she said.

We walked away from the camp, sat on a low wall, and opened the backpack. I was braced for disappointment, figuring the weasel who had stabbed Oliver Maloof might have sold us a bag of bricks or trash. But the first thing my hand fell on was a torn wallet, inside of which was a driver's license belonging to Jarrod Maloof. A thump of adrenaline hit my system. I'd do a more thorough examination of all this when we got back home, but for now I took a preliminary glance through the bag's contents, the detritus of Jarrod's life. Baby pulled out a battered notebook bound with elastic bands as I picked through candy wrappers and sweat-stained clothes.

"Ugh." She pushed the back of her hand against her nose as I worked. "The smell is *foul*."

Another jolt hit me. Not as sharp as before; something half recognized, darker.

"What?" Baby sensed it.

"The clothes," I said. I lifted the nearest item, a pair of shorts. "They're all filthy. They reek of cigarette smoke. Body odor. Even the wallet stinks." I sniffed it, which awakened the nausea the run had given me.

Baby brushed cigarette ash from the notebook pages as she flipped through a mess of notes and sketches. The notebook was stuffed with random scraps of paper—parking tickets, takeout menus, concert flyers, and water-warped postcards—all of them doodled on. "Dude had no home," she pointed out. "Hard to score a shower out here. Laundry's a special occasion."

"Right," I said. "So where did that nice clean football jersey in the trophy box come from?"

We sat quietly. I thought about the jersey that had been rolled up tightly and tucked into the plastic zip-lock bag. It had been spotless, pristine. Had it been washed before it was placed in the bag? Preserving that memory of the missing youth without letting the street-life stink infect the rest of the collection? Was that the reason for the zip-lock bags? I was about to share this theory with Baby when she tapped my arm.

I looked over. Baby pointed to a sketch in the notebook that sprawled over two pages, a streetscape of the alley where we sat.

I saw the Muscle Beach camp's lean-tos and the souvenir shops they nestled behind. I saw a telephone pole with dark, deliberate lines reaching from it that seemed to depict wires sagging in the heat. A sharply etched figure of a repairman in a harness hung from the pole, working on the wires.

I looked down the alley and saw what seemed to be the pole from the drawing. Twenty feet up, a Public Utilities Commission box was bolted just beneath the crossbar, the shiny new steel gleaming in the red and blue lights.

CHAPTER 22

IT WAS MIDNIGHT BEFORE Baby walked back up the rickety stairs of Arthur's house. She'd waited until Rhonda had gone to her bedroom with the trophy box and the contents of Jarrod Maloof's backpack before she'd slipped out of her bedroom window and called an Uber. She was tempted to stay home, where it was familiar and safe. But she was trying to prove something to herself, to Rhonda, and to Arthur. She could and would survive outside the nest.

Baby knocked on the front door of the old house on Waterway Street, then tried the doorknob and was surprised to find it unlocked. "Hello?" she said, and Arthur called out that he was in the kitchen.

She had to stop for a moment in the near darkness of the

corridor when she saw him sitting there, hand on the side of a coffee cup—he reminded her so much of her father, it made her heart ache. Earl Bird was someone who'd charged around the world like a raging bull, chasing loan sharks, skewering bond-skippers, cornering fence men and thieves. But through her childhood, there'd been rare moments of stillness like this, when Baby would walk into the mansion on the beach to find the huge man waiting quietly for her. When Arthur turned at the sound of the floorboards creaking under her feet, she half expected him to smile at her and say, "Hey, li'l Baby," just like her father.

But Arthur said nothing. She slid into the chair across from him and let her bag slump to the floor under the table.

"Hell of an hour to be walkin' in," the old man said.

"Better get used to it."

"Uh-huh."

"All right, spill," Baby said. "Who's got it in for you, old man?"

Arthur tapped the cup. His wedding ring clinked on the porcelain. "It can't be as bad as that," he said finally.

"You know it is," Baby said. "That's why you wanted a big scary man to help you out. Because you *know* it's that bad."

"But they wouldn't kill me. That's ridiculous. That kind of stuff only happens in movies."

"Who are we talking about?"

Arthur glanced out the window at his side yard and the fenced houses beyond. "Almost every house around here has been bought by a company called Enorme," he said.

"Enorme?" Baby said. "Who are they?"

"Some megacorporation." He shrugged. "You know the type. All the executives have their own yachts."

"But what do they do?"

Arthur shrugged again. Baby took out her phone and googled, saw all that she needed to see. Sprawling tech communities. Cinematic aerial shots of factories the size of football fields. Glossy investor videos with beautiful happy people in suits.

"They own pretty much the whole block," Arthur said. "That's why those other houses are fenced off and boarded up. They're prepped for demolition. Enorme's gonna put one of their factories here. Or a skyscraper or...I don't know. I didn't read the paperwork."

"But they don't own your place?"

"No."

"You're the last holdout." Baby sat back in her chair, felt a flower of dread blossom in her chest. "They're heavying you to sell."

"They're heavying me." Arthur nodded and put his hands on the table with his withered palms up. "But it's like I told my wife, Carol: When you got a bully after you, you just hunker down and carry on and wait for them to get bored."

"Or," Baby said, "you fight back."

"I'm too old to fight back."

"These Enorme people—did they throw money at you?"

"Sure."

"Why didn't you take it?"

"What am I gonna do with the money?" Arthur looked around. "Everything I want is right here. Except Carol. And money can't bring her back."

"How did Carol die?"

"Heart attack," Arthur said. "Start of the year. It happened in the kitchen."

Baby stiffened. The old man flapped an impatient hand.

"I know what you're thinking." He sighed. "But you're wrong. She didn't get shocked by anything. She was sitting right where you're sitting now, at the table. I saw it. She grabbed her arm suddenly and fell on the floor. Didn't say a word. She had diabetes. And heart problems."

"She did?"

"Yeah," he said. "She must have forgotten to take her heart medicine or . . . " He trailed off.

Baby raised an eyebrow. "Did she tend to forget things like that? Was she a forgetful person?"

Arthur didn't answer.

"So you called 911, right?" Baby said.

"Yeah. Of course. Immediately."

"And what happened?"

"Carol was eighty, okay?" Arthur's hands were shaking. He tried to disguise it, but Baby could see the tremors. "They didn't do an autopsy. And the EMTs, they took all her medications with them. So if there's something hinky about all this, like you're trying to suggest . . . "

He paused, held on. Baby gave him a moment.

"I can't face that." Arthur stared at his hands. "If they did something that killed her... if they... I don't know if I could face something like that."

They sat in silence together, the night outside absurdly quiet.

"I could," Baby said. "I could do it for you."

Again, the silence. Baby was used to that, to loaded male silence. It didn't dissuade her.

"Arthur," she said. "I want to help you. If these Enorme fuckers have been messing with you, then I want to catch them and wipe the floor with them. But you're not safe here."

"Well, I ain't leaving."

"I knew you'd say that."

"So what do we do? You got any ideas, whiz kid?" Arthur asked.

Baby grabbed her bag and plopped it on the table, making the coffee in Arthur's cup ripple. She unzipped it, and some of the equipment she'd brought from home tumbled out.

"Of course I do," she said.

CHAPTER 23

AFTER WE'D GOTTEN HOME from Santa Monica, Baby had retreated to her room, and I went to mine. I strapped an ice pack to my knee and looked over the bizarre trophy collection again. I had Jarrod Maloof's jersey and the newspaper cutting about the missing troubled youth on the bed.

As I was lifting the grimy backpack, I heard three muffled pops come from the front of the house. I turned. Three more. I hesitated, then went downstairs, noting the light in Baby's room was off. It was well after midnight, and I was glad that she was getting some sleep. I had a feeling the next few days were going to wear us down in a way that hunting for missing pets and photographing adulterers in motel parking lots had not.

I opened the front door, stepped out—and narrowly missed being hit with an egg that smashed on the wall beside me. By the time I realized what had happened, I saw the egg-hurlers already legging it up the hill away from the beach, toward the Pacific Coast Highway.

"Jesus." I sighed. I might have chalked this up to random kids pranking random homeowners if I hadn't spotted a drone hovering above the adjacent house. That gave the game away. Our home was being targeted by web sleuths who were angry at me for being on Team Troy. I slumped with exhaustion and cynicism. These kids were incensed by true crime but reacted to it by filming themselves vandalizing someone's house like they were trick-or-treaters.

I drew myself up. I refused to let the case and the weight of everything resting on my shoulders get me down.

I changed into my workout gear, went to the roof, and stepped out into the dim blue light coming off the enormous pool. Whatever else I could say about my dad, his house was a winner. The glittering city of Manhattan Beach sprawled around me, the moonlit sea in front.

Leg day could wait. I loaded the barbell for a gentle chest-press set, a hundred pounds. I sat on my weight bench, drew another huge breath, tried to clear my mind. I lay down and wrapped my gloved hands around the barbell resting in its hooks two feet above my face. I told myself I would finish my night with a win of some sort if it killed me.

Then I felt the hard nudge of a gun barrel against the top of my skull.

CHAPTER 24

PANIC WALLOPED INTO ME, raw and wild and electric, an explosion of pain in my sternum.

There was a man standing over me in the dark, in my own home, aiming a gun at my head. I had no time to wonder whether he'd been waiting for me there on the roof or if he'd snuck in when I responded to the eggers at the front door.

I gripped the barbell and looked at the figure, upside down to me, his extended hand gripping the pistol butt. I could tell it was a man in a dark hoodie, but all I could see of his face were his eyes.

I must have jerked involuntarily.

"Freeze," he barked.

Every muscle in my body clenched. My brain was

screaming with worry about Baby, asleep in her bedroom below. Terrifying possibilities coursed through my mind—that this man had already murdered my younger sister or that she would come through the rooftop door any minute and he'd kill her before my eyes.

I gripped the barbell as the man held the gun against my head.

I waited for a sickening bang. The end.

It didn't come. He reached into the pouch pocket of his hoodie and came out with a cable tie. I watched, bug-eyed, as he skillfully slipped the tie one-handed over both the barbell and my right wrist and yanked it tight. He found another tie and did the same on the other side, zipping the plastic tight against the back of my bare wrist, just below my weight glove.

"Listen good, lady," the man said. Having secured me, he seemed to relax slightly. He slid the gun up so that it was pressed against my forehead. "You gonna drop the case. Okay?"

"Wh-what?" I stammered. Something was rising in me, overcoming my terror the way a bank of dark clouds eats the night sky. A billowing plume of anger grew so big, it seemed to bulge inside my ears, stifling all sound. "What did you say?"

"You gonna *drop... that... case,*" the man said. "Make whatever calls you gotta make. Do whatever it is you gotta do. But you gonna *drop it* tonight or I'll be back here."

I breathed, fury bending my bones outward to make space for itself. The man stepped around and stood between my knees at the end of the bench, a hooded silhouette against the night sky.

"You back away for good or I'll be comin' around again with my li'l ties." He nodded at the cable tie on my right wrist. "I can have a lot of fun with those. You saw how fast I put 'em on. I got plenty of tricks where that came from. I'll have you and that li'l teenage beauty all trussed up before you—"

He didn't get to finish. The balloon of rage burst in my chest. I heaved the barbell up off the hooks holding it, brought it to my chest, then used all my strength to simultaneously jump up and launch it at him. My tied hands carried me, and I smashed the bar horizontally into his chest, knocking him backward. We tumbled together to the ground, landed with the barbell pinning him, me straddling his chest. The gun skidded across the tiles and into the pool. I braced my thighs, lifted the barbell, twisted it vertically—and drove it down onto his chest.

The huge surface of the stacked weights attached to the end smashed into his torso. I heard a colossal crunch, felt a wet expulsion of air. I stood and as he rolled away, I dropped the weights and put a foot against the bar. I braced myself, then snapped the cable ties off my wrists like they were dental floss.

My attacker was crawling for the stairs, coughing blood. I marched over, picked him up by the ass of his jeans and the collar of the hoodie, and threw him through the open door down the stairs. He landed in a crumpled heap on the landing like a human bag of laundry, leaving blood smears on the walls.

CHAPTER 25

BABY SLAMMED THE DRILL into the toolbox on top of the ladder, thumped the lid closed, and examined her work. The camera she'd just installed on the pillar of Arthur's porch was big and encased in white, a glistening black eye with a view of the entire front of the property. It was a showy piece, the kind of camera designed to be seen, the kind hooked up in stores to discourage shoplifters. Baby and Rhonda had used them a couple of times in the exact type of operation that Baby was about to pull.

The night was quiet all around her. The frogs and crickets in the long grass must have been scared off by the sound of the drilling. Arthur had gone to bed. She got down, folded the ladder, leaned it against the porch, and carried the toolbox to the back of the property. She checked the Ubers in the area. Six minutes for a pickup. When she got home, she'd sneak back into the mansion, try to catch a few hours of shut-eye.

Baby rounded the corner of the back porch and saw a figure in the moonlight just off the steps, a big man with close-cropped hair. He stood poised, waiting, listening. Baby guessed he'd been planning to enter the house until he'd heard her drilling up front.

Baby thought about yelling. She didn't. Instead, she stepped around the side of the house, intentionally dropped the toolbox, and cursed loudly. Then she crept forward and, as expected, saw the man had spooked and bolted for the back fence.

She silently followed, the tall grass brushing at her hips, prickles catching in her jeans. She vaulted the fence a few seconds after he did, then trailed him through the overgrown garden of the house behind Arthur's. The man turned right and headed toward a strip of apartment buildings. She was ten yards behind.

As the man climbed into a small gray Honda, Baby stopped by a tree, slipped her phone from her pocket, and prepared to take a picture of the license plate. She growled in frustration as a call from Rhonda flashed onto the screen, making the camera vanish. By the time she'd declined the call and tried to snap a picture of the trespasser's license plate, it was almost too late, and the photo was blurry.

"Where are you?" Rhonda demanded when Baby answered her second call.

"In my bedroom?"

"That's funny." Her older sister's voice was strained. " 'Cause I just killed a guy right outside your door. You didn't hear anything? You didn't think to come out and help?"

Baby's mouth opened and shut, the words caught in her throat. The hairs on the back of her neck stood up when she heard sirens wail on the other end of the line. "You *what*?"

"Get your ass home, Baby," Rhonda snarled. "Right now."

CHAPTER 26

A PLAINCLOTHES COP LEANED against the ambulance beside me and peeled the lid off his coffee, which was still steaming. He was maybe pushing forty, fit, with a short-cut beard. I hadn't even let him introduce himself before I launched into my statement from where I sat on the tailgate of the ambulance. The police officers stomping in and out through my front door eyed the eggshells on the steps suspiciously as they passed.

"I feared for my life, and I acted with the force I believed was required to defend myself," I concluded my third run-through of the story. I was trying not to look at my hands, at the cuts the cable ties had left on my wrists. The comedown from the adrenaline and rage was giving me the twitches. "If you want more detail about what happened, it'll have to be in front of an attorney in a formal setting."

"You're a lawyer, huh?" The detective sipped his coffee.

"How'd you guess?"

"I know who you are," he said. "I'm not here because of the home-invasion homicide. I was actually on my way here anyway, even at this late hour. Hence the coffee." He lifted the cup. "A call like that? A woman beat a guy to death in her home gym with a barbell? Hell, you know I hit the gas. I'd just picked up this coffee when I heard, otherwise I'd have skipped the caffeine injection."

I stared at him. The confusion must have been plain on my face.

"I'm Detective William Brogan." He shook my hand warmly. "I'm heading up the Troy Hansen investigation."

"Oh, Jesus." I held my head.

"You said the intruder told you to drop the case," Brogan said. "Did he mean the Troy Hansen case? Is that what this was about?" Brogan gestured to the front door of my house where the EMTs were wheeling the dead intruder out on a gurney. I wondered how many of my neighbors had been awakened by the commotion and were now watching from their windows.

"I don't know what this was about," I said. "I told you three times—I don't know the guy. Never seen him before."

"What's your best guess?"

I tried to organize my thoughts. Brogan gave me time, waiting, leaning, watching.

"The Troy Hansen case has captured everybody's attention."

I shrugged. "You must know better than anyone that the internet crazies are out in force."

"They are," he conceded. "But it's a big leap from throwing eggs at your door to sticking a gun in your face."

"My sister and I—we're still a pretty new outfit," I said. "We haven't dealt with a case like this yet. The rest of our cases have been pretty mild."

I fell into my own thoughts, pondering my hesitation to tell Brogan the truth. In fact, there were a few active—albeit slow-burner—cases on our books at the 2 Sisters Detective Agency that, at a stretch, might have inspired someone to threaten me and Baby. Cheaters. Frauds. Bail jumpers with violent pasts.

But I couldn't ignore the sense that whoever the man I'd killed was, he was likely to be connected to Troy, to Daisy, to the ten missing people and the box with their things that Troy had found under his home.

I hesitated to reveal any of my thoughts to Brogan. I didn't know him, didn't trust him.

"Were you able to ID the guy?" I asked as the second ambulance, the one carrying my victim to the morgue, headed out.

"His name is Martin Rosco," Brogan said, his eyes wandering over my face. "I've seen his work before. Career crook. Thug for hire. Got a couple of priors for sexual assaults. The cable ties—guy loves them. Or *did* love them." He shrugged, seemed to see something in my expression. "Don't break your heart over him, Ms. Bird. You said it yourself—you were acting in self-defense."

"I thought my kid sister was...in the other room." I swallowed. "If I'd known that she wasn't here, that it was just me, maybe I—"

"But you didn't know," Brogan said.

I gathered myself. It wasn't easy.

"Where is she?" he asked. "Your sister."

"She snuck out," I said. I tried not to let my fury infect my words. I'd save it for when Baby arrived back home. "I called. She'll be here any minute."

"Maybe you should get out of town for a while," Brogan said. "The two of you. We'll be laying charges on Troy in the next couple of days for his wife's murder. After that, this will die down."

"So you were on your way here to try to convince me to drop Troy as a client?" I asked. "Did you see what happened to the last guy who tried to get me to drop a case?"

He gave a quarter of a smile.

"It's a free country," I said. "I have every right to look into this case, to help the truth come out, whether for my own interest or for financial gain."

"And it's not that I don't appreciate it, Ms. Bird." Brogan put a palm up, reasonable. "Dave Summerly told me about the security camera mix-up. That was a good save."

I smirked. "Never underestimate people's ability to mishandle technology."

"Well, it changes our timeline," Brogan said. "But you've probably worked out already that it's not a silver bullet. Troy still could have come home right after Daisy, got into an argument with her, and killed her. He could have put her body in the back of his truck and driven her to a dumping site that night. He might have just driven the *other way* out of his driveway and down the street, missed the camera. So you can stop helping now."

"What if it's not that simple?" I asked, trying to match the patronizing tone of his last few words. "What if, for once, it's not the goddamn husband?"

"Tell me why it's not."

I looked up at the third floor. My bedroom. I thought about the box of trophies still spread out on my bed. About Jarrod Maloof and nine other missing persons. I hoped the crime scene techs were leaving my room alone. "I just think there's more to this case than meets the eye."

Brogan looked smug. "Sure is."

"What?"

"Did Troy Hansen tell you about his big win?"

I almost said *What big win?* but stopped myself, not wanting Brogan to know my client wasn't being wholly forthcoming with me. But it was too late. My face gave me away. Brogan smiled and drained his coffee.

"You know what, Ms. Bird? You've been so helpful with all this so far, and after a night like tonight"—he nodded at the ambulance—"you seem like you could use a break. So I'm just going to cut out the middleman."

He took a folded sheet of paper out of his jacket pocket and handed it to me. Then he saluted me with his empty coffee cup and wandered off. I unfolded the paper, saw it was part of a bank statement from Troy and Daisy Hansen's joint account.

There had been a direct deposit from an unidentified account about two months before Daisy went missing.

A deposit of $250,000.

CHAPTER 27

IT WAS THREE A.M. when I finally heard Baby's footsteps on the stairs. I was on my knees outside her bedroom with a cloth and a bucket of soapy water washing blood off the wall. She hovered uncertainly behind me for a few seconds, then put a 7-Eleven iced coffee with a huge whipped-cream topper down by my side. I smelled caramel sauce through the metallic stink of blood. I didn't look at her or the coffee-flavored olive branch.

"Thanks for rushing home," I said sourly. "Traffic must have been awful. Culver City's usually only a half-hour trip in the middle of the night."

"Culver City?"

I stopped scrubbing, tossed the cloth into the bucket.

Baby was looking at the cuts the cable ties had left on my wrists.

"Waterway Street in Culver City," I said. I stood and met my sister's gaze, trying to contain my anger. "Looks like your bestie has really slipped down in the world, judging from the Google Maps Street View. Are you even going to ask me what the hell happened here? Whether I'm okay?"

"You're tracking me," Baby said. The tendons in her neck stood out, her anger rising too. "Just like we tagged Troy Hansen. You've been tracking me, like I'm some...some *mark*?"

"In case you haven't noticed, Baby, we are eyeballs-deep in a case involving a potential serial killer." I was teetering on the edge. "Eleven people might be dead. It could've been either one of us instead of Oliver Maloof stabbed earlier, and someone just broke into our home and threatened to murder me. And you're lying about where you are and what you're doing in the middle of the night. Of course I'm fucking tracking you!"

Her mouth quivered, bewilderment fighting outrage.

"You almost got us shot by *pet-nappers*," I continued. "So, yeah. When I saw how big and how dangerous the Troy Hansen case was going to be, I put a tracker in your purse. I did that because you're unpredictable and you're defiant and you're my responsibility. And I'm glad I did it! I only wish I'd kept a closer eye on the signal. If I had checked it earlier, when you said you were going to bed, I might not have killed a man in our house!"

"Stop." She put a hand up. "Just stop. This is not my fault."

"I thought he was going to murder you! He knew who you were, what you looked like! He'd been watching us! He got in here, and— "

"And you took care of it," Baby said. "Look, the dude came in here tryin' to fuck around and found out what happens when you mess with us. You showed him."

I couldn't speak. Baby seemed to have gotten hold of her emotions, and I was surprised and envious of her for it. I was standing in front of a woman who had collected herself completely, and it made me feel like the disheveled, tired, unpredictable one in the relationship.

"What happened tonight was not your fault," Baby said in a calm and convincing voice. "And it wasn't mine either."

She picked up the coffee and held it out. I took it.

"So here's what's going to happen," she said. "I'm gonna get Jarrod Maloof's diary and look through it for any solid ties to Troy Hansen or anyone else. And I'm also going to check out Maria Sanchez's online world. She's the one who went missing just before Jarrod, right?"

"Right," I said stiffly.

"You're going to get some sleep," she said. "And when you wake up, you're going to figure out what to do."

I stared at my coffee. The cream was melting into a foamy soup between the ice cubes.

"I want to know why you were in Culver City," I pushed.

"That's nice." She patted my shoulder. "But you're not getting that information. You're not even getting an apology.

Me sneaking around isn't any worse than you being a purse-bugging super-creep."

"I'm— "

"You're not my mama, Rhonda." Baby put a hand up again. "I got all the way to the day I met you without needing a mother. I sure as hell don't need one now."

"But I'm your legal guardian. You're only sixteen, Baby. You need *someone,*" I pleaded. "And I'm all you've got."

"And I'm all *you've* got," she said. She poked me in the chest. It hurt. Not only because I was bruised and exhausted from what had happened but because she was right. I'd cut ties with everyone from my life in Colorado to be with her, and the closest I'd gotten to expanding my social circle since I'd moved to LA was a collection of contacts in the private-investigation world. And Dave Summerly. I had a sudden strong impulse to text him.

"Lay off me," Baby warned. "Or I'll be gone faster than you can snap your fingers. Got it?"

She snapped her fingers in front of my nose. I nodded reluctantly. It was all I could do. She turned me by the shoulder and pushed me toward my bedroom.

"Get some sleep," she said. "And try not to bludgeon anyone to death on your way to bed."

CHAPTER 28

AFTER A FEW HOURS of sleep, I awoke with a plan to meet with Troy Hansen and find out about the money in his bank account before he had a chance to cook up some bullshit story about it. He didn't yet know that I knew. I had the element of surprise in my pocket.

Speaking of surprises, when I arrived at the café in Burbank where Troy Hansen had told me to meet him, I saw Dave Summerly outside. It was as if thoughts about my ex had summoned him. He was leaning against the café wall, his phone pressed to his ear, a notebook in his hand.

Presumably Troy Hansen was already inside the café, tucked in among the prettily dressed diners. Burbank on a weekday morning: TV meetings and tourists. I parked the

Impala and tried to decide if courtesy called for a person to stop and chitchat with her ex-boyfriend or if it was acceptable to go right in to consult with the suspect said ex was shadowing.

While I was debating, Summerly saw me, ended his call, and walked over.

"You okay?" he asked as I exited the car. "Brogan told me about last night."

I shrugged. "I'll survive."

"What about Baby?"

"She wasn't there."

"Brogan also said he gave you the tip about Troy and Daisy's windfall," Dave said.

"He seems like an okay guy, Brogan," I said, not willing to admit that I hadn't known about Troy's money.

"He is." Summerly nodded. "It's good to have a boss who lets you run your own program. He's a country boy from up north." He seemed like he was considering something. Then he came closer to me, looking conspiratorial, and I smelled his aftershave. Familiar. Stirring. I kept my eyes on my feet. "I'm going to throw you a bone, Rhonda. I've got back-end data from Daisy's socials. You said you wanted it. I'll email you the files so you can take a look."

"Why?"

"Oh, I don't know. Because you had a hard night last night?" He shrugged. "Because you're going to have a worse time today? Because I care about you and I think you deserve the full picture? Troy Hansen's a killer, Rhonda, and being tangled up with him is dangerous for you and the kid. I really think you should ditch this case."

I thought about the man I'd killed the night before.

Drop. That. Case.

"I don't need your pity, Dave." I shifted away, cheeks burning at my own hypocrisy. "I got this."

He backed off.

But before he could turn away, I asked, "Why am I going to have a worse time today than last night? Last night was pretty bad."

Something twisted on his face. "You haven't seen the video?"

"What video?" I asked. Summerly thought for a moment, then looked in the café window.

"Like you said"—he shrugged and opened the door for me—"you got this."

I found Troy Hansen hunched over at a corner table, a dark hoodie pulled up, sweating over the menu. When I sat in front of him, I realized he wasn't reading the menu at all, just staring at it fixedly, his eyes blank.

"You know, don't you," he muttered.

"Yeah." I gave a humorless laugh. "I know. I know about the deposit, at least. A quarter of a million dollars, Troy? Two months ago? When were you going to drop that little bombshell on me? That's motive right there. Once that information gets out, the internet is going to have a field day with it. Wherever Nancy Grace is, she'll be doing backflips."

Troy looked startled. He lifted his head, the corners of his mouth turned down hard. I felt all the air leave my lungs.

"There's more, isn't there," I said. "What's this I hear about a video?"

"You're gonna need to try and stay calm," Troy said. "Take out your phone and google me."

I did as I was told, my finger beading sweat on my phone screen.

CHAPTER 29

IN THE VIDEO, Troy Hansen stands in a drugstore. He's wearing the same hoodie, pulled up, but it's easy to know it's him from his stooped posture. He's in the beauty-products section, a basket on his arm, staring at bottles. From somewhere else, I hear the soft clatter of cardboard on the linoleum. The camera dips, comes back up. Troy is suddenly holding a box of condoms. He hands it to the person behind the camera.

"Whoops. Thanks." A woman's voice.

"No problem." Troy gives an awkward smile. He tries to go back to his shopping. She doesn't let him.

"Gotta stock up." She shakes the box. He looks. "You never know when there's gonna be another pandemic."

Troy laughs his weird, tittering laugh. "Essential items only."

"Right. Right." She shows the camera the box of condoms. "You, uh, you go through a lot of these?"

"Me?" Troy's smile twitches. "No. I don't tend to."

"Oh. So you don't use 'em at all?"

Troy grins down at his basket, eyes mischievous. "Well. Not *that* size, anyway."

I fished around on the internet on my phone at the café table while Troy squirmed in his seat. It didn't take me long to find out that the condom video was in the process of going viral. The original poster's follower list on TikTok was spinning like the reels on a slot machine. Stills of Troy standing in the grocery-store aisle smiling and holding a box of condoms were trending on every news chart in the country. The video had been uploaded barely thirty minutes ago.

"When was this video taken?"

"About an hour ago."

"Jesus, Troy," I said.

"I was just buying shampoo!" He gave a dark growl. It was the first genuine, complex emotion I'd seen him exhibit. "It was morning. I thought the stores would be empty."

"So you thought you'd go out and get some scalp cleanser and flirt with some random woman?" I asked. "Are you nuts?"

"I wasn't flirting!"

"It looks like you were flirting," I said. "She *made it* look like you were flirting. How did you not see it?" I slapped the table. "A woman recording a video saunters up to you in public and accidentally drops a box of rubbers at your feet, and you don't clock that as a setup?"

"I wasn't thinking!" Troy pleaded. "She wasn't holding the phone like a camera. She had it tucked in her front pocket. And it wasn't flirting, it was…it was *question* and *response*. She said, 'Do you use these?' I said, 'No,' and then it was like—"

"The punch line was right there," I said. "You couldn't help yourself."

"Yes! Exactly!"

"You're either an idiot or a sociopath, Troy," I said. "I'm trying to figure out which. Your wife has been missing for a week."

"Maybe I'm both." Troy clawed his scalp. "But I'm not a killer."

We sat in silence.

"Rhonda, I said something stupid. Really stupid. But this video…this isn't me. I don't go around bragging about my… my penis size to random women. Something came over me."

"It doesn't matter, Troy," I said. "It doesn't matter if you really were flirting or if you went on autopilot or you panicked or you were tired or…whatever, Troy. It doesn't matter what you were actually doing. I'll repeat what I just said: It. Looks. Like. You. Were. Flirting."

"Oh, Jesus. Jesus." Troy hung his head.

"Let's get on to the other thing." I stared at the top of

Troy's head. "A quarter of a million dollars was deposited in your and Daisy's bank account two months ago. Where did it come from, and why didn't you tell me about it?"

The waitress came over, asked if I wanted coffee, returned with a mug. Once she left, Troy lifted his head and looked at me. "We won the lottery," he said. "Daisy buys a lottery ticket every week. She's done it since college. You know what Daisy's like, right? You've been looking into her life. You know Daisy's an eternal optimist."

"Why didn't you tell me about it?" I repeated.

"Because it's motive. Like you said." He squirmed in his seat. "I wanted you to help me."

"When people find out about this," I said, "they're going to see a sociopath who won the lottery and began dreaming of a new life. A life without his spouse."

"They're going to find out about the box too." He wrung his hands, looking at the windows at the front of the café. I followed his gaze and saw Dave Summerly and two plainclothes cops out there. "The police are gonna have to arrest me soon or people will riot."

"Troy." I took a deep breath, then put my lawyer voice on, prepared for a hard sell. "Maybe you getting put away just for a little while is not a completely bad thing."

He turned to me, his pupils huge.

"Out here, you're damaging your reputation minute by minute, day by day," I said. "Even when you're not bragging about your dick size on camera—"

"I didn't—"

"—any and all footage of you looks terrible. You stand awkwardly. You walk awkwardly. It's not fair, but people interpret that stuff and see what they want to see. They see guilt. None of this is going to help you if you end up going to trial. At least if you're in the county jail, you'll be away from the public eye."

"I can't go to prison," Troy said. "I won't."

"Listen, county is not—"

He shot up from his seat, knocking the table with his thighs and making my coffee slosh over the rim of my cup.

"I feel sick," he said. He certainly looked it. His lips were white as paper and his left eye was twitching. "I'll be right back."

Troy headed to the café's restroom. I watched Summerly's wide back leaning against the front of the café and thought about county jail, about how someone as weird as Troy Hansen would fare there. A weird vibe could be useful in prison. If Troy kept his mouth shut, he might be avoided, an unknown quantity in the midst of more obvious prey. Because there would always be prey. The prison system was jammed full of the vulnerable, the young, and the naive. I mopped up my spilled coffee, mentally rehearsing what I would tell Troy to prepare him for his first-ever incarceration, when his words suddenly echoed in my ears as clearly as if they were bouncing off a canyon wall.

I can't go to prison.

I won't.

I hurried to the restroom at the rear of the café and found

what I'd thought I'd find—a locked door and a horrific silence in response to my frantic knocking.

I turned and saw the back door of the café just past the restroom. I went out the door, glanced back up at the bathroom window, saw it pushed all the way up on its rusty hinges.

I eased back into the café as calmly as I could and called Baby.

"We have a problem," I said. "Troy just did the worst possible thing an innocent man can do."

"What? What did he do?"

"He ran."

CHAPTER 30

BABY MET ME IN the parking lot of a strip mall in Toluca Lake. I pulled in just long enough for her to jump out of her Uber and into my car. I'd been circling the blocks, spiraling wider and wider, looking for Troy. He'd ditched his truck and, with it, our tracker and the police bugs on the vehicle.

"Did Troy get himself another burner phone?" Baby asked by way of greeting.

"He must have," I said. I was sweating; my heart was hammering. I forced myself not to drive erratically, but my foot was heavy on the accelerator. "The burner I gave him wasn't a smartphone, but Troy knew about the footage of himself in the supermarket going viral. He must have gotten a new phone."

"If that's true," Baby said, "why didn't he tell you?"

"Maybe he's been thinking of running since day one."

"Stupid." Baby's jaw clenched. "You never run. Everybody knows that. This is going to look terrible."

"It won't look like anything. We're going to find Troy before anyone realizes he's gone."

Baby was texting like crazy.

"You're supposed to be looking out the windows."

"I'm texting Jamie," she said. "If Troy bought a burner, maybe we can track it somehow."

"Hell of a long shot."

"You got a better idea?"

I didn't. We drove and drove, our heads swiveling. We hit traffic, and it was all I could do not to scream and beat on the steering wheel.

At one point I pulled over so Baby could run across the street to check out someone who looked like Troy at a bus stop crowded with people. An incoming call from Dave Summerly flashed on my phone.

"He slipped us?" Summerly barked.

"Look, he didn't slip you," I lied. "The stress is getting to my client. You and your team hanging around like vultures waiting for an injured rabbit to die isn't helping his mental state."

"I'm not trying to help Troy, Rhonda," Summerly said slowly. "I'm *trying* to breathe down his neck so Troy will do something that leads us to his wife's body."

"He needs a few hours to himself, that's all."

"Rhonda, I—"

"Sorry, Dave."

I hung up as Baby got back in the car. She shook her head. The bus stop had been a bust.

"Tell me what you found in Jarrod Maloof's diary," I said, my tires screeching as I pulled out. "I need something to get my mind off this wild-goose chase we're on."

"I didn't have a lot of time." Baby was scrolling through her phone. "And I didn't find anything helpful. Jarrod apparently thinks Uncle Oliver is working for the CIA and that he recruited his parents for some kind of seditious scheme. There's a lot of stuff about the president. It's all completely cuckoo."

"No mention of Troy specifically?"

"Nope. The only thing that might be related is an undated entry about someone coming and fixing the phone wires near the Muscle Beach camp and the sketch of the man up the pole." She sat back and sighed. "It could be Troy. I mean, that's what Troy does, right? But who knows. Jarrod Maloof is such a conspiracy nut, he probably thought it was government spies or the illuminati or whoever the fuck, trying to listen in to the camp's business."

"What about Maria Sanchez? You said you'd look at her too."

"Totally different. Maria's online life was dedicated to her makeup and hair tutorials," Baby said. "She was trying to grow a following online." She sniffed. "I had, like, a hundred times more followers when I was doing fashion influencing full-time, but she's not bad."

Baby showed me a screenshot of Maria Sanchez. The girl was posed in a gold-filtered shot, caught in the process of dividing her long, luscious hair into sections, presumably so that she could style it. Spread out before her on a white table were the tools of her trade.

"There's the hairbrush from the box." I pointed at the screen. "The one with the rabbit."

"Right," Baby said. "You can see her using it in a couple of her videos."

Traffic began rolling again. "Here's what I don't get, Rhonda. The only thing Maria Sanchez and Jarrod Maloof have in common is that they're both teenagers. She's not crazy. She's, like, a beautiful, put-together, ambitious young person. He's a messed-up homeless kid with zero grip on reality. They come from completely different parts of LA. She never mentions him on her socials. He never mentions her in the diary. Where's the link?"

"Maria was last seen entering Franklin Canyon Park. Was she a big hiker?"

"Sort of," Baby said, her attention caught by a guy in a black hoodie waiting at a taxi stand. She took a good hard look, then turned away. "She went hiking, but she didn't like it. She wasn't fit. She complained on her channel about how hard it was. Grueling. I feel like it was something she did just for the likes and follows."

This conversation wasn't bringing down my stress levels.

"Okay," I said, changing tacks. "You're Troy Hansen, accused murderer. You've decided to run. Where do you go?"

"Mexico." Baby was texting. "We're, like, two hours from the border. He's seen it in the movies. If you're a middle-class white boy with no priors fleeing the law, you go to Mexico."

"This isn't a movie. As far as we know, all Troy has on him is his wallet and maybe a phone. He can't use his credit cards without being tracked. Even if Mexico is the plan eventually, it isn't the plan today. Today he needs shelter. He needs help. He needs . . . " I trailed off, thinking. Troy's words from the other day floated back to me.

I have one buddy, a guy from work.

"I know where he's going." I swung the wheel.

CHAPTER 31

BABY AND I SAT in the Chevy and watched the wire-fenced parking lot of the Public Utilities Commission hub just north of Skid Row in downtown Los Angeles. Of the twenty-seven vehicles in the lot, sixteen were regular cars and eleven were pickups, vans, or trucks. Of those eleven, only one was rigged with a foldout ladder and a huge spool of electrical wire. We figured that one belonged to George, Troy Hansen's work buddy.

A guy left the building and crossed the parking lot, and as soon as I laid eyes on him, I knew it was George—I recognized the big, bearded Black guy from the photo in Troy's living room. He had Troy Hansen's same uncomfortable, stooped walk and downcast eyes, plus weirdly delicate hands that looked silky soft even from a distance. He and Troy were kindred spirits. I watched him get in the truck with the ladder, and Baby snorted in the seat beside me.

"That's him," she said. "Dude moves like a kicked dog."

I started the car and followed the pickup at a good distance. The bearded guy was talking on the phone the whole time, driving edgy and distracted, not noticing when the light turned green, not remembering to signal. He pulled into a mall parking lot, and I had to shunt the Chevy into an unofficial space against a wall so we could get out and keep up with him.

He walked into a Walmart. Baby and I followed the guy into the store full of visual clutter—shelf stackers wearing blue vests, heavy with lanyards; bright lights; hundreds of bikes on racks; a big inflatable monkey nodding over the toy section. We stood near the women's clothing section and watched George rake T-shirts and pants off the stands in the men's section.

"Clothes for Troy," Baby said.

We followed George to the sporting goods section. The big man snatched a backpack off a shelf without even stopping.

He headed for the gun counter, and I noticed a movement behind him. Dave Summerly was marching down the party-supply aisle, his eyes on his phone. I realized with stomach-churning clarity that Summerly had had the same idea we had and was probably following directions given to him by a police team tracking Troy's pal.

"Oh, jeez." Baby spotted Summerly at the same time I did. She didn't say anything. Neither did I. We moved in tandem, a machine with interlocking parts. Baby rushed forward to intercept Summerly while I sprinted toward the gun counter and grabbed George's arm. He jerked it away hard and whirled around to look at me.

"If you really want to help Troy, you'll leave this store with me right now," I hissed.

CHAPTER 32

THE BIG GUY EYED my tattoos and pink hair, then left his collected items on the gun section's counter and followed me without hesitation. Maybe Troy had told him about me. Or maybe George had decided I was a trustworthy member of the weirdo club. I've always dressed and styled myself for me exclusively, but in my previous time as a defense lawyer, I'd found that my visible tattoos opened as many doors as they closed, particularly in my work with young criminals.

As we traversed the sea of checkouts, I told George to switch off his phone, and he did. I looked back across the store and glimpsed Baby and Dave talking animatedly, him trying to push forward, her trying to convince him to stay put.

I walked Troy's friend to a far corner of the store. "Where is he?" I said to the big guy. Despite his size, he backed away, and I suddenly realized how young he was. Mid-twenties at most.

"I don't know where Troy is." George shook his head, his eyes on the ground. "I haven't seen him since—"

"Nope," I snapped. "Don't play dumb. We don't have a lot of time. I need to get my hands on Troy and convince the police assigned to watch him that he hasn't run off. Otherwise they'll order a BOLO and the world will hear about it, and it won't be pretty."

"I just—"

"You were buying clothes for him just now," I said. "Supplies. He called you at work and told you what to buy for him. Where to meet him."

The big, bearded guy just kept shaking his head. Then, without warning, he burst into tears. I was stunned. His exterior—the heavy brow, dark beard, shoulders as wide as a refrigerator—had spoken of an inner stoicism that wasn't actually there. I was in the presence of a big kid pushed right to the edge.

"Listen." I put my hand on his arm and watched him wipe tears away with the back of his hairy hand. "I'm Team Troy. Okay? I'm here because I want to help him too."

He looked at me, his eyes huge and wet.

"I'm his private investigator." I put my hand out. "Rhonda Bird."

"George Crawley. Troy and I work the callouts together."

"You're okay, George." I rubbed his arm. The urge to console the upset, overgrown boy was hitting all my newly formed mother triggers, raw and ragged since Baby came into my life. "You're all right, buddy."

"Troy didn't do this," he whispered. Nearby shoppers were trying, though not very hard, to avoid staring at us. "He didn't kill Daisy. I'm his best friend. I *know* the guy. He's innocent."

George drew a huge breath. "This is all Daisy," he said. "The escape. The box. Everything."

CHAPTER 33

I WALKED GEORGE TO my Chevy Impala, keeping an eye out for Dave and Baby, and told him, reluctantly, to hold off on what he was saying about Daisy Hansen until my sister could hear it. I trusted Baby's instincts, her ability to read people's emotions.

The big guy took up most of the back seat; my suspension labored audibly as we both got in. We watched shoppers crossing the parking lot, happily pushing carts of electronics and kitchenware to their cars, and a mother trying to wrangle her toddler into a car seat while two older boys fought in the back seat of an SUV. I eyed George in the rearview mirror. He was biting his already savaged fingernails.

Suddenly, Baby slipped into the passenger seat, drummed the dash, and told me to go.

"How did you lose Dave?" I asked Baby after we'd peeled out of the parking lot and I'd introduced her to George.

"I told him you'd already bounced," she said. "I faked getting a text saying you were halfway to the safe house where we'd stashed Troy."

She turned in her seat and skewered George with a look. "Now's the time to spill it, dude," she said. "Tell us where Troy is, or we'll take this rig up to a hundred and ten miles per hour on the freeway and kick you out the door."

"We're not going to do that." I twisted Baby back around by her shoulder. "But I admire your faith in this car. I'd have to strap on a rocket to get us to a hundred and ten." I looked at George. Not even a glimmer of a smile. "We're going to treat George like what he is, Baby. Our ally. He was just about to tell me why he thinks all of this is Daisy's doing."

George shifted in his seat, heaved another exhaust-blast sigh. I felt it on the back of my neck.

"I don't... I'm not saying I know for sure." He nibbled his nails. "It's just... Troy is a straight arrow. Okay? He's—he's not what the people on the internet are saying he is. There's a whole channel on YouTube devoted to finding out who he's having an affair with right now. Because it's only dudes who have affairs, right? Not true."

"Get specific," I said. "You said Daisy was behind this. What did you mean exactly?"

"I mean Daisy was the one having an affair," George said.

Baby and I looked at each other. Then the inevitable text from Dave Summerly flashed up on the screen of my phone, which sat propped in the ashtray.

Not cool, Rhonda.

Los Angeles rolled by us, shadows of palm trees streaking the little gray stores of the jewelry district with their gates and barred windows. The trees made dark silhouettes in the gold haze.

"Troy called me a few days ago," George Crawley said. "The cops were starting to come down harder and harder on him, like something was wrong over there at the house. At first they sat him down for a bunch of talks, and it was all very low-key. But Troy said that things were becoming hostile. Their tone was changing from, like, *Oh, man, you're overreacting. She's an adult. She'll probably come home soon* to *So what were you doing that night?* and *Why didn't you call us earlier?* Troy asked me to come over and hang with him. He was freaked out. We were both freaked out."

I felt the atmosphere in the car closing in.

"We tried watching a movie, but we just couldn't stop talking about Daisy and what had maybe happened," George said. "Troy still had his phone and stuff back then, but he had a feeling that the cops were going to confiscate his electronics and he wanted to be able to keep in touch with me. So he fished out an old phone from a drawer. It was Daisy's old phone, from before she upgraded. He told me to go plug it in, charge it up. But when I went to plug it in, I saw it was already charged. It was just switched off. And it even had a new SIM card."

My stomach sank. Baby was still as a stone.

"You already had suspicions," I said, trying to keep my tone even, non-accusatory. "It would take more than an unexplained second phone to bring you all the way to 'She's having an affair.' You found messages that proved it."

"Did you go through the call log?" Baby asked.

"It was empty. There were no messages either. But I poked around on the phone and I found the messaging app she'd installed. It was hidden."

"Seems like overkill to have a hidden app on a hidden phone," Baby said.

George wiped his puffy, tearstained cheeks. "Daisy's a very beautiful woman. She was, like, prom queen. Troy and me, we're sort of... you know. The last guys picked for the team. The two of them, Troy and Daisy, met online. Texted for months before they actually met. I think that was the only reason he had a shot with someone like her. Hooking her before she found out how weird he was in person."

"Why would Troy hire my agency and not tell me that Daisy was having an affair?"

"He doesn't know."

"He doesn't *know*?" Baby whirled around. "You didn't tell him?"

"Chill!" I turned Baby around again.

"The guy's wife disappears, and you know who she likely ran off with, and *you don't tell him*?" Baby's voice filled the car. "It doesn't make any sense!"

"I didn't know how to tell him!" George's face crumpled

and he burst into fresh tears. "Troy's my best friend! He's my only friend!"

"You do realize, don't you, that whoever she's bangin' on the side might have buried her in the desert somewhere." Baby was relentless, her eyes wild. "Or the two of them might be by a pool in Palm Springs, sippin' margaritas and wearin' fake mustaches, while Troy stares down the barrel of a murder rap."

"I didn't—"

"You're an idiot!" Baby yelled. "You're not a good friend, you're an idiot!"

"Everybody, chill out!" I roared. Baby glared at me. I locked eyes with George Crawley in the rearview mirror. "Tell me you have the messages, George. Please, God, tell me you didn't delete them."

"I did delete them from the extra phone," he admitted. "I didn't want Troy to find them. But before I did, I made a screenshot and sent them to myself. Just in case."

Silence descended on the car.

"The whole affair thing, it just about slipped my mind when we found the box," George said.

Baby and I exchanged a look.

"You were there that night too?" I asked.

"I was there when he found the box." George nodded. "We were searching the house, top to bottom, trying to find something. It was Troy who went down into the crawl space to sniff around. He came up with the box and . . . we realized this was much bigger than just Daisy."

"Is there anything about the box in the messages between Daisy and her lover?" Baby asked. "Jesus, dude. Whoever this person is, he might be the killer of all those missing people. Maybe Daisy was holding the trophy box for him. Maybe Daisy was *in on it*."

"Just slow down." I put a hand on Baby's leg. I had to be the rational head in the car. "Let's figure all this out when we get to Troy. George." I looked back at him. "You have to tell us where he is."

George rubbed his bleeding nails. He wiped his cheeks and met my eyes in the mirror.

"Turn left here," he said.

CHAPTER 34

NOTHING ABOUT GEORGE CRAWLEY'S apartment surprised me. Just inside his front door was a huge glass-fronted cabinet stuffed with Star Wars memorabilia and Sasquatch collectibles; manuals on how to locate the mythical beast were shoulder to shoulder with hand-painted 2-M Hover Tanks. We walked down the hall and passed a tidy room with a neatly made bed and a dressmaker's mannequin by the window with some kind of velvet cloak hanging from its shoulders. There was an elaborate map spread out over a card table, with tiny painted figurines and symbol cards strategically placed on the fictional landscape.

"Maybe you guys should wait here." George hovered uncertainly in his kitchen, which was full of fancy cocktail-making equipment. "The hiding spot's not far away, but we might need to use it again if— "

"Forget it," Baby snapped. "We're slapping an ankle monitor on Troy after this. *Two* ankle monitors. Now hand him over, nerd burger, before I start playing rough with your toys."

George glanced worriedly at his cabinet, then led us back out into the apartment building's hallway. We followed him three apartments down, then turned a corner.

"You have a second apartment?" I asked.

"No." George sighed. "But I know this one is empty. The real estate agents have been showing it for weeks, and I noticed that they never lock the sliding door to the balcony. I told Troy that if he went out on my balcony and climbed from balcony to balcony, he could get into that apartment. Even if the cops came looking for him at my place, they'd never check an apartment down the hall."

"Jesus." Baby glanced out a window to the street. "We're fifteen floors up!"

George shrugged. He stopped outside apartment 72 and knocked. "It's me," he said.

Troy opened the door. His eyes widened when he saw me and Baby, and he looked over at George, who seemed to be on the verge of tears again.

"I'm sorry, man."

Troy swallowed an angry grunt and let us in. We stood in the bare living room surrounded by the stink of carpet cleaner. I gestured at George, who pulled his phone from his pocket. He tapped and swiped a few times, then handed the phone to Troy.

"There's more bad news," George said.

CHAPTER 35

TROY SAT IN THE passenger seat of the Chevy Impala, a silent, lean specter, sometimes napping with his head against the window. I held the wheel and turned over the consequences of Daisy's affair in my mind.

The lottery win and her infidelity opened up whole new realms of possibilities. Daisy might have decided to take her half of the lottery winnings and run off with her lover. Or Troy might have learned about the infidelity and struck out in a rage. Or the mysterious lover might have been the one to lash out in jealousy.

I'd sent Baby to take George back to his workplace before the guy faced a penalty for walking out. I had to accept the fact that Dave Summerly would also catch up to George in time, but for now, I was a step ahead. Troy huffed a small, dark laugh in the quiet of the car as we entered the outskirts of Glendale.

"What?"

"Oh, I'm just reading about Daisy's apparent love of film noir in these messages to her boyfriend." Troy was slowly swiping through the message thread he'd sent himself from George's phone. "Daisy hates those movies. Film noir is my thing."

"You shouldn't read those," I told him. "We'll get them to the police. They'll tell you if there's anything relevant in there."

"Do we really have to share these with the cops?" he asked.

"Yes. We do."

"These will just strengthen the case against me," he said. "It'll look like I found out and I killed her."

"Holding back the trophy box is enough of a risk," I said. I took a deep breath. "And I need to talk to you about that."

"Oh?"

"It's not right for me to hang on to it any longer," I said. "The families of those missing people should know anything that relates to finding their loved ones." I told Troy what had happened with Oliver Maloof, that the man was in the hospital recovering from stab wounds. "The Maloof family deserves to know what's going on. I've had the box for long enough."

"I'll be arrested as soon as the police get hold of it."

"Yes."

"And the internet will know. There's clearly a leak in the

cop camp. The stuff about the lottery win went up about half an hour ago."

"Cops and journalists." I nodded. "Sometimes enemies. Sometimes friends."

"Well, Rhonda, I guess that's it," he said. I looked over and saw him staring at me. "I thought when I hired you that I would be partnering with an ally. Getting help. But you haven't helped me at all. I won't be requiring your services any longer."

We stopped at the roadblock at the end of Troy's street. The two cops manning it turned to us, and I could see their smug smiles even in the dark.

As Troy reached for the door handle and said, "I'll walk from here," I grabbed his arm.

"Don't get out yet," I said.

"What? Why?"

I pointed down the street at the golden glow from hundreds of candles.

CHAPTER 36

I KNEW WHAT I was seeing even from a hundred yards away. This was a candlelight vigil. The soft radiance of the lights on the faces of families gathered in the night, some of whom had brought their dogs on leashes, might at first have made someone think, *Street party*. But it was silent. Reverent. Expressions were serious. Children were wide-eyed, nervous. Troy and I watched as a couple pushing a stroller turned the corner and walked toward the vigil, a framed photograph of Daisy tucked under the guy's arm.

"They're not going to let you get to your driveway," I said. "Let's just go. You can crash at my place."

"No," Troy said. "Just drive me home."

"Troy."

"It's my house." He sat up in his seat. "I'm tired, and I want to go home."

"You assholes were supposed to keep the public back," I snapped at the checkpoint cops. "What's the point of blocking off the street if you're going to allow something like this?"

"We can't stop people who live on the street from inviting their friends over," one of the cops said. He looked at Troy. "Your neighbor across the way organized this. Says there should be about two hundred guests coming. She can't remember all their names, though."

They laughed as I rolled up my window and drove through. Troy was gripping his seat belt tight.

"Mrs. Drummond," he said. "I backed my work truck into her mailbox once. She's never forgiven me."

We drove slowly toward the mass of people. Some of Troy's neighbors were sitting on their porches or standing on their lawns in small groups. Some were arranging flowers and teddy bears and photographs of Daisy in a huge mound in the Hansens' front yard. People turned to look at us, pointed, whispered. The wall of bodies shifted, blocking the road.

I pulled over as close as I could get to Troy's house. We both got out. I couldn't let him walk into that scene alone.

The crowd was so silent, I could hear the crickets chirping nearby. I had a strange instinct to take Troy's hand or arm, but I didn't want to appear to be either a girlfriend or someone leading him unwillingly. White lights—photo flashes, phone flashlights—sparked to life between the golden candle flames. Dozens of cameras and hundreds of eyes watched us unsuccessfully try to skirt the edges of the crowd on the way to the house. The crowd shifted and swelled around us. In their midst, I could hear the whispers.

"Murderous pig..."

"Dirtbag piece of shit..."

"Where is her body..."

A little girl watched anxiously as we walked by. She shrank away from me, moved close to a woman's leg as Troy passed her. "Mommy, is that him?"

At the back of the crowd were Daisy Hansen's parents, Mark and Summer Rayburn; I recognized them from their public appeal. Her mother, Summer, lean and bronzed and fine-featured, was kneeling by the flower pile reading a letter pinned to a teddy. Daisy's father, Mark, broad-chested and silver-haired, watched Troy and me work our way to the house.

Suddenly a woman stepped into Troy's path. She was small with frizzy hair and dark-rimmed glasses. She held out the candle clutched in her fist like it was a microphone.

"Hey, Troy!" she snarled. "This is for Daisy." She jabbed the candle at him.

Troy stumbled back as the hot wax hit his face. "Oh, shit!" he cried. The crowd was immediately divided—half the people trying to maintain calm and dignity, the other half hurling abuse and flicking their candles at us. Hot wax scorched my arm, neck, and face. The crowd became black silhouettes in the near dark. I shoved Troy through the press of bodies and up the driveway to his home.

The shouts of the crowd had grown too loud for me to hear Troy's parting words before he shut the door, but he'd looked tired and afraid. I went back down the driveway, thankful that only a handful of people were still spitting abuse at me. The rest of the crowd had turned inward, probably to dissect Troy's appearance, his body language, the fact that he hadn't addressed them.

As I reached my car, two figures emerged from the crowd: Mark and Summer Rayburn. Their approach zapped electric fear through the relief I'd felt when I gripped the door handle.

"You're Rhonda Bird, right?"

I turned. Mark was blank-faced. Summer was clutching his arm like it was the only thing holding her up.

"That's me," I told the man, sounding less steady than I would have liked.

"We want to talk to you," Mark said. "Hopefully you've got the decency to grant us five minutes."

"I respectfully decline." I put my hands up. "I'm sorry. I'm extremely tired. And I'm guessing you don't want to sit me down and tell me all the reasons why you're on Team Troy."

Daisy's parents looked at each other.

"You guessed wrong," her father said.

CHAPTER 37

WHEN ARTHUR OPENED THE door to Baby, he was wearing a chocolate-brown suit with a navy-blue tie, a huge Windsor knot riding below his Adam's apple. It was clear to Baby that he'd lost a lot of weight since the last time he'd worn the suit; he looked like a shriveled tortoise in its shell. But his eyes held the kind of veiled vulnerability Baby had seen on Earl a hundred times, as he went out to meet a lady dressed in his ill-fitting best. So she told Arthur the same thing she'd always told her dad.

"You look like George Clooney."

Arthur straightened slightly, popped his cuffs.

"Thanks, sugarplum," he said. He sucked air down the sides of his dentures. "I feel like an idiot without a hat, though."

"It's eight o'clock at night." Baby took his arm. "What do you need a hat for?"

They walked to the ancient station wagon he'd cajoled out of his garage that afternoon. Baby had left George and Troy and Rhonda and all that business behind, literally showering the day off, then putting her makeup on, trying to get into a whole other frame of mind. There was a man to protect here too and evildoers to stave off.

Arthur looked at her high heels and pencil skirt and whistled. "We're gonna be the talk of the town."

"You betcha."

When they arrived at the restaurant, Baby wondered how long it had been since Arthur had gone out for dinner. He had a sparkly gaze, but the menu and ordering system had him flummoxed. He let her handle everything, just nodded along and pretended to understand as she explained to him what a QR code was. Within an hour, though, with two drinks under his belt, he was downing dumplings like an expert and doing George Clooney impressions.

"The electrician came today, fixed everything. He said I was lucky that I'd called him—not sure how he meant it," Arthur said. He nodded at Baby's phone on the edge of the table and asked, "Any nibbles?"

Baby picked up her phone and opened the app that let her check on the four cameras she'd installed at Arthur's house. They were all blacked out. She smiled.

"Not just a nibble," she said. "Got 'em hook, line, and sinker."

She stood, went around the table, and slid into the booth next to the old man so she could show him the phone. Baby wasn't oblivious to the stares of other diners—the tall Black teenage girl and the elderly white dude were a combination as perplexing to onlookers as the concept of PayPal was to Arthur. She ignored the looks and rolled the video back until she had the footage she wanted:

Baby and Arthur leaving, locking the door behind them, and walking arm in arm down the porch steps. The evening breeze made the long grass at the front of the property shiver. Not long after, a figure in a hoodie approached from the end of the street, walking swiftly, head down.

Baby and Arthur watched the figure on the video march quickly up the porch steps, hop up onto the rail, and pull a can of spray paint from his pocket. The image darkened. They watched more footage of the guy in the hoodie traversing the porch, again hopping the rail, and jogging down the side of the house to hit camera number two.

"See how he jumped down from the rail like that?" Arthur sipped his whiskey. "I used to be able to do that."

They watched as the hoodie guy blacked out all four cameras. Baby noted the time stamp. "Eight oh seven p.m.," she said. About an hour and a half ago.

She opened a second app on her phone, the one for the hidden cameras, and scrolled the tape to 8:07 p.m. Just as Baby had expected, as soon as the man in the hoodie finished blacking out the fourth and final decoy camera, he raked back his hood, giving the hidden camera a full view.

She snapped a screenshot of his lean, bearded face.

"Gotcha." She smiled.

"So now what do we do?" Arthur asked.

"We take our orders to go," Baby said. "You're gonna want something to nosh on in the car. We're going for a world record in intergenerational learning here tonight, Arthur. My job is to explain facial-recognition software to you. Your job is not to have a stroke while you're trying to grasp it."

"You saw what kind of trouble I got into trying to use the microwave, right?" Arthur sighed.

"I believe in you, man."

"Can't I do my learning here? I'm comfy."

"No," Baby said. "We've got one more stop tonight."

CHAPTER 38

THE ANIMAL SHELTER WAS a sprawling place, a low brick compound ringed by trees and hidden from the lights of nearby Koreatown, a dark pocket in a glowing city. Baby could hear barking from where she stood at the roadside brushing down the front of her pencil skirt and adjusting the collar of her crisp white button-down shirt in the side mirror of the station wagon. Arthur watched her from the front passenger seat, one elbow slung over the windowsill, his cheeks flushed in the warm night.

She hit the buzzer on the intercom, shook tingles of nervousness out of her fingertips.

"Yeah?"

"We're here for the pickup," Baby said. There was a pause.

She glanced at the cameras over the cyclone fence. The intercom crackled.

"Sorry, what pickup?"

Baby flashed a badge at the camera over the fence like she didn't know there was a more accurate camera on the intercom panel. "Got approved this afternoon. It's on the schedule."

"What schedule?" Arthur asked. Baby shushed him and waved at the car. She waited, her breath a hard ball caught in her throat. The cyclone fence buzzed and slid back.

"Don't blow it, Arthur," she warned him as she got back in the driver's seat.

"I might be the only guy in LA who's never taken an acting class," he said. "Wasn't a problem until now."

"So keep your mouth shut and we'll be fine." She slapped his chest lightly. When he didn't smile, she slapped his chest a little harder. She heard her father's words come from her own lips, as if Earl were riding along with them: "Come on. Where's your sense of adventure?"

The monster dog dragged itself to its feet when Baby and Arthur appeared before its cage, lumbering to its full height one heavy limb at a time like a wounded elephant rallying. The animal was a saggy, probably drugged, and definitely demoralized version of the one Baby had seen in the thieves' den earlier this week, but the dog stirred something in her. She had been terrified the first time. Now she was curious. Arthur's eyes nearly bugged out of his skull until Baby knocked his shoe with her own, reminding him to keep cool. The shelter's night attendant scoured the heavy, tattered logbook lying open on his desk in the concrete hall full of cages.

"I got nothin' in here about a pickup," he said. "Certainly nothing about a visit from any cops. Makes me nervous, letting a dog go without the proper outtake forms and all."

"We're not cops, we're feds." Baby squared her shoulders. "And the fact that your manager didn't note the transport approval down is not my problem. This dog is coming with us whether you're emotionally and administratively prepared for it or not." She jerked her thumb at Arthur. "My partner's put twelve months into this case. Without the dog, the whole thing sinks."

"I don't get how a dog can be a witness," the attendant said, watching with trepidation as Baby opened the cage and Arthur attached a leash to the beast's thick collar. "You gonna put that thing on the stand or what?"

Baby didn't answer. She observed the huge animal as it lumbered out of the cage. The shiny black dog gave the weakest tail wag she'd ever seen, and she tried to hide a smile.

"This dog's going to do what he was born to do." Baby stroked the dog's head. "He's gonna make bad guys run for their lives."

CHAPTER 39

DAISY HANSEN'S PARENTS FOLLOWED me to the 2 Sisters Detective Agency office. They were staying at a hotel in town while they looked for their daughter, but I didn't want to go to a public place with them. Talking with the Rayburns about their daughter's disappearance and possible murder over drinks in a bar might look uncomfortably celebratory if it was captured by web sleuths.

Our two vehicles drove in somber convoy through the empty streets. I unlocked the glass door through which their son-in-law had shuffled uncertainly not so long ago and settled them in the chairs in front of my desk. The Rayburns had the drawn, bloodless pallor of parents with a child in peril, a look I'd seen a thousand times when I'd represented wayward kids.

"First of all," Mark Rayburn said, "while we consider ourselves, uh, on Troy's team, as you put it"—he glanced at his wife—"it's not because we think he's a great guy."

"Troy has an anger problem," Summer said bluntly. She tucked a strand of silver-streaked blond hair behind her ear.

"What kind of anger problem?" I asked. I was honestly curious. It didn't match what I'd observed about him so far. "Have you seen signs?"

"Yes. He snapped in front of us once." Mark's lips tightened. "It was a few years back. We live out in Vegas, and Daisy and Troy were at our place for Christmas. Some neighbors were over too. A kid who lives two houses down sprayed Troy in the back of the head with a water pistol, and the guy just lost it."

"It was embarrassing." Summer shifted in her seat. "Okay, so it was Christmas, and emotions were high. We know that Troy's family, the Hansens, are not a tight-knit group. They're from some small town in the middle of nowhere in the north of the state. There's always been conflict in his family. So for Troy, Christmas and Thanksgiving and that sort of thing are... you know. Stressful."

"And that Sanderson kid is an asshole. Everyone thinks so. But you keep it together." Mark stabbed a finger on my desk. "Especially at the in-laws' place."

"*Especially* at the in-laws' place," Summer echoed. "We

recognize that Troy was triggered somehow, but we don't sympathize with how he reacted."

"What did Troy do?" I asked. "When the kid sprayed him with the water pistol?"

"He threw a lawn chair." Mark brushed invisible lint from his knee. "Yelled at the kid a little. It really soured the afternoon. Nobody felt very comfortable or festive after that. But that's Troy. He dampens the mood. Gets sullen or brooding. Everyone will be having a good time and then Troy will say something or do something strange, and suddenly it's crickets."

"He's the kind of guy who cracks a joke at a funeral." Summer winced. "And falls asleep at a wedding. He just… makes the wrong choices."

I sat there quietly, thinking.

"Summer was more concerned about the Christmas incident than I was. To be honest," Mark said, "I don't know any man who hasn't yelled at a kid at least once in his life."

"You seem to be apologizing for your son-in-law," I said to Mark.

"For his anger, yeah. But Troy's just kind of… odd." Daisy's father sighed. "We've never disliked him—we just didn't really get him or his goofy friend George. And we couldn't ever understand what our daughter saw in Troy. They just didn't seem a match, you know?"

"Troy wasn't Daisy's usual type," Summer said. "In high school, in college, she always dated high achievers. Team captains, class presidents. Popular kids." She made an upward ramp with her hand. "Or at least, she dated boys who seemed more like her. So when she brought Troy home just after she graduated and moved out to LA...we met him and we thought, *Oh*."

"Oh," Mark echoed, nodding, his eyes wide.

I tried to keep my tone even: "Well, there are worse things to be than slightly offbeat." Mark Rayburn's eyes flicked over my pink hair and tattoos, and he kept nodding.

"We weren't happy when we discovered that Troy had waited more than a day before reporting Daisy missing," Summer said. "But we weren't surprised."

"You weren't?"

"It was in keeping with the kind of person we've known him to be. He's not alarmist. He's logical to the point of ridiculousness."

"But Troy doesn't deserve this circus that's following him around," Mark said. "The things people are saying. Including the police."

"You believe the police are wasting their time by looking at Troy?" I asked.

"Yes." Summer gripped the edge of my desk. I saw the hard mask she was wearing to hide her terror of losing her child start to slip. "The last time we spoke to Daisy, she was in love. But it wasn't Troy she was in love with."

CHAPTER 40

IT STARTED WITH A snicker. A snorting, mischievous snicker, the same kind of noise Daisy had made as a teenager in her bedroom, holed up with a bunch of other beautiful blond girls, plotting heartbreak for high-school jocks. Summer Rayburn hadn't heard that snicker in years, but she heard it again six months ago when Daisy stood in the corner of the kitchen tapping away on her phone and snickering with delight. Troy had been out helping Mark in the yard. Summer asked her daughter what all the secrecy was about, but Daisy came back with some vague stuff about a joke a friend had made. Summer didn't buy it. And she noticed the phone her daughter was holding wasn't the same one she'd had when she arrived at the house.

The snickering turned to wistful sighs, and then one afternoon Daisy drove out to Vegas for a visit and wrapped her mother in a big, juicy hug. It was unexpected. Unexplained. But Daisy was happy. Like she was in love.

"Do you know for certain whether Daisy was having an affair?" Mark asked me. He skewered me with a look. "The police won't tell us anything, and we've been advised not to speak to Troy."

"I can't confirm anything right now about Daisy's personal life." I held my hands up. "I got some new information only a couple of hours ago, before I dropped Troy off at the house. I haven't had a chance to look at it yet."

"I think she was." Summer's voice was thin, breathless. "The lottery win confirmed it for me."

Daisy had been talking about putting a deck on the back of the Glendale house ever since she and Troy bought it. She'd painted vivid pictures of the two of them sitting out there on Adirondack chairs, watching the sunset. She'd do her morning yoga out there. Film her Instagram reels. Plant fragrant jasmine to run around the handrail.

"I was sick of hearing about this damn deck," Mark said. "I would have built it for her myself if my back weren't so bad. Then they get that cash. And suddenly I'm listening to *Troy* trying to convince *Daisy* to put the deck in."

"She blew off every suggestion," Summer said. "She didn't want to spend a dime of that money. 'Just use a little and come to Vegas!' I told her. 'Have a big weekend. Don't go crazy, but celebrate! You've won the goddamn lottery!' "

"Do you think she was thinking about leaving Troy?" I asked. "And holding on to the money until she had a plan?"

"Maybe." Summer nodded. Her lip trembled, and she swiped carefully at her eyes. "Or maybe whoever she was with, you know, on the side... maybe Daisy told him about the money. And he wanted some of it. Or all of it. And got threatening."

A sharp rap on the office's glass door behind the Rayburns made us all jump. I stood and opened it to find Dave Summerly standing in the hall. He slapped a sheet of paper into my palm.

"Hello, Rhonda." He smiled tightly. "Mind if I come in?"

"What is this?" I unfolded the paper. The word WARRANT screamed off the page.

"This is a raid," Summerly said.

CHAPTER 41

DAVE SUMMERLY LEANED AGAINST the wall in the hall with his arms folded in that smug and superior and undeniably sexy way while I made my excuses to Mark and Summer Rayburn and promised we'd talk again tomorrow. They left and I let Summerly in but only as far as the guest chairs, which I blocked so he couldn't sit down.

"What the *actual hell,* Dave?"

He lifted his hands in mock helplessness. "You tell me, Rhonda. You tell me why I have to play dirty like this. Because I don't want to. I want us to help each other out here. But you want to play cat-and-mouse games. So I've had to cook up some bullshit to come over here and turn your life upside down."

"What reason could you possibly have to enter these premises?"

"I got a dead guy on my hands," Summerly said. "Martin Rosco. The Cable-Tie King. Remember him? You killed him in your house. Now I've got to put that case to bed. I gotta decide whether I'm going to file it under self-defense or homicide."

"You're not going to charge me with homicide." I leveled a fierce gaze at him. "You might be trying to piss me off, but you're not that big of a time-waster."

"I told the judge I'd feel better about calling it self-defense if I could just get a look at your files. I need to find out which case Martin Rosco was trying to dissuade you from working on." Summerly smiled. "Clever, right?"

"What baloney. That judge must have owed you a huge favor to sign such a garbage warrant."

"He did. I looked the other way on his nephew's possession charge a few years back."

"Dave, you're not going to touch a single sheet of paper inside this office," I said. I lifted a finger in warning. "You're not going to unstick a single Post-it note or open a single manila folder. I've been clearing my dad's stuff out of this place for months. Everything is exactly where it's supposed to be and it's staying there."

"Rhonda," Summerly growled, his eyes locked on mine. He took a step toward me. "I am going to absolutely trash this office. I'm gonna make it look like a hurricane swept through here. And I'd just love for you to try and stop me."

He took another step forward. I refused to be backed into my desk. I stood with my arms folded until he was within reach.

Then I grabbed him and kissed him hard.

CHAPTER 42

BABY SAT IN THE driver's seat of the station wagon, the big dog beside her. It was three a.m. She'd dropped Arthur off at home hours ago and changed out of her nice outfit into a dark T-shirt and jeans. Baby and the dog—whom she'd named Mouse for the same reason bouncers are called Tiny—were watching a neat little house on Truslow Avenue behind the museum in Fullerton. Nothing moved in the quiet neighborhood.

Baby opened her phone again and looked through the criminal record belonging to Chris Tutti, the man who had blacked out the cameras she'd hung at Arthur's house. A list of burglaries the length of her arm, a couple of extortion beefs. If Chris Tutti had ever killed a person, he'd gotten away with it.

The place was cuter than Baby would've expected a guy like Tutti to have. Blue weatherboard with white trim. Potted plants. She recognized the small gray Honda in the driveway.

She unzipped the pouch on her belt and took out a dog treat, something she'd been doing every few minutes for the past half hour or so. The huge black monster dog stared at her with yellow eyes the size of golf balls.

"Let's do a bit more of our homework, Mouse," she said. She twisted sideways and locked eyes with him, the treat clutched in her fingers.

"Shake," she said.

The dog put a paw the size of an oven mitt in her hand. She gave him a treat.

"Danger," she said.

The dog's lips twitched.

"*Danger,* Mouse," she said. "It's *danger.*"

The dog gave a low growl.

"Good," Baby said. She gave the dog another treat, then wiped the slobber off on her jeans.

She repeated the training a couple more times:

Danger. Growl. Treat.

Danger. Growl. Treat.

Baby was impressed with how well the animal was responding after a scant few hours of training. She stealthily exited the car, then went around and quietly popped open the passenger-side door. She clipped on the dog's leash and walked the huge animal to the pretty blue house.

The back door was unlocked. She went in—moving fast so that Mouse's big toenails clacking on the kitchen tiles wouldn't wake Tutti before she was ready—full of fear and exhilaration. She noted but didn't really think about the cross-stitched tapestry hanging on the wall in the corner of the living room, the afghan over the couch, the floral slippers by the back room. She followed the Odeur de Douchebag drifting from the front bedroom, a mixture of cigarettes, dollar-store deodorant, and wet towels.

When Baby and Mouse entered the bedroom, Chris Tutti sat upright in the bed, knocking the table lamp off the nightstand and onto the floor, scattering water bottles and burner phones plugged into chargers. The room glowed neon green from a big fish tank filled with sad silhouettes of guppies bubbling in the corner.

"What the fu—"

"*Danger!*" Baby gave Mouse's leash a gentle tug to get him listening. "Look, puppy. It's *danger*!"

The monster dog exploded, thrashing and hurling himself at Tutti so hard, Baby had to get two hands on the leash and dig her feet into the carpet to hold the animal back. The barks rattled the windows, made her eardrums pulse.

"Chris Tutti!" Baby yelled over the barking. "I'm here about you harassing the owner of the house on Waterway Street!" There was a scream from the back of the house. Baby ignored it. Chris Tutti was cowering on the bed, cornered by the vicious dog. "You're gonna tell me who at Enorme sent you there!"

"I don't know what you're talking about!" Tutti clearly didn't know whether to hold his hands out to protect himself or tuck them defensively by his side to prevent his fingers being chomped off. "Jesus Christ, keep that thing away from me!"

"Get the danger! Get the danger!" Baby told Mouse. He ramped up the noise until fever-pitched hell-barking fired out of his throat. The dog stood on his hind legs, twisting and thrashing. "Tutti, you got three seconds before I let go of this leash."

"Oh God! Don't do it! Don't do it!"

"One."

"Oh, please! Please!"

"My hands are getting tired."

"I don't know anything!"

"Two."

"Su Lim Marshall!" Tutti's terrified face was lime green in the light cast by the fish tank. "She's head of—of land acquisitions or some shit!"

"Put a shirt on," Baby barked. "You're gonna sit here and tell me everything she asked you to do. We're gonna get it on camera."

"Fuck that shit!" Tutti tried to shuffle to the end of the bed, but Mouse pawed at the blankets, his jaws inches away from Tutti's bare feet. "I ain't coppin' to no murder rap!"

Baby smiled. "Who said anything about murder?"

Then she heard a sound she recognized, barely audible above the dog's barks—the hammer of a gun clicking. Baby turned. There in the hall was the almost comical sight of a small, frail older woman in a nightgown with a sizable revolver shaking in her little fists. Baby yanked the dog into the hallway with her and backed up a couple of feet toward the front door. Though Baby couldn't see the old woman's face, she knew impossible equations must be running through her mind. Should she shoot the dog and take her chances with the girl, or shoot the girl and take her chances with the dog? With a revolver, the milliseconds between shots made either choice a potentially fatal one.

"Nana!" Tutti cried. "Don't shoot her, for Christ's sake! I'm on parole!"

Baby threw herself at the front door, opened it, yanked Mouse through it, and slammed it behind her. A shot blasted through the stained glass above the door; the shards made pretty tinkling sounds in the street as she ran for the car.

CHAPTER 43

ABOUT SIX YEARS AGO in Colorado, I worked a case defending a teenage girl who was accused of planning to take a rifle to school and shoot as many of her classmates as she could. The girl was guilty, and she admitted it.

During long nights working on strategy and researching prior cases to get her the best sentence possible, I'd basically lived in my cramped little office, a gas heater by my feet and the coffee machine working its ass off. The day before the sentencing hearing, the girl's mother showed up at my door. She hadn't slept in three days, the worry over her daughter's fate writhing in her brain like a snake.

I couldn't let the woman drive home, and I couldn't put her in a cab. She needed help, and I needed her to be fresh and bright and ready to read her appeal to the judge. I borrowed a foldout couch from a neighboring office, put the woman in it, and went back to my desk. The mother of the would-be school shooter slept soundly for eighteen hours while I filed motions and wrote reports and emailed colleagues.

Since then I've always kept a foldout couch in my office. When I moved to Los Angeles and took over my father's business, I found he had one too, but his was tattered and coffee-stained and full of mouse holes. So when I woke at six a.m. to the sound of Dave Summerly stirring, we were in the clean, fresh, and barely used foldout in my office that I'd bought to replace my father's. Turns out, a foldout in the office is handy not only for after-lunch naps and clients desperate for sleep but for banging your ex-boyfriend when he attempts to conduct a raid on your premises.

Summerly and I got dressed in opposite corners, sneaking looks at each other. We both had guilty smiles. His softened into a reflective one. He stopped looking at my body and started searching my eyes.

I held up a hand. "Before you say anything, I don't know what last night meant. And I sure don't want to try to figure it out right now. I need coffee and a shower and I have to check in with Baby and make sure she got home safe last night."

"Why does it have to mean anything?" Summerly sighed. "This is what you do, Rhonda. You assign meanings to things, then you decide you don't like those meanings and you run off, trying to put as much distance as possible between yourself and those terrifying, arbitrary meanings."

"A plausible theory."

"You ever think of *consulting* with the other person to decide what a thing means?"

"Dave, listen. Whether we do it together or I do it alone, it ain't happening right now."

He rolled his eyes and grabbed his phone from my desk. Some paperwork I had sitting there caught his eye. "Dorothy Andrews-Smith?" he said, pointing.

One of the names from the trophy box, the sixty-two-year-old who'd disappeared from her house in Redondo Beach. I felt a shiver run up my back. "What about her?"

"I know this case." He picked up a sheet of paper. I could see from where I stood that it was her MISSING poster. "Dorothy Andrews-Smith. Last seen at home. Front and back doors left hanging open, no sign of Dorothy or her cat. Has her family hired you to find her?"

"Uh." I raked my fingers through my hair. "I mean... I'm making some inquiries." It was the vaguest thing I could think of to say. "I've got confidential papers on that desk, Dave. Would you mind not sniffing around my cases?"

"I have a warrant to sniff around your cases." He put the poster back down. "So you're trying to prove Troy Hansen's not a wife killer, *and* you're rubbing shoulders with gangs? You've got a real bucketload of thankless jobs here, Rhonda."

"Gangs?" I asked. "Dorothy was mixed up with a gang?"

Summerly's phone pinged. Something shifted in his

face when he read the message. Without a word, he turned toward the door. He was about to walk out, brow furrowed, when I called, "Hey!" The word jolted him out of a deep, intense focus. "You gonna say goodbye or what?"

He came over and pecked my lips, then left without saying anything.

A feeling of unease settled in my chest. I hadn't shaken it when I got to my car, or when I arrived home, or when I jumped in the shower. I thought about texting Summerly but didn't know how to explain that some extrasensory flicker in my brain hadn't liked the way he'd walked out and hadn't liked how he'd looked when he read that text, whatever it was. I checked social media and all the news sites, but there was nothing new about Troy or Daisy. I called Troy on his burner, but he didn't answer. The GPS tag I'd placed on his truck said it was still in his driveway, but I knew that didn't mean much.

I looked into Baby's room and saw her bed hadn't been slept in. I swore out loud and checked to see if she'd replied to the text I'd sent as I left the office. She hadn't. The neatly turned down sheets and the blankness of my phone screen deepened my sense that something bad was about to happen.

When the doorbell rang, the sound was like the whump of a bullet taking me in the chest. I went to the front door, knowing even before I put my hand on the knob that whatever terrible thing I had sensed was waiting for me on my stoop.

CHAPTER 44

DETECTIVE WILL BROGAN WAS holding a cell phone down by his side, and his eyes were set and hard. His jacket was dusty, and the lines in his face seemed deeper than they had two days before.

The phone and the hard eyes told me all I needed to know.

He'd been taking and making so many calls that morning, he'd simply grown accustomed to carrying the phone around. And he'd shut off his own emotions completely because there were other people to devastate now. The public, through an address to the media. Daisy's family. Me. Brogan couldn't afford to show whatever it was he felt. So his gray eyes, when they fell on me, were empty. And when he spoke, his voice was even and flat.

"Rhonda."

"She's dead, isn't she?" I asked. "Daisy Hansen."

He flicked his head toward his car, which was parked just down the street.

"You better come see the body," he said.

CHAPTER 45

I DIDN'T ASK HIM anything about the body I was going to see. I needed time to think, to work up to handling it.

Though I'd never met her, I'd seen enough to imagine that I would have liked Daisy Hansen. Sure, she was flawed. She was a cheater. She was unreliable and secretive, and her optimism was probably relentless. But I'd seen her mother's barely contained, minute-by-minute terror that her daughter was never coming home. I'd seen fear and sadness in the candlelit eyes of Daisy's friends and neighbors outside her house. For hours, I'd scrolled Daisy's social media pages and learned her little quirks and eccentricities. How she squealed at random dogs on leashes in the park. How she hated Fridays because she liked to work. I knew the sound of her long-suffering sigh when she didn't get enough sleep. I knew the wheeze she made when she laughed hard.

Good and bad, Daisy had been a real and genuine person.

I sat in the car beside Brogan and watched Manhattan Beach become Sepulveda and then the 105 East. The sight of an In-N-Out Burger made me simultaneously nauseated and desperate to go inside and order everything they had.

"Look, Rhonda," Brogan said eventually. "I know Troy Hansen killed his wife."

"What makes you so sure?"

"Because I know what kind of man he is and what kind of wife he had."

I waited, feeling tired. Brogan seemed to age as he thought, as if the memories he was turning over were draining something from him. He was probably only in his mid- to late thirties, but they'd been hard decades.

Brogan ran a hand through his hair, seemed to weigh his words even when they were out of his mouth. "I know him because I've been him. I've been the guy with the star wife. Daisy Hansen was a bubbly, vivacious woman. If she wasn't chitchatting with the yoga gals, she was changing the lives of her diet-program followers. She was emailing, calling, texting, studying, hunting for opportunities, doing good deeds, paying it forward, being a good friend, a good colleague, a fierce competitor." He shook his head. "It exhausts me just thinking about what it was like to be Daisy Hansen."

"You said you'd been him," I pressed.

"I was the turkey vulture married to the swan for

ten years." He glanced at me. "She ran marathons to raise money to cure cancer. She installed community gardens in run-down neighborhoods. And here I was, the bozo cop who hadn't had the grades for law school."

"Oh, wow."

"Yeah. She was a fucking saint." Brogan took a pack of cigarettes from the center console and lit up. "She ran a charity that cared for orphaned baby elephants. She started it when she was in college. In the beginning, you hate yourself for being such a piece of garbage. Then you hate the other person for insisting on being so amazing all the time."

I said nothing.

"Troy Hansen is an awkward loser from a family of duck hunters up north," Brogan continued. "I don't know if it was sheer luck or a twist of fate or a glitch in the universe, but somehow, Troy Hansen landed Daisy Rayburn, and she was the best and worst thing that ever happened to him."

"You think he envied her," I said.

"Wouldn't you?"

I thought about Daisy and Troy's beautiful home. The meals in the Tupperware. The magazines on the coffee table. The artfully filtered Instagram shots.

I thought about my high-school years. I'd been nearing two hundred pounds at age fourteen and on the fringe of a goth group of drama and literature nerds. Girls like Daisy hadn't deliberately set out to make my life a nightmare, but they didn't need to. I'd loathed the ease with which they navigated the world.

But I hadn't wanted to see them dead.

"It's okay to discover that, actually, you hate your wife." Brogan shrugged and exhaled through his open window. "But you don't kill her. You do what everybody does: You get a divorce."

"There's no evidence that Troy Hansen hated his wife," I said.

Brogan snorted humorlessly and kept driving. "We're not there yet."

CHAPTER 46

DETECTIVE WILL BROGAN DROVE us to a dirt road leading into scrubby bushland at the base of Mount Wilson, an hour east of Pasadena. Two patrol cops saw Brogan behind the wheel and waved us through. There were three more checkpoints before the white Crown Vics and crime scene tape appeared through the trees. I rolled down my window and smelled smoke and motor oil on the wind.

"We shot a drone down about an hour ago," Brogan said. "Didn't want to do it, since it was flown by the same internet kid who'd tipped us off. He's the one who told us that Troy left the house in the middle of the night. But I can't have pictures of this floating around out there until I've got a proper ID. Then I can inform Daisy's parents."

"What do you mean?" I said. I felt like I couldn't catch up, like the conversation was traveling at a hundred miles an hour while the car slowly rolled along the dirt road. "You weren't watching Troy's house last night?"

"Oh, we were watching the house." Brogan glanced at me. "But Troy snuck out the back at about two a.m. He hopped a neighbor's fence and stole his car."

"Why?"

"To come here," Brogan said.

"Troy snuck out of his house, stole a car, and came here?"

"Exactly."

I forced myself to breathe.

"The kid with the drone followed him halfway here," Brogan said. "Then he thought he better call us. So we put a new tail on Troy and told the kid with the drone to back off. Those drones are amazing. Can fly for hours, some of them."

I held my head. "Jesus."

"Kid wouldn't take the hint, though, once it was clear where Troy was going. He wanted to get the scoop. So we had to bust his toy."

I squeezed my temples.

"We knew Troy would lead us to Daisy eventually." Brogan sighed. "They always do."

We passed a squad car nosed into a bare spot in the brush between two large eucalyptus trees. I recognized Troy in the back seat, facing away from us. Brogan pulled into a space fifty yards down the road and we got out.

Dave Summerly was standing by a burned-out car I

recognized as Daisy's little red Honda Civic. There was a gurney beside the car with what I assumed was a body on it, already bagged and tagged and zipped up.

Most of the cops on the scene were doing their jobs—securing the cordons, taking measurements or photographs, making notes. But here and there, an officer stood crying. I've never gotten used to seeing cops in uniform shedding tears. I was the only civilian on-site (except for Troy), and when the officers saw me, the mood immediately changed. The tearful cops turned their backs to me. Others threw angry looks my way.

Brogan straightened and sighed and started to step away from me, a signal that his task was complete and he had to get back to work. For the second time in my investigation, the lead detective had extended a friendly hand, and I was grateful for it. Brogan could have let me find out about the discovery of Daisy's remains from the news, but here I was, at the scene. I knew I was pushing it, but I asked anyway. "Can I talk to Troy?"

"Be my guest," Brogan said. "The squad car's not bugged."

I didn't believe that, but I nodded. "Thanks. Did he tell you how or why he came to this place? Did he say how he knew that Daisy's body was here?"

"He did," Brogan said. "But if you believe what he says, you're an even bigger idiot than he is."

CHAPTER 47

TWO OFFICERS STOOD NEAR Troy in the squad car, one leaning against a tree smoking a cigarette, the other texting. I was ten yards away when the one who was smoking got a radio call; he listened, then nodded to me. I slid into the back seat beside Troy. He looked even more deflated than he had the last time I'd seen him, when he was bleary-eyed and slamming the door on an angry mob. His hands were cuffed to a bolt in front of the seat, so he wiped his wet eyes on the shoulders of his shirt.

"I found a note," he told me. He grimaced, shook his head. I knew and he knew that whatever he was about to tell me was ridiculous.

"Just say it," I said.

"I found a note," he repeated. "Just sitting there in my kitchen. It was... it was after midnight. I heard a noise, so I came out, and there was this note on the kitchen island. All it had written on it was a location."

"Troy."

"They have the note." Troy squeezed his eyes shut. "The police. I left it in the car."

"You're trying to tell me," I said, "that whoever killed Daisy snuck back into your house last night and left a note in your kitchen telling you where to find her body?"

I waited. Tears ran down Troy's face.

"I knew I couldn't bring the note to the police. Not until I knew what it referred to. I knew the police weren't watching the back of the house, otherwise how could I have—"

"Troy!" I roared. *"Stop!"*

He wouldn't look at me. I punched the metal grille dividing the front of the squad car from the back. The skin on my knuckles split. The pain was good. I hit it again three more times, roaring curses. I wanted to hit Troy. The temptation was overwhelming.

"They'll have the note," Troy repeated softly. He was speaking to no one. "I left it in the car when I... when I ran to see if Daisy was..."

I got out. The patrol cops watched me march back up the road to the crime scene. Brogan saw me coming and peeled away from a conversation he was having with a photographer.

"Was there a note?" I asked.

"No, Rhonda," Brogan said. "We searched his person. We searched his car. We searched the scene. I even had two officers walk the trail back toward the highway in case it had flown out the car window. There was no note. There was never a note."

I turned and walked away. I followed the dirt path back through the three checkpoints, turned right, and headed toward the off-ramp from the highway. When I was out of sight of the officers, I crossed to a concrete barrier, sat down in the shade of it.

I took out my phone and texted Baby. **Tell me exactly where you are right now.**

She sent me a pin for 101 Waterway Street, Culver City.

I calculated the time it would take me to get there, told her I was on my way, and ordered an Uber. I put the phone away and sat back against the concrete barrier.

Then I cried for Daisy Hansen.

CHAPTER 48

ABOUT AN HOUR LATER, I walked up the steps of 101 Waterway Street as though I were in a dream. I was aware but unquestioning of my curious surroundings: The weed-smothered front yard. The big security camera above the porch, its lens spray-painted black. Behind the screen door, an extremely familiar-looking enormous black dog started up a hellish clamor at my arrival, which Baby silenced with a single word. I drifted into the old, creaky house and sat at a big kitchen island. Baby took the stool on the other side, and a small, elderly man with thinning white hair sat at the table.

The story poured out of me. Telling it emptied my mind, which was what I needed. As I shook it off, I gently woke up to my surroundings. I was drawn out of my sadness for

Daisy and my hopelessness for Troy and into the puzzle of the circumstances I had just walked into. As Baby took in the information I'd given her, I realized her shoulder was bandaged, and the big dog snoring loudly in the corner was a beast I'd encountered before.

"Why didn't Troy just call you when he found the note?" Baby said through gritted teeth. "If there ever was a note, it's long gone now."

"Baby," I said, glancing at the man at the table who'd been listening quietly to everything I'd said without comment. "What the hell is going on here?"

Baby tried to buy herself time. She cleared some bloody tissues and gauze from the kitchen island in front of me and swept them into a trash can she produced from under the sink. She was clearly familiar with the house. Her silence was making the temperature under my collar rise.

"Baby."

"What?"

"I asked you a question."

"This is Arthur." Baby gestured at the old man. "He's being harassed and threatened by psychopaths from a megacorporation who want to buy up the whole neighborhood and are trying to squeeze him out. It's possible they killed his wife, and there's no doubt they tried to kill him. I'm halfway to solving the problem but I hit a snag last night when I got into it with a dumbass from Fullerton and his gun-toting grandma. I'm fine. I wasn't shot, it's just glass from a door that exploded."

She rubbed her bandaged shoulder, looked around, spotted the dog on the floor. "And, uh, yeah. That's the dog from the pet-nappers' apartment. We took him, Arthur and I. For protection. I've named him Mouse. Anything else you want to know?"

Some minutes passed; I don't know how many. I sat silently reviewing what I had heard, mulling it over, examining it. I turned on my stool and looked at the man, then the dog, then the kitchen in the rickety old house. I put what I had heard together with what I'd just learned about the Daisy Hansen case. Tried to connect the scenarios. Then I gently placed my hands on the kitchen island.

"Baby," I said. "This is a joke, right?"

"It's— "

"You're out of your mind," I said. My voice rose quickly to an earsplitting volume. "You're out of your goddamn mind!"

Baby sighed, folded her arms, dropped a hip.

"What are you thinking, getting involved in something like this?" I roared. "You took this whole thing on by yourself? You confronted a murder suspect *by yourself*?"

"She wasn't by herself," Arthur said.

"Oh, don't you start." I whirled around, stabbed a finger at him. "I've got nothing but *flaming contempt* for the kind of guy who would let a teenager get mixed up in a mess like this!"

Arthur was unrattled by my tirade. "Lady," he said. "You're the one who needs her head examined here."

"What!" I yelled.

"You're handlin' this kid all wrong." He gestured at Baby. "You're basing everything you do with her on how many years she's been running around the earth, not on what she's been through and what she knows. Keep doing that and you're gonna end up wondering what in the world *you* were thinking."

I gripped the kitchen island to keep myself from punching someone.

"Barbara hadn't been in this house five minutes before she saved my ass—stopped me from being fried to death in my own damn kitchen." Arthur pointed at Baby. "Took her a single day to figure out that someone's trying to kill me, who that person is, *and* what she plans to do about it. I was impressed enough with that. But just now, I learned she's been doing all that stuff while also trying to track down a serial killer or whatever the hell it is you were just saying." He waved a dismissive hand at me. "Seems to me that you ought to cut the kid some slack."

"She's *my* kid!" I shouted, tapping my chest. "Did she tell you that? I'm all the family she's got in the world. If some... some psychopaths from a megacorporation kill her and bury her in the concrete foundations of the eco-tech-village they plan to build here, it'll be my fault."

"Sure." Arthur shrugged. "But maybe that won't happen. Maybe instead she'll run off on you. She'll get tired of you not seeing what she's worth and disappear on you in a different way. She's already flown the coop, right?"

I looked at Baby, caught her watching the old man in a

way that made my heart ache. She was smiling. Blushing. I'd spent a lot of my teenage years in that same state—basking in the fantasy of fatherly connection with men who were not my father but who for whatever reason took on a paternal role. Earl Bird had run out on me when I was thirteen. He'd packed his things, and I'd never seen him again. For a long time, I'd gotten a fix when older men encouraged me, saw my potential, provided an ear, said they were proud of me. I felt for Baby now. Because this man, Arthur, was not her father, and eventually the spell she was under would be shattered. She would realize what I had realized—that she could never have Earl back. And the more men she sought for her fatherly fix, the sooner she'd run into one who would use it against her.

I walked out of the house. Baby followed. She slid into the Chevy next to me.

"I am going to help Arthur," she said. Her tone was firm. "I'm not dropping his case."

"It doesn't sound like my approval matters," I said. "But even if it did, this wasn't the way to get it."

"Why?"

"The secrecy." I gestured to the house. "The sneaking around. The lies. That doesn't fly with me."

She looked at me. I could tell she was surprised that my calm tone matched hers, that I'd collected myself so fast. I felt a tickle of self-pride in my chest. Maybe I was getting better at this whole parenting thing.

"I think what you're doing is dangerous." I held her eyes.

"I think you're going to fall. I hope that doesn't happen, believe me. And maybe it won't. You're smart, and you're capable, and you've got good instincts."

Her eyes shimmered. She swiped at them, hid the emotion.

"But, Baby, it's my job to catch you when you fall." I tapped my chest. "And I can't do that if I don't know you're out on the ledge in the first place."

"Okay," she said. "I get it."

"Can this wait?" I nodded at the house. "Is he safe in there until tonight?"

"I think so. I'm running all the cams to my phone. And the dog is there."

"Good, because right now, Troy Hansen is likely on his way to the county jail." I looked at my watch.

"You still want to help him? You believe him?" Baby was incredulous. "He just led police directly to his wife's body. His story about finding a random note in his house is…is…"

"It's hard to believe." I nodded. "But I don't turn away from stuff because it's too hard. Text our favorite tech nerd, Jamie. Tell him to run the number Daisy was texting on her secret phone. I want to speak to her lover."

CHAPTER 49

DR. ALEX BRINDLE'S psychology clinic was run out of a stylish multilevel house with glass balconies at the front on a hill near Dodger Stadium. I was familiar with the street, having waited in the traffic to get into the stadium when I first moved to LA, batting merchandise peddlers away from the windows like flies.

Today there was no game, and the street was clear. Baby sat reading aloud to me the highlights of Daisy and Alex's conversations from the messages George had sent us the other day. I parked under a big tree and Baby sat with her elbow on the sill and big sunglasses covering her tired eyes.

"From Alex," Baby said. "'I just sat with a client for an hour and a half, walking her through her divorce, and all I could think about was you. My mouth was moving and I was saying all the right stuff, but my brain was disconnected. I was wondering if you were having a good day. What you were doing for lunch. Whether it's safe for you to meet with me this afternoon. Maybe I could surprise you with a cheeky Negroni between appointments? Might help me focus on what I'm doing here.'"

"Jeez," I said.

"Gross," Baby decided.

"Lucky he's not a neurosurgeon, since he can't keep his mind on his job," I said. "Pretty wordy texts. That was a real love letter. I mean, who doesn't want to hear that they're driving someone to distraction?"

"She's wordy too." Baby scrolled. "I guess you've got to be when you're stepping out on someone. Risky to call. Gotta text all the time."

"Actually, it's riskier to text," I said. "Leaves a trail. Though it's useful for us. When was that message from?"

"Three months ago."

"What are the messages like after the lottery win?"

Baby scrolled. I watched a puffy-eyed woman in a floral dress leave Alex's clinic and walk down the hill past our car. She tucked a fistful of used tissues into her handbag.

"Lots of *We need to talks*," Baby said.

"From Alex or from Daisy?" I asked.

"Both," she said. "When things are good, they write about it. When they're bad, they talk about it. So they don't say anything they'll regret in writing."

"Listen to the armchair psychologist over here." I sighed. "Let's go talk to the real one."

We got out and walked up to the house. There was a brass nameplate bolted above the knocker with Dr. Brindle's name and title stamped on it. I could see just inside the door the usual paraphernalia of a clinic trying to masquerade disarmingly as a family home—potted plants, generic knickknacks, inspirational quotes in brushed white frames.

A curvy Black woman with red-framed eyeglasses opened the door.

"We're here to see Dr. Alex Brindle," I said. "Is he in?"

"I'm Alex Brindle." She smiled at me, then at Baby. "Are you two my eleven o'clock couples session?"

Baby's lips quirked. I found myself hitting high revs to try to keep up.

"No, we're not a couple. I'm Rhonda Bird." Brindle and I shook hands. "We're here about Daisy Hansen."

I'd never seen a person's demeanor flip so quickly. Brindle's hand shrank in mine, and her posture stiffened; her lips pressed tight against her teeth. Her eyes searched mine.

"She's dead, isn't she?"

When I didn't answer, Dr. Brindle let go of my hand and gripped the door frame. "Oh God, I've killed her. I've killed her. I've killed her."

CHAPTER 50

ALEX BRINDLE'S LEGS WERE so wobbly, she barely made it to a big beige armchair in the room at the front of the house. I had to help her there. Baby stayed outside to tell the actual eleven o'clock couple who had just arrived that the doctor was unexpectedly indisposed.

I watched the psychologist crying in her armchair and tried to keep a neutral-to-sympathetic expression on my own face while I determined if her behavior was genuine. I decided that the tears were real. But the words *I've killed her* rang in my ears, and I was impatient to find out what she'd meant.

"Do her parents know?" she asked.

"If they don't, they will soon," I said, sitting down on the couch across from the therapist. "The police are doing their best to inform them before the internet breaks the news."

Brindle sucked in a deep breath, looking like she wanted to gag.

"How did she . . . I mean, did they . . . did they find . . . "

"They found her body this morning. They'll be doing an autopsy soon."

"Oh Jesus." Brindle put her face in her hands.

"You said you killed her," I pressed. Baby came into the room and sat beside me. "What did you mean by that?"

"I told her to leave him." Brindle swiped at her eyes, leaving a streak of mascara across her right temple. "It was him, wasn't it? Troy?"

I glanced at Baby. Her eyes were narrowed, suspicious. "We're not sure yet."

"This is all my fault. I told her to— "

"You told Daisy quite a few things that you shouldn't have told her over the course of your relationship," Baby interrupted, taking out her phone.

"Like what?"

"Oh, I don't know." Baby smirked. "Like her ass reminded you of polished stone? Like the smell of her shampoo on your pillow turned you on? Like that you held whole sessions with clients here while your mind was completely tangled up with her?"

"My messages." Brindle put her hand over her mouth. "You . . . you've read those? Did you . . . oh God."

Baby powered on. My heart was in my throat. Brindle

seemed to be assuming Baby and I were cops. She was probably too upset to notice how young my sister was. Well, we needed to keep her not thinking about it too much for as long as possible.

"Let's see what else we have here," Baby said, scrolling on her phone.

Alex Brindle looked like she was about to be sick.

"Two weeks ago," Baby said, "you texted, 'We need to talk.' It was in response to Daisy telling you in a text message that she loved you. You called her. The two of you spoke for an hour and forty-seven minutes."

Brindle sat back in her chair. The color had drained from her cheeks, and sweat was beading at her hairline.

"In fact, Daisy said she loved you several times across your message history." Baby flicked the phone screen with her thumb. "You never said it back."

"I feel sick," Brindle said. "Just... just give me a second."

"This is all very—" Baby started, but I hushed her. My sister had gone in hard, and she'd done a good job. But she was still learning when to ease off the accelerator. I'd had enough practice with clients to know that a physically incapacitated suspect couldn't provide a solid story, whether that story was fact or fiction.

Brindle put her head in her hands.

"I loved her too," she said. "But I had so much more to lose than Daisy did."

"Like what?"

"Like my license and my practice." Brindle wiped sweat

from her brow. "I was Daisy's psychologist. She started coming to me about a year ago, wanting to talk about her marriage to Troy. She'd tried getting Troy into couples counseling but was having a hard time convincing him that there was a problem. And apparently he's not much of a talker. So Daisy and I would meet alone. We grew close during the sessions. She was bright and funny, and that's a bit of a rarity around here. Most of the people who walk in that door are struggling to find some peace in their lives. I counsel trauma victims. Rape victims. I specialize in broken marriages."

"You're a hero." Baby rolled her eyes. "We get it."

"There's a phenomenon that occurs sometimes between patients and therapists." Brindle tore a tissue from an ornate silver box on the coffee table. "It's called transference. You come in here, you open up, you form an emotional connection. Sometimes a patient confuses that connection with romantic feelings. When Daisy told me she was thinking about me outside the sessions..." Alex Brindle shook her head. "I should have stopped things then."

"Yes, you should have," Baby said. "You're looking at the loss of your psychologist's license and up to six months of jail time. California Business and Professions Code, division two, chapter one." My sister leaned toward me and whispered, "I looked it up in the car."

"Less vinegar, more honey," I murmured, then turned back to Brindle.

"I should have told the police as soon as I heard that Daisy was missing." Brindle rubbed her eyes. For a moment, she gripped her head as though trying to squeeze out the fear. "I just couldn't. I didn't want to put myself in the public eye like that. I've been sitting here for days now, just hoping that Daisy kept our relationship secret, that she'd be found safe and everything would blow over."

"Well, it didn't," Baby said.

"When did you and Daisy become intimate, Alex?" I gave Baby a warning look.

"It's been about five or six months." Brindle twisted the corners of her tissue into little points. "Troy blew up at a neighbor kid when he and Daisy were at her parents' house at Christmas. Daisy didn't like that. She came in wanting to discuss it. She wasn't talking about leaving him then. She was just . . . questioning her choices with Troy. The truth was that she didn't know him that well. That there were things from his past, his childhood, that worried her. There were a lot of closed doors."

"What do you mean, closed doors?" I asked.

"Things he wouldn't talk about," Brindle said. "Whenever Daisy tried to deepen the connection, you know, be vulnerable, he'd shut down. Say the past was the past. Daisy was worried about what kind of past that was."

Silence in the room. Baby was chewing her nails.

"But look." Alex Brindle sighed. "Daisy was also just questioning her life path in general. I thought she was bored, to be honest. That can happen. He worked. She worked. They had a nice home. She tried to go digging around in his past for drama and couldn't get anything. She needed conflict. There was no jeopardy in her life. No risk. No thrill."

A shimmer of energy seemed to pass through the room. Baby felt it too. She nudged my Vans with the side of her designer boot.

"What do you mean by *thrill*?" she asked. "Like, Daisy wanted to do something dangerous?"

"She just wanted something to give her life a spark," Brindle said miserably. "I think our affair was, you know... the risk she was chasing. That's what I was trying to work out with her, all those times we said we needed to talk." She nodded at the phone in Baby's hand. "Did she love me? Or did she love the taboo?"

"Then the money came into the equation," I said.

"That just made her question things more." Brindle shook her head. "And it made *me* question things more."

"Were you thinking of running away with Daisy?" I asked.

"No," Brindle said. "Not at all."

"So what were you questioning?"

"What Daisy wanted to do with the money," Brindle said. "It turned me off. It was too intense for me. Here she is, telling me that she loves me, right? That she's thinking about leaving her husband for me. Then she tells me she wants to go to graduate school, get a degree in psychology. She runs her thesis idea past me. And guess what?" Brindle gave a sad laugh. "Her thesis topic was my area of expertise. My *exact* area."

“Sounds like she was becoming obsessed with you,” I said.

“She was.” Brindle nodded. “And I was in too deep. I was trying to back off.”

“What’s your area of expertise?” Baby asked.

Dr. Brindle laughed, a small, embarrassed sound.

“When I started out, I didn’t do this kind of domestic stuff, couples therapy.” She gestured to the coffee table, the fluffy throw on the couch, the whole pretty but sterile setting. “But I learned after ten years of trying to change the world one monster at a time that you make a lot more money and you sleep better at night when you counsel normal people about normal problems.”

Baby and I looked at each other.

“I used to work in prisons,” Brindle said. “My doctoral dissertation was on serial killers.”

CHAPTER 51

BABY WALKED NUMBLY TO the car beside me, her face blank and her eyes on her feet. I felt the way she looked. We sat in shell-shocked silence in the sun-warmed Chevy for a good five minutes before either of us spoke.

"Daisy found a serial killer," Baby said.

I held the steering wheel.

"She did it to impress Alex," Baby went on. She gestured to the house we'd just come from. "She was obsessed with her lover, obsessed to the point that she would leave her husband. That she would leave her job. That she would leave her *life*. She wanted to bring Alex something that was right up her alley. Maybe a project they could work on together. So she hit the internet and scratched around until she found an unsolved crime. Then she got to work on it, and—"

"And what?" I asked.

"And she found what she was looking for." Baby shrugged. "You stick your finger down enough spider holes, eventually you're gonna get bit."

I couldn't untangle my thoughts. My phone bleeped.

"Question is, how far did she have to look?" Baby asked. "Maybe all she had to do to find a serial killer was roll over in bed."

The message on my phone was from Dave Summerly. I opened it.

We need to talk, it said. **Your place. Urgent.**

CHAPTER 52

DAVE SUMMERLY WAS WAITING on my front steps when I arrived, once again talking on his phone. He wrote a number on the back of his forearm with a pen while the device was clamped between his ear and shoulder.

I'd been so distracted by Dave's text that when Baby asked me to drop her on a corner so she could get an Uber and go to Arthur's, I did, not really thinking about it. Back home, I parked and opened the door for Dave, who was still on his phone. He hung up and immediately powered out a quick series of messages without saying hello or even looking at me. He smelled of sweat and dirt and there were fine scratches on the backs of his hands and mud on the soles of his boots.

"What the hell happened to you?" I asked when he finally looked up from his phone.

"I went back out with a couple of crews looking for the note," Summerly said. "I walked the brush. I climbed down into a goddamn ditch. We found some old pieces of a handgun and two dead raccoons but no note at the scene or anywhere nearby. If it ever existed."

"Pretty thorough," I said.

"Yeah, well, I did it for you." Summerly put his hands on my shoulders. "Rhonda, I know you believe in this guy. I didn't want you coming back to me telling me I didn't search hard enough."

I didn't know what to say. Every inch of me was sizzling at his touch.

"What was so urgent?" I asked.

For a moment, the big man struggled. "Brogan gave me the death-knock job. I came straight here after seeing Daisy's parents. I just..." He shook his head, chewed his lip. "I'm sorry. I know it's selfish, and you and me, we're sort of... "

"What?"

"I just needed to see you, Rhonda."

We tore each other's clothes off. It gets like that with me, at least sometimes. When I'm hurt or sad or furious, I'm driven to binge on food or work or exercise or men. I shoved the both of us into the shower and then into the bed, and for a while I was able to think about something other than what we'd both seen out at the foot of the mountains, something other than Alex Brindle's guilt and panic, George Crawley's innocent loyalty, and Troy Hansen's raw, raw pain. I was able to focus on my hand gripping Summerly's hair and not on that body bag on the gurney. I pulled Summerly into me and kissed him and forgot all about what kind of hell Mark and Summer Rayburn were walking through at that very moment.

The escape didn't last long. Twenty minutes later, I was standing in the kitchen rustling up something for us to eat. Dave came in and ran a hand up my back, then headed for the fridge.

"We actually do need to talk," I said.

"About what?"

I pointed to the cardboard box I'd put on the kitchen table, the box Troy had given me.

"That," I said.

CHAPTER 53

BABY STEPPED OUT OF the Uber, flipped her sunglasses down over her eyes, and smoothed the front of her skirt. In heels, she was well over six feet tall, and the blazer she wore was sharp-shouldered and nipped in at the waist. When she reached the automatic doors at the front of the Enorme offices, she drew the attention of all three security guards, but she walked right past them to the black marble reception desk in the foyer. Behind it, a huge LED screen was showing an Enorme promotional trailer.

Business-expansion solutions that harness nature-taught growth. I thrive with Enorme!

The receptionist was on a call when Baby arrived, but Baby spoke anyway. "Barbara Bird for Su Lim Marshall."

Hearing Marshall's name galvanized the receptionist. She tore out her Bluetooth earpiece and hit a button on her computer. To be surprised, to be caught off guard, was to be vulnerable, and the company couldn't afford that. Ever. Baby bet that hearing Marshall's name gave people around here the twitches.

"Ms. Bird! Of course. This is, uh, this is regarding..."

"Regarding a contract for the sale of Arthur Laurier's property."

That got things rolling. The receptionist asked for ID, and Baby handed over one of her best. Then she stood back and pretended to fire off a batch of communications on her phone. The receptionist, still smiling, made a call, maintaining the facade that she'd been expecting Baby. Only forty-five seconds passed before she popped up from her seat and showed Baby to the elevators.

Su Lim Marshall's office was on the third floor, down a long, empty hall from the elevators. Baby's first impression of Marshall was a small, insectile woman. She came around her desk with the same calm, poised charm the receptionist had exhibited. Completely unfazed by her unexpected visitor. Ready for any obstacle. *That's what we do here. We refocus, adapt, neutralize.* Baby didn't return the smile.

"It's a real pleasure to meet you," Marshall said smoothly, showing Baby to a seat in front of her almost comically large and bare desk. The thing commanded the room like an altar, yet it was empty save for a cell phone and an iPad. "I'm so glad that Mr. Laurier has decided to accept our offer on Waterway Street."

"Oh, he hasn't," Baby said.

Marshall stiffened microscopically. Baby saw a tendon in her throat go taut, then instantly soften again. The iPad gave a light musical note. Baby assumed it was announcing the arrival of a brief workup on herself, whatever the receptionist had been able to scramble together as Baby rode up on the elevator.

Baby placed her phone on the edge of the black glass sea that was the surface of Marshall's desk. She pulled up a video, put the phone on speaker, and hit play. The sound of Chris Tutti's voice fluttered around in the big room like a moth in a jar:

"Su Lim Marshall! She's head of—of land acquisitions or some shit!"

"Put a shirt on. You're gonna sit here and tell me everything she asked you to do. We're gonna get it on camera."

"Fuck that shit! I ain't coppin' to no murder rap!"

Marshall lifted her eyes from the phone to Baby. One of her thin brows rose slowly. "What *was* that?" the small woman asked with a tight smile. "A clip from a movie?"

"That was one of your Enorme employees, Chris Tutti, admitting you paid him to murder Carol and Arthur Laurier," Baby said. "Took about thirty seconds for him to give you up. And I didn't even have a gun on him. All I had was a dog on a leash. Imagine what police detectives in an interrogation room would do."

"I don't know who—" Marshall went for the iPad.

Baby held a hand up. "Don't go through the motions of

pretending you don't know who Tutti is. He worked security in the staff parking lot here for a year, then got bumped up to corporate valet. I assume that's when you met him. I bet you saw the tattoos on his knuckles, ordered a background check, and decided he might be useful in solving a little problem you were having over at Waterway Street. You saw him as the kind of lifelong bottom dweller who could use the extra cash."

Marshall's hand was still on the iPad.

"If you want to read the brief on me that your receptionist just sent you, go ahead," Baby said. "You'll find all it says is that I work for a private detective agency based in Koreatown."

"Wow." Marshall took a minute, shook her head. "Wow."

Another minute passed. Baby waited. Su Lim Marshall looked through the huge windows out at the LA skyline. At the brown smudge of afternoon heat haze.

Baby had been expecting more denials, for which she had responses prepared. She'd tell Marshall that hiring an idiot like Tutti to rub out Arthur had been a grave mistake. That a solid connection between Marshall and Tutti existed somewhere, whether it was in an internal email, a message between burner phones, a handwritten address on a napkin, a slice of the two of them conversing on security camera footage. So if Baby's security cam footage of Tutti vandalizing Arthur's house wasn't enough, and Tutti having been employed by Enorme wasn't enough, and Tutti admitting that Marshall had hired him for the murders wasn't enough—*something* would be enough. And Baby would find that thing, whatever it was. That witness. That bank deposit. That overheard clue.

She would find it.

She would connect Marshall to Tutti.

But none of her responses were needed. Marshall simply looked at Baby and smiled.

"Okay, Ms. Bird," she said brightly. "You wanna play? Let's play."

CHAPTER 54

BY THE TIME I finished telling Dave Summerly about the trophy box—how I'd come to acquire it and what I knew about its contents—he was standing before the collection of ten sad little zip-lock bags, each with the newspaper article pressed against its surface, spread out on my dining-room table.

Summerly stood there emotionlessly, his hair still wet from the shower we'd taken together, his mouth clamped shut and his jaw muscles twitching. Jarrod Maloof's greasy backpack and a printout of Alex Brindle and Daisy Hansen's messages over the months of their affair were also on the table. I'd come clean on everything. It had taken me half an hour to get it all out. Summerly licked his teeth and looked at me in a way he never had before.

"Tell me what you're thinking," I said, though I was terrified to hear it.

"I don't even know where to start." He shook his head. "I can't...I can't fix on anything. It's all swirling around. The...the utter disappointment I feel that you didn't trust me with all this. The fucking *blinding rage* I feel that you would jeopardize a chain of custody this way."

"I kept the box back until now because I wanted to know how it connected to the case," I said carefully. "And I knew it would blind the police team to the possibility of Troy's innocence. Make their tunnel vision even narrower. The chain of custody isn't any more corrupted than it would have been if a suspect handed evidence to his lawyer. No one has touched the box except me. It's been with me the whole time."

Summerly's fists were clenched and shaking. He picked up each bag by its corner and placed it as carefully as he could into the box. But even though he was being as gentle as possible, the anger was fighting to get out of him. He fumbled Dorothy Andrews-Smith's bag. I went for it. He snatched it away.

"Dorothy Andrews-Smith was killed by a fucking gang, Rhonda."

"How do you—"

"I *know*," he said. "I know she was. And you will too when you examine the facts. How closely have you looked at these cases?"

"Maybe you haven't noticed, but I've been a little busy," I said. "When I started, I went for Jarrod Maloof. He went missing most recently. His uncle is— "

"I don't care." Dave rubbed his brow. "I don't care what happened to him."

"Yes, you do." I tried to keep my voice gentle. "Baby and I are wondering if Daisy's affair with Alex Brindle might have sparked this. The therapist was pulling away. She felt the relationship was too intense, too risky. It could be that Daisy wanted to connect with her on a shared interest, and she went looking for— "

"Rhonda, you gotta stop talking." Summerly slapped the message printout on the top of the box.

"Alex Brindle— "

"Is a ruined witness," he barked. He picked up the box and headed for the door. "The thing you should have done when you discovered Daisy was having an affair was *tell me* so I could get Brindle's story while she was fresh. Now I gotta wonder what you've suggested to her in your untrained, unsanctioned, possibly manipulative interrogation."

"What?" I slipped by him and grabbed the doorknob before he could. "What did you just say? You think I don't know how to preserve the testimony of a witness? I was a lawyer for twelve years!"

"Exactly." Summerly hugged the box to his chest. His eyes were fierce with contempt. "You go into every interview knowing which side you're on, what answers you want. I'm a detective, Rhonda. I'm trained to make sure that doesn't happen." He shook the box in his arms. "These people? They aren't paying me to be on their side," he said. "Every dollar you make off Troy Hansen is a reason for you to ignore the truth."

"You really think I'd do that?" I asked. "You think I'd protect Troy if I thought he was guilty just to make a buck?"

"What am I supposed to think, Rhonda? Isn't that what lawyers do?"

I tore open the door. "Get out," I snarled.

He did.

CHAPTER 55

THE PILE OF WEEDS Arthur had dumped beside the rusted gate of 101 Waterway Street was bigger than the crouched man himself. Baby could just see the old dude's wicker sun hat bobbing as he worked. Before she was half-way across the street, Mouse charged off the porch and ran to the gate, eyes aflame, to ascertain if she was who she appeared to be or an afternoon snack. She nodded toward the porch, and the dog lifted his chin, turned a wary circle, and trotted back up there.

Mouse was easy to train—she entered commands in his brain, and, like a computer, he performed them. But she wasn't surprised. Baby had learned that with dogs, it was all about incentive, and she had two incentives to offer him. The first was snacks, a previously foreign concept to the abused and neglected hound. And the second was a life free of beatings. Baby had no intention of ever raising her hand to the dog, but she could tell from the way he winced whenever she moved too suddenly that the dog wasn't sure of that yet. Mouse was probably on the longest beating-free streak of his life, and she guessed he was eager to keep it that way.

As Baby neared the old man, she saw he was concentrating on pulling out a three-foot-tall flowering weed. It made a ripping sound as it came free of the dry soil and sent up a puff of delicate seeds. Arthur, on his knees in the dirt, spotted Baby's heels, moved his gaze up to her legs, then squinted at her face.

"You look nervous," he said.

"I'm not nervous," Baby scoffed. "Why would I be nervous?"

"Because you just made a move," he said. He grabbed the base of another weed, gave it a wiggle to test its grip on the earth. "You're dressed to kill. I'm guessing you just went to the Enorme people to give them what for."

"Even if I did," Baby said, "what makes you think I'd leave all rattled?"

"I've seen their work."

Baby snorted.

"I'm thinking about just taking that money and getting out of here, Barbara," Arthur said. His shadow was small on the cracked concrete path. "Your sister coming around here reminded me that you got people. I don't. What you're doing for me and this house, it's nice. But it's not worth it. I should cut my losses."

"Arthur, you're not doing that," Baby said.

"Why not?"

"It's like this, okay?" she said. "Su Lim Marshall hired some two-bit thug to come after you. Chris Tutti is a loser. He lives with his grandmother. He's been in and out of jail since he could walk. He's a career fuckup. Su Lim Marshall hired him only because he was there. He was convenient. A guy who doesn't have what it takes to maintain a *fish tank* is the person she hired to run a scare campaign against an elderly man and off him if necessary."

Baby waited. Arthur said nothing.

"You know why she did that?" Baby asked.

"No."

"Because she's lazy," Baby said. "She's complacent. Do you know how a person gets lazy and complacent about killing people?"

"How?"

"By doing it a bunch of times," Baby said. "I'm positive that Su Lim Marshall has done this before. And if we shut up and take the money, she'll keep doing it. We're here, now, dealing with this because the folks before you shut up and took the money and cut their damn losses."

Arthur put his hands on his knees. He stared at his own shadow, which was imperceptibly growing.

"We're going to find out who the last guy was," Baby said.

"And the guy before that. And the guy before that. That's how we take these people down, Arthur."

A car pulled into the street, about six abandoned and fenced-off houses away from where Baby stood. Mouse growled, came trotting down the porch steps again. The car was a huge black Escalade with tinted windows. One of the windows rolled down when the car was two houses away.

Arthur got up and stood beside her. The car approached, its darkened interior impenetrable in the afternoon sun. Baby felt sweat break out on her upper lip.

As the car passed, Mouse let out a hellish round of barks, throwing his weight at the rusty gate, making it rattle in its frame. The window of the car slid up again. The car drove on and disappeared around the corner. Baby realized she'd been holding her breath.

"Okay," she said. "So maybe I'm a little nervous."

CHAPTER 56

I WAS PUTTING MY overnight bag into the Chevy Impala when Baby called. The surf was up, crunching hard beyond our row of houses, and I could hear kids squealing and dogs barking out on the esplanade.

There was a hipster-looking couple on the opposite corner who'd been there when I emerged from the house, and from their theatrically casual gestures, I'd known immediately that they were web sleuths or citizen journalists trying not to get made. Half the skill of being undercover is staying relaxed. The guy yawned, then the girl copied him, then they laughed too hard about it. By the time Baby called, they'd given up the ruse and were openly filming me on their phones.

"Hey," I said.

There was a pause, then Baby asked, "What happened?"

"You hear me say 'Hey' and you immediately know something happened?"

"I'm your sister."

"Yeah, well." I got into the car and started fiddling with the phone. "Dave was at the house and I...I figured it was time to tell him everything. So I did. He blew up. He took the box, the backpack, the messages, all of it. I was about to call you."

"What was Dave Summerly doing at the house? You two are back on? I knew that would happen."

"That's what you wanna know? Whether Dave and I are banging again?"

"I'm your *sister*, Rhonda."

"Fine, we were." I put the phone on speaker and pulled out. "But the whole 'He thinks I'm covering for a possible serial killer' thing snuffed us back out. I'm leaving now to go north. I want to speak to Troy's parents. I mean, where have they been in all this?"

"True. And what's the deal with his childhood?" Baby said. "Daisy told Alex there were too many closed doors. Was she right to be worried?"

"Look, no offense," I said. I took a deep breath. "But I really feel like going alone. I need some time to think."

"I get it."

"Talk later."

"Drive safe."

For two hours I drove in silence, just my wheels on the

road and the sound of traffic ebbing and flowing around me. Red lights, billboards, overpasses. Dry, rocky mountains. I called Men's Central Jail to speak to Troy, already knowing the response I would get—inmates weren't permitted to use the phones after five p.m. It was useless, but I had to try. Next, letting my impulses carry me, I dialed Mark and Summer Rayburn. I hung up halfway through the first ring, cursing myself for being so insensitive. After a minute, I got a call back from the same number. I winced as Mark came on the line.

"I'm sorry," I said. "It's Rhonda Bird. I just realized it's a terrible time to call."

"Don't worry about it." I heard the sound of people talking, then a door sliding shut. The other voices were cut off abruptly. "I needed an excuse to go out and get some air. The house is full of people. Everybody's crying."

I listened to Mark's gravelly voice and willed myself to keep it together.

"I'm all cried out myself," he said. "I was going to call you, actually."

"You were?"

"Yeah," he said. "They're doing the autopsy on Daisy. Getting it rushed through because of all the public interest. They don't know everything, but there were some things they were able to tell us. Her body was burned inside the car, but it looks like she was already dead."

I didn't know what to say, so I just listened.

"If it was Troy, why would he do that?" Mark asked. "I

mean, there was no need to hide evidence, right? Fingerprints and stuff. Troy used Daisy's car all the time. Would make sense for traces of Troy to be there."

"Look." I took a deep breath, feeling like I was on unsteady ground. "The psychology behind all this stuff is... there are mixed opinions, okay? Sometimes killers cover their victims with a blanket to hide what they've done. That happens particularly when it's a known victim. Could be that burning the... the scene... was driven by shame."

"So now you think it could be him?"

"I don't know," I said. "But, Mark?"

"Yeah?"

"I'm not gonna stop *until* I know."

Mark Rayburn gave a hoarse grunt. I didn't know if it was appreciation or derision.

"Personally, I think we should be looking harder at that George Crawley guy," he said. "The man makes me uncomfortable. Always has. Never known him to have a girlfriend. Maybe he got jealous, went to the house, made a pass at Daisy."

"Maybe," I said. I thought about George Crawley weeping from stress in my car. "I don't want to discount anything yet, but I'm following other leads."

I saw a cluster of lights approaching, a gas station flanked by fast-food joints. I started shifting lanes. "Tell me, did you ever meet Troy's parents?" I asked Mark.

"No," Mark said. "They didn't come to the wedding. Troy said they were elderly. Limited mobility. But I think that was bullshit. From what Daisy told me, they're hicks from some backwater place up north somewhere."

"Outside Ukiah, up in Mendocino County."

"Right. I'm thinking the kids just didn't invite them. Didn't want their big day to turn into an episode of *The Beverly Hillbillies*."

I said goodbye to Mark, pulled the Chevy up to a pump, and started filling it with gas. The site was identical to a thousand highway oases I had stopped at. A dusty, ruddy-faced panhandler begged for change on the edge of the lot. A mom and dad with sleeping kids in the back seat of their car checked their tires, calculated the time left before they hit LA.

In the attached convenience store, I grabbed snacks without much thought—nuts, chips, jerky, whatever I could eat one-handed. As I was filling a forty-four-ounce slushy cup, the attendant grabbed my arm. I was so startled, I dropped the cup, spilling chunky sludge everywhere.

"Yo, lady," the guy said. He was looking out the big dark windows to the lot. "Don't go to your car yet, okay? Some dude just crawled up and snuck into the back seat."

CHAPTER 57

BABY TAPPED AWAY AT her laptop at Arthur's kitchen table, the sunset bleeding into night. Arthur brought her a glass of water, but she ignored it. As she tapped and clicked, the water was joined by a cup of coffee, then a slice of cake, then a cookie, then a hard candy wrapped in shiny foil and served on a little porcelain plate. He was carting over a second cup of coffee to replace the one that had gone cold when she looked up.

"You're gonna bury me alive in a pile of drinks and snacks here," Baby said.

"I need something to do."

"Play with the dog."

They looked at the dog. Mouse was snoring in the corner,

his big pink belly sagging on the floor, all four legs stretched out and stiff, roadkill-style.

"Tell me what you've found out." Arthur sat down beside her.

"I haven't got a lot to work with." Baby sighed. "On the record, Su Lim Marshall joined Enorme as an administrative assistant in 2012. Now she's head of the California acquisition division. Seems to have worked her way up the ranks pretty naturally, if quickly. No weird promotional leaps that might suggest she was being rewarded for doing the company some murderous favors," Baby said. "The company has two other eco-villages in the state, and they were both set up by Marshall. But they were on vacant land. Marshall didn't threaten or bully anybody out of their houses there, at least. She didn't need to."

Baby brought up Su Lim Marshall's LinkedIn profile, turned the screen toward Arthur. Marshall was classically posed—three-quarters to the camera, hair shiny and perfect, shoulders relaxed, chin up. She looked like a million other corporate types who silently oiled the gears of commerce in dark gray power suits, driving dark gray power cars to dark gray power towers. Baby showed Arthur the two other California eco-villages, clusters of glass buildings, one in the desert and one in the forest.

"So who was Su Lim Marshall before she became an Enorme attack dog?" Arthur asked. Baby was so distracted, he had to ask a second time.

"Why is that relevant?"

"Because who a person is deep down inside is always relevant," Arthur said. "It's why anybody does anything."

"Look, Arthur, I'm not trying to tap into Marshall's psyche," Baby said. "I'm not trying to find out if she was picked on in high school or if she's ever been married or what kind of guy her dad was. I'm trying to find out how many times she's done *this specific thing*." She tapped the kitchen table. "Because that's all I can use against her."

"Maybe." He shrugged. Baby waited. When he didn't go on, she threw her hands up.

"I hate it when you say 'Maybe' like that. Like you don't mean 'Maybe,' you mean 'You're wrong.'"

"Carol used to hate it too." Arthur smiled. "All I'm saying is, you don't know what's relevant until it's relevant."

He pushed the coffee closer to her. She relented and drank, then rubbed her tired eyes.

"You and your sister, you're also chasing a serial killer, right?"

"Could be."

"Carol used to watch those documentaries on the TV." Arthur nodded. Sat back in his chair. "Those crime ones. I never got into that stuff. If we were in bed and there was a bump in the night, she'd kick me out to go find out what it was. So I didn't need to have my head filled up with crazy stories about guys waiting for me on my back porch with a butcher's knife. But I still picked some things up from all her watching."

"Where's this going?" Baby huffed.

"Seems to me, Barbara"—he gave her a warning look—"there's usually an awful lot of interest on these shows about who the killer was and where he came from. People want to know if he was picked on in high school. If he was ever married. What kind of guy his dad was."

Baby thought about it. "You don't know what's relevant until it's relevant."

"Uh-huh."

Mouse sprang up from the floor as if he'd gotten an electric shock, rushed to the back of the house, and smashed into the screen door, throwing it open. Arthur and Baby followed the dog to the back porch. To the right, across the fences of the neighboring properties, they saw movement. Two houses down, men emerged onto the back porch, pointed at Arthur's yard, and looked around. Someone flicked on a light. Music with a heavy, grinding bass began to thrum out into the night. It was so loud, Baby could feel the rhythm in her chest.

"Who the hell are those guys?" she asked.

"I don't know. What I'm wondering is, why's the power on?" Arthur said. "There hasn't been power to any of these other houses in months."

Mouse was barking at the fence on the right side of the yard, the side where the men had appeared. Then he rushed across the overgrown garden to bark at the opposite fence. Baby and Arthur looked. Lights were also coming on in the house on their left side. A man in a hoodie shoved open a window on the second floor, looked out at them, and grinned. There were thick gold chains around his neck and a set of grilles sparkling in his bottom row of teeth. As they watched, the guy took a pistol from his waistband and leaned casually on the windowsill while holding it.

“Well, howdy, neighbors!” he called.

CHAPTER 58

THE CONVENIENCE-STORE ATTENDANT and I stood by the slushy stand, watching the night. Beyond the automatic doors, the world was carrying on. A trucker pulled an eighteen-wheeler into a spot by the highway, its brakes hissing loudly. The family with the sleeping kids loaded up and moved on. People queued for the fast-food drive-through. My Chevy sat by the pumps.

"Tell me exactly what you saw," I said.

"Dude came round the pumps from that side." The attendant pointed to the darkness beyond the reach of the overhead lights mounted on the store's awning. "Crouched by your car, then snuck in the back door."

I was convinced by the alertness of this young man. His name tag said RAYMOND.

"You ain't got nobody traveling with you?" Raymond asked, his scalp sweating between his cornrows. I could see his pulse ticking in his neck. "Like, this ain't a prank?"

"No," I said. "I'm alone." I felt a weird rush of emotions—terror, gratitude, rage. My skin crawled, my mind shuttling through a thousand terrible possibilities, all of them beginning with the young store clerk *not* noticing a man sneaking into the back seat of my car.

Raymond shook his head. "Fucking tweakers all up and down the highway pullin' this shit. I'm calling the cops."

I followed him to the counter, keeping my eyes on my car, watching for movement.

"You think he's still in the back right now?" I asked.

"Hell yeah, I do."

I stood quietly wanting to hug the kid as he dialed and explained the situation to the 911 operator.

"Fuck that." Raymond slammed down the phone. He brought a baseball bat out from behind the counter. "There's a crash up at the next interchange, about five miles from here, and every cop in the county is tied up with it. We gonna handle this ourselves."

"No, no, no. Let's just wait," I said. I caught up with Raymond and grabbed his T-shirt as he headed out the automatic doors. "Wait."

"I'm sick of these tweakers stealing my beers, pissin' on my damn dumpsters, threatening my customers," he muttered. He kept walking and raised his voice as he approached my car. "Hey! Shithead! Get your junkie ass out of that car right now before I open it up and drag you out!"

I stood by Raymond's side, frozen by his sudden ferocity. A few yards away, the trucker paused mid-descent from the eighteen-wheeler, one boot still on the step, his head twisted around to us. Nothing in my car moved. It seemed impossibly dark inside, the overhead lights blocking my view into the windows with icy reflections.

"I've got a gun in a bag in the car," I told Raymond.

"Oh, shit. We better move quick, then," he said. He rushed up to the car and yanked open the back door with one hand, brandished the bat with the other.

A whump of dizziness hit me, a cold rush of adrenaline dumping into my system. Raymond and I stared at the empty back seat of the car. The baseball bat clunked to the ground loudly. Raymond leaned forward and examined the front seats, then reached for the foldout panel in the back seat that led to the trunk.

"What the—" I started.

"What the *fuck*?" he finished for me. Raymond went to the driver's side, popped the trunk, walked around, and threw it open. He stared at my bags, then at me. My face must have told him something about the thoughts in my head.

"Nah, nah, nah." He held a hand up. "Don't do me like that. I'm not crazy, ma'am. Okay? There was a dude. He got in your car. I swear to Jesus, man."

"Those cameras." I pointed to the cameras over the automatic doors. "Do they work?"

"Yeah, but the system's password-protected. Only the manager can use it." He sighed, picked up the bat. "I can't access it."

"What about you?" I called to the trucker. He jumped down from the bottom step of the truck. "You see a guy get into or out of my car?"

"I weren't lookin'." The truck driver shrugged.

"I swear, lady," Raymond said, "there was a dude in your car."

"Okay." I put a hand on his shoulder, which was warm and damp with sweat. "Well, he's gone. We must have taken our eyes off the car long enough for him to slip away. But now I just want to get out of here. I'm creeped out enough."

"I feel that. I'm sorry."

"It's okay. Thanks for looking out for me, Raymond," I said. He walked to the automatic doors, his shoulders slumped and the bat hanging by his side. He looked like a struck-out Little Leaguer. I slid into the car and turned the engine on.

I smelled cigarette smoke.

The hairs on the back of my neck stood on end. I looked in the rearview mirror at the darkness beyond the reach of the gas station's lights, but there was nothing but blackness and stillness there. With nothing to tell me that the cigarette smoke hadn't drifted in from outside the vehicle, I did what most people would do: I told myself not to be crazy.

Then I locked the doors and headed back to the highway.

CHAPTER 59

ARTHUR AND BABY SAT on the low brick wall in front of 101 Waterway Street idly watching different goings-on. At another time, in another place, they might have been a father and daughter observing the roll and tumble of suburban life, watching their neighbors peacefully watering their lawns, enjoying evening drinks on their porches, calling the kids in from play as the streetlights flickered to life. But here, tonight, they were watching something else. Baby's gaze was on a drug deal happening only twenty yards away, the third she'd witnessed in the past ten minutes. Corner boys loitered on the house's lawn, hands in their pockets and heads down, talking trash while they waited for customers to roll up. Arthur's attention was captured by an argument slowly intensifying on the porch three houses down in the other direction. There was a scream, and a woman involved in the argument was thrown down the steps; her tiny denim shorts did nothing to protect her legs from the concrete path. Already bleeding, she was picked up and tossed again through the rusty gate into the street.

The air around Baby and Arthur was vibrating with competing stereo systems and potential violence.

They'd given up letting Mouse roam the property, fearing he'd leap the front fence and attack someone out of sheer confusion. He sat behind the locked front door now, bellow-barking and scratching at the wood. Baby felt the dog's helpless bewilderment. The world outside was filled with obvious danger, and his new owners were clearly distressed by it, and yet they'd chosen to go out *into* it. And without him! He had one instinct: Protect Baby and Arthur. And they weren't letting him do that.

Two Escalades pulled up at the end of the street. Men in leather jackets exited, consulted with their men on the ground. They did a tour of three or four houses, spoke to different crews, then embarked again, rolling by Arthur and Baby slowly. Baby stood up, defiant. She was still standing that way, rigid and hard-eyed, when a group of men strolled along the sidewalk toward them.

"This one looks all right," one of them said to another, his gaze on Arthur's house. "Got screens on the windows."

"This house is occupied," Baby snapped. "Keep it movin'."

The man leading the pack, a redhead with sunken, glazed eyes, took her in. "What did you say, bitch?"

"Keep it movin'," Baby told him. "You deaf?"

The pack of guys snickered and guffawed. Baby kept her gaze locked on the leader as he passed, shouldering her on the way.

A police squad car pulled in at the other end of Waterway Street. Arthur and Baby watched it roll toward them. When it was within a few yards, Baby stepped out into the road. The female officer in the passenger seat buzzed down her window and leaned out.

"I've been wondering when you'd show up," Baby said. "I called this in an hour ago."

"Called what in?"

"This!" Baby gestured to the street. "These houses are owned by a company called Enorme. All these people are trespassing here. And aside from that, they're blatantly conducting criminal activity. There's a drug deal happening right there in front of us."

"Where?" The officer squinted through the windshield.

"There!" Baby pointed. The dealer, who was maybe thirty feet away, looked over. He tucked a wad of cash into his pocket and snapped a salute. Baby watched the dealer go back to his stash to re-up; he had the kind of detached confidence that made her stomach knot.

"I can't be sure of what I just saw." The officer shrugged at her partner. "You?"

"Nah. I left my glasses back at the station."

"Ma'am," the officer said, leaning out again. "I'm not seeing anything here that suggests to me that my colleague and

I should bother these people, who seem to be going about their business peacefully."

Baby scoffed. "Look, if you can't spot a drug deal in progress when it's happening within throwing distance of your squad car bumper, that's your problem. But these people are trespassing. Okay? You can at least clear them out if you're not going to arrest them."

"Do you know who any of these people are?" the officer asked.

"No."

"So how do you know the homeowners haven't permitted them to use the premises?"

Baby gritted her teeth. "I don't know that."

"Hmm." The officer nodded. Baby gave it one last shot.

"I could call the cops again," she said. "Try to get a different pair of officers out here. Maybe I'll even get hold of your boss. Your chief might be interested to know how you've responded to this scene."

"Oh, I don't think he would be," the officer behind the wheel said. He grinned. Baby eased a breath through her teeth.

"Come on." Baby felt the desperation rising from her stomach into her chest. She gave a laugh that was almost a sob. "I mean, come on. Don't you have . . . " She had no words. Let her hands fall by her sides.

The female officer eyed Baby. "Ma'am, you seem edgy to me. Have you consumed any illegal substances?"

"No way, don't even." Baby backed away from the car. "Don't even try to pull that one on me."

"Is there anything else we can assist you with?"

"No." Baby winced. The word was like acid in her throat. "We're good."

She walked back to Arthur. The old man's eyes were full of dread.

"This is bad," she said. "Real bad."

CHAPTER 60

I CHECKED INTO A little roadside motel around midnight. I'd called ahead, and the clerk had left the key for me under a potted plant by the door to the darkened reception office. I went into the room, dumped my bags, and showered.

I stood for ages under the water-saving showerhead, forcing scalding-hot water needles into my skin. It wasn't an entirely bad sensation, but no amount of physical discomfort could alleviate the guilt galloping around in my chest after the confrontation with Dave Summerly. Or the uneasiness I felt after Raymond's insistence that he'd seen a man sneak into my car. Truth was, I believed the guy. And though I'd managed not to dwell on my violent altercation with Martin Rosco in my home, I wondered if someone had been hired to finish what Rosco had started. There'd been no sign of anyone suspicious when I stopped at a roadhouse for dinner. Nor at the next gas station I stopped at before arriving here. But I felt watched all the same.

My emotions were tangled. I lay on the bed and stared at the dusty stucco ceiling and tried to talk myself down from that catastrophic ledge. My senses jolted at every sound outside the motel room. I'd never been afraid of the dark, but as I reached to turn off the bedside lamp, a horrifying thought occurred to me. There had been no cars parked outside when I arrived. What if I was the only guest at the motel tonight? This isolated place was nothing but a tiny office and a row of six rooms. The clerk probably forwarded calls to the motel's number to his own phone at night.

I realized that if I screamed, no one would hear me.

When my cell phone rang, I did scream. It took me a few long, urgent seconds to catch my breath.

"Something you want to tell me, Ms. Bird?" Detective Will Brogan asked when I picked up the phone and turned the bedside lamp back on.

I heard my own sigh rattle on the line. "The box," I said.

"The box, the messages, the backpack," Brogan said. "Hell of a twist in the tale, all of this. And I'm surprised it's come this late in the story."

"I thought I was protecting my client," I said, "and the truth. And you know what? I stand by my decision, Brogan."

"I get it," Brogan said. His tone was reasonable. I held the phone and felt a tiny amount of comfort.

"You're taking this better than expected," I said.

"Well, I'm tired." He gave a small, warm laugh. "It's been a hell of a day. Maybe eight hours ago I would have been pissed as hell at you for holding this back. But to be honest, I've had a lot going on. The crime scene. The autopsy. The press. I'm kind of relieved I didn't hear about the box until all that was over."

"Well, you're welcome," I quipped. "Dave sure got angry enough for the two of you."

"He's an emotional guy. I've been around longer. I'm more grizzled and jaded. I'm not surprised anymore when people do things like this—hide evidence. Lie. Protect the bad guys. It takes a bit more than that for me to really pop my lid."

I smiled. I couldn't deny a tiny stirring in my chest at Brogan's measured composure. Unshakable men had always attracted me. It was probably a throwback to growing up with an unstable and then absent father. I heard him shifting in his chair.

"Anyways, I'm sorry to tell you that I'm calling because I'm on a streak of delivering bad news, and it's your turn."

"Okay?"

"Troy Hansen got beat up this evening at Men's Central."

All the air left my chest. I lashed out, kicked the nightstand over. The lamp rattled to the floor and threw abstract shadows on the walls.

"They couldn't see that coming?" I yelled. "Are you serious?"

"Well, they probably did see it coming." Brogan sighed.

"But you know what these good ol' boys who go into corrections jobs are like. They want to see justice done, even if it's the in-house kind. Either the guards smacked Troy around or they put him in a cell with someone who would and turned the cameras off. The saving grace is that it's nothing permanent. He's been through the infirmary and he's already back in his cell sleeping it off."

"They'll kill him in there," I said.

"Maybe."

"Until he makes bail, he's in the lion pit," I insisted. "You get that, right? And it won't matter if you think he killed Daisy or murdered all those other people or both. You will never know the absolute truth because there'll be no trial, no confession, no hearing of—"

"I know, Ms. Bird. I know," Brogan said. "But I'm doing my job here. I ordered Troy's arrest. I had to. The guy led me to his wife's body. And nothing you've done today has made me think twice about that order."

"There's always tomorrow," I said.

"That's the spirit."

"Brogan, I helped you out by surrendering that box," I said. "It's your turn."

"Are you kidding me? I'm calling you right now to update you. Giving you the twenty-four-hour news cycle on this case. I don't have to do that."

"But you are, because you're trying to keep me on your side in case I get something more. In case I can be useful to you later."

“I’m also just a genuinely nice guy, Rhonda.”

“So throw me another bone, Mr. Nice Guy. I’m in the middle of nowhere, clutching at straws.”

“In the middle of nowhere?”

“Uh-huh.” I took the phone away from my ear when I heard what sounded like footsteps on the gravel outside. “And I don’t think I’m alone.”

I went to the curtain, pulled it back, and looked out. The lot was empty. The road beyond and the woods bordering it were quiet. I double-checked the lock, then took a chair and wedged it under the door handle.

“Let me think.” Brogan sighed. “Our techs have analyzed Troy’s cell phone locations over the past several months. I could maybe send you that.”

“Good. And I want the official files on all the missing people from the box.”

“Big ask,” he said.

“You’ve got nothing to lose.”

The silence stretched, both on the line and outside my dark little pocket of rural California.

“Let me see what I can do,” Brogan said.

CHAPTER 61

IT WAS A HELLISH night on Waterway Street. Baby had never read Dante's *Inferno,* but she saw scenes out her window overlooking the front of the house that she presumed belonged in its pages.

Three houses down, one of the vacant dwellings seemed to have become a makeshift brothel, cars arriving every twenty minutes or so. Baby watched as men held up their phone screens to a guard at the door, were let in, then came out anywhere from ten minutes to an hour and a half later. While the system seemed orderly, it was a rowdy bunch. Girls fighting. Johns arguing over payments and girls. She saw one man get thrown clean over the dying hedge at the front of the house and another get punched in the stomach and stuffed in the trunk of his own car.

The sex work seemed to be relegated to one end of the street; the other end was where the drugs and partying were going on. One party had begun in a pretty two-story brick place, then spilled across the street to the opposite property. A guy passed out in the gutter, and a group of men came over, surrounded him, took whatever was in his pockets, then filmed themselves urinating on his sleeping form.

As the night went on, the dealers, the pimps, and their drunken and drugged clientele grew louder, more violent. The same cops who'd done a drive-by in response to Baby's call came by again, but they didn't exit their vehicle. They stopped to talk to a couple of men. They pointed half-heartedly at the passed-out guy in the gutter.

Baby assumed Su Lim Marshall had somehow arranged for the street to be available for whatever goings-on the bad men of Culver City and the surrounding area wished to conduct. Apparently, the only rule was that no one was allowed to die. A death would raise questions, bring unwanted attention. So, ten minutes after the second drive-by, an ambulance arrived to carry the unconscious guy off. The bewilderment on the faces of the paramedics at the happenings around them was obvious to Baby even from a distance.

With months of stress already weighing down his bones, Arthur put wax earplugs in his ears and went to bed around eleven o'clock. Baby stayed awake to fend off anyone who approached. Arthur's house, the only one on the street without booming music or steady traffic in and out, became a curiosity for the street's visitors, so soon some of them knocked at the front door to see what was up. Mouse's wild performance behind the door discouraged them. But before long Baby was following the aggravated dog out back, where a shadowy figure had decided to investigate the porch. Once he'd been chased away, a group of drunk girls from the house on the left decided it would be fun to see if they could sprint across Arthur's yard without the dog catching them and mauling them to death. Baby locked Mouse inside again, aware that the game could have fatal consequences.

When the visits stopped, around two a.m., she lay on the couch and stared at the purple and red lights from the street party dancing on the ornate ceiling moldings. She wondered if Arthur's life had been better before she entered it. One way or the other, it was only a matter of time before Su Lim Marshall's minions set up some catastrophe leading to Arthur's violent but apparently accidental demise, and at least before she'd shown up, he'd been able to get some sleep at night.

Maybe Mouse was better off without her too. In other circumstances, Rhonda would never have let Baby get a dog. She would have said Baby was too young for the responsibility. And Baby hadn't exactly provided a safe and stable home for the abused animal—she'd drafted him as a soldier in a war he couldn't possibly comprehend. Was she any better than the pet thieves who'd used him to guard their animal-trafficking den?

At three a.m. someone hurled a brick through one of the

front windows, and Mouse went charging around looking for the perpetrator, growling and snapping his jaws. Baby settled him, then started sweeping up the glass. As she knelt on the carpet and worked, tears sprang to her eyes. She swiped at them angrily. Baby had told Rhonda she could handle this situation, and damned if she would let Marshall turning Arthur's street into a Pop-Up Gangland break her.

Baby cleaned up the mess and dragged a bookcase over to block the broken window, which exhausted her but also gave her a sense that she wasn't completely failing. She fell into a half-sleep on the couch at four a.m.

The screaming woke her at 6:17.

CHAPTER 62

SEEN FROM A DISTANCE, the house on the corner seemed no different than those around it. Every window and doorway was lit up, and there was movement inside. But as Baby moved with the crowd toward the weatherboard building, she smelled smoke on the wind. A primal energy coursed through the people converging on the house. Fear. Excitement.

It was a fire lighting up the building.

Two windows on the bottom floor exploded. Baby could see flames between the silhouettes of people crowding around the property. Smoke billowed out of the broken windows, upside-down waterfalls of coiling blackness. She pushed to the front, nudged a guy out of the way so hard, he toppled over on the grass, clearly drunk. People were watching the house burn and taking videos on their phones. She didn't see a single person calling for help.

"Call the damn fire department!" she yelled. Nearby, someone cackled. She heard some mutters of refusal. These people weren't the type who called 911 for anything, ever. Emergency services meant problems. It meant witnesses. Rock-solid proof of whereabouts and times. The ambulance earlier had been bad enough.

Baby hoped the light from the fire or the smoke on the wind would alert someone more responsible a few streets away. She looked through the open door of the burning house and saw flames stroking the walls of the hall on both sides. She turned, planning to dash back to Arthur's and grab her own phone. She saw the old man at the edge of the road. His glasses were orbs of gold light from the inferno.

Then the scream came again, the same skin-tingling sound that had snapped Baby awake. It came from the second floor. She rushed forward, realizing with weird, panicked clarity that her feet were bare. The porch boards were warm. She looked down and saw glowing embers dancing beneath them through the gaps in the wood. The hall was blocked by fire.

"Up there!" someone yelled. Baby staggered back, narrowly missed being clobbered with a wooden plank that had fallen from the second floor and bounced off the porch awning. Someone was kicking boards away from a window. A hand shot through the gap, waving.

"Somebody help us!"

Baby looked at the crowd, saw lazy red eyes. Grins. Grimaces. Stupefaction was the best thing she saw, people's bewilderment at what to do to answer that cry. The fire was so loud, Baby couldn't tell if there were sirens coming. She hoped there were. She hoped normal people beyond the reach of the houses bought up by Enorme were on their phones, calling for help. But she couldn't wait to find out.

She raced through the yard to the back of the house, praying the fire hadn't reached there yet. She got lucky. It had begun in the front room and gone up. She scaled the awning over the back porch and clambered up the exterior cladding, her fingernails biting into a window ledge and her bare toes scraping the paintwork. Baby had popped a few windows in her brief time as a PI. She braced her shoulder against the top of the window frame, tucked her arm into her T-shirt, and smashed the window with her elbow. A shard of glass scraped the outside of her thigh as she squeezed into the house and hurried across the empty room.

The hall was black with smoke. Her eyes and nose ran. Baby fought her way through, coughing, to the front. A teenage boy and girl were crouched at the window, waving their arms. They must have gone upstairs when they saw the flames on the first floor, thinking they'd pop out the window and instead finding themselves trapped. Baby marched over, grabbed them by the backs of their T-shirts, and hauled them toward the back stairs.

"Come on! Come on! This way!"

It felt like a minute or less had passed since she'd entered the house. The flames had been one floor down. Now they were here, melting the cheap plastic frame of a picture that had been hanging on the wall, making it drip like melted ice cream onto the floor. Baby turned the couple around and shoved them toward a bathroom. There was one window, long and covered with frosted glass. She shoved it open. Hot air blasted past her.

"It's too high! I can't! I can't! I can't!" the girl squealed. She clung to Baby like a drowning person, a frantic, painful, skin-cutting grip. There was nothing else to do—Baby punched the girl in the stomach. When she doubled over, Baby turned her and shoved her head-first out the window. The girl tumbled and landed flat on her back on the soft grass, groaning.

Baby turned to the guy. He went willingly. The consequences of not getting a move on were plain. Baby watched him slide carefully out the window, legs first, and drop onto the grass below with a grunt. With her T-shirt held to her mouth and nose, her head already spinning from smoke inhalation, Baby closed her eyes and jumped out the window.

CHAPTER 63

ARTHUR FUSSED OVER BABY all the way back to the house. There was blood running down her left leg, enough to leave a row of bare footprints on the sidewalk. The kids she rescued had disappeared into the crowd, seemingly unharmed. Firefighters had finally shown up.

The front door was hanging open and Mouse was standing at the gate barking when they arrived back at the house. The old man and the girl froze at the sight of the hall light spilling out onto the path.

"Did you . . . ?" Baby said.

"No," Arthur said.

They went in through the gate, closed it behind them. The dog snuffled at Baby's fingertips, whimpering, as she and Arthur went inside. At least it was clear they were alone. If there had been someone else around, Mouse's focus would have been on the intruder.

In the kitchen, every cabinet door was hanging open. Arthur strode forward but Baby stopped him. "Don't touch anything," she said.

"We better turn the power off, I guess, in case something's wired up again." He sighed. Baby went back out, opened the fuse box, and shut the electricity off. The relief she felt was minuscule. When she returned, she found Arthur lighting candles and placing them around the kitchen. The air seemed changed, somehow tainted.

Baby took her phone from the coffee table in the living room and opened the security-camera app. She rolled the footage from the hidden cameras and found what she was looking for. At the front of the house, a small female figure in a black hoodie appeared, walking with confidence, hands thrust deep into her pockets. She slipped silently through the gate, shut it behind her, then went and pushed the unlocked front door open. Instead of going into the house, she bolted around the side. Mouse appeared, rushing out the front door, his attention immediately captured by the crowd in the street. The figure in the hoodie went around the back of the house, disappeared inside, came out again in mere seconds, and jogged off into the dusk.

Arthur joined Baby and the two of them stood in the candlelight and watched the footage a few times in silence. Baby could hear firefighters at the property on the corner of Waterway Street trying to disperse the crowds. She could hear Mouse in the kitchen munching kibble from his bowl.

"She was in the house for only a few seconds," Arthur said. "Maybe she was just getting the lay of the land."

"No, that's Su Lim Marshall, and she's done something," Baby said. "Look at the way she walks. Look at the purpose. She lured Mouse away, then came in and did something. And we have no idea what. She might have sprayed contact poison on our pillows or towels. She might have put something in the food. We need to throw out everything, Arthur. Empty the cabinets. We'll have to wash all the plates and glasses and cutlery. Better yet, throw them out too. Throw out everything from the bathroom. All the medications. The soap and shampoo."

"Wait, wait, wait. We don't know for sure it's Marshall," Arthur said. "Could have been some kid from the street looking for our wallets while we were out."

"It's her," Baby said. She had watched the footage a dozen times. "I saw her at the Enorme offices. I recognize her size and her shape. But it's more than that. I told you she made a mistake when she hired Chris Tutti to take you out, Arthur. She's not gonna make the same dumb move twice. Su Lim Marshall came here herself. She lit the fire down on the corner as a distraction and then came in here. We've just gotta make sure that whatever trap she set for us, we don't fall into it."

Baby went into the kitchen and grabbed a garbage bag. She tugged open the fridge and started loading items into the bag. Arthur opened the cabinets and began doing the same.

They both turned when Mouse gave a retching cough.

CHAPTER 64

MY SLEEP WAS FITFUL, full of nightmares cut short by panicked wakefulness. Living so close to the ocean since I moved to LA less than a year ago, I'd gotten spoiled by the comforting night music—the crunch of the waves, the chatter of gulls, the sound of people clumping along on the esplanade. Here, there was only ringing silence that gave way to sinister suggestions of danger—a scrape, a scuttle, a squeak.

I gave up on sleep at six thirty a.m., washed my face, and dressed. There were fewer overnight voicemails to the 2 Sisters Detective Agency about the Hansen case than there had been before Troy was arrested, but there were still fifteen or twenty, and some of the numbers had intriguing international codes. I listened to a few while I brewed coffee in the sticky little machine.

"My name is Etienne Durand. I'm calling from Pierre Fonds, in France, about the Troy Hansen case—"

"This is Sarah from Nashville—"

"Bob Thompson. I'm a resident of Cape Town—"

There were two cars in the lot when I left my room at seven. A tired-looking couple unloaded bags from a camper van into the room closest to the reception office, and the clerk had arrived for the day. I returned my key and stood looking out the front windows while he finalized my payment.

Across the street from the motel, parked by the edge of the woods, was a beat-up Ford pickup with flaking army-green paint. The morning sun was at such an angle that it bounced off the windshield and made it impossible for me to get a view of the driver.

"That truck," I said to the clerk. "Was it there when you—"

Before I could finish, the truck started up and drove away. I paid my bill and left.

But the truck was in my rearview mirror again as I pulled into Ukiah around seven thirty. It sent a cold tingle up my spine, an instinct I didn't fully trust, given how tired I was. I told myself that the driver was probably a local farmer or hunter just using the same roads I was. But I took the license plate number down anyway. As I followed the GPS to the Hansen house outside of town, I used voice command to send a text to Jamie.

Can you run a plate for me? And yes, before you ask, I'll deposit the money right into your account. Fifty dollars for a plate check, as usual, but I'll double it for a response in under an hour.

I had the burning sense that I'd just wasted a hundred dollars on my own paranoia.

Not long after, I knocked on the door of a little log house on Camber Road. I could smell coffee and woodsmoke coming from inside, so I assumed the Hansens were awake. The door was opened by a man who was Troy's spitting image: dark-haired, stooped, and with hard gray eyes. He surveyed me, unsmiling. Behind him, a small woman with stringy blond hair peered out from the shadows.

"Barney and Reina Hansen?" I asked.

"You people aren't supposed to be here until this evening." He looked at my Chevy parked in the driveway. "We're in the middle of breakfast."

Struck dumb by the greeting, I glanced at Mrs. Hansen, whose large, exhausted eyes and upturned nose gave her the appearance of a worried church mouse from a children's book. She offered me a smile that was there and gone in a flash, little more than a facial tic that I sensed she got away with only when her husband's back was turned.

"I'm sorry," I said. "'You people'?"

"RealFeal Productions." Barney grimaced at my Van Halen T-shirt—or my breasts, I wasn't sure which. "That's you, ain't it?"

"N-no," I stammered. "Uh, no. That's not me. I'm Rhonda

Bird. I'm a private investigator your son hired, and I was hoping to speak to you about him."

"Well, you should have called ahead." Barney smirked. "Don't tell me you drove all the way from LA thinkin' you'd just march in here and we'd sit you down and give you coffee and tell you everything we know."

I felt my eyes widen. That was exactly what I'd thought. "Maybe that was…arrogant. But I just assumed you'd want to help your son with the…the *murder charges* he's facing," I said. "I should have called ahead. Yes. And I'm sorry I've interrupted your breakfast. But, Mr. Hansen, I'm trying to help Troy. I'm trying to find out what the hell happened to your daughter-in-law."

Reina looked like she wanted to speak. Barney didn't let her.

"I'll talk to you." He shrugged. "Sure. And I got plenty to say too."

"Good."

"I know exactly who killed my daughter-in-law."

A bolt of exhilaration whumped into my stomach. Barney Hansen stepped back. I moved to step forward, but he held out a hand to stop me from entering.

"The RealFeal people are paying us fifty-five thousand dollars for an interview," he said. "You top that, and you can have all the time with us that you want."

I felt my mouth fall open.

"Come back when you have the contract all written up," he said.

He slammed the door in my face.

CHAPTER 65

I STOOD ON THE porch and laughed. Because there's a point you reach when you're so tired, and so hopeless, and so far from home that your misery dries up completely and you're left with a weird, unstable kind of hilarity.

I felt like I was on a boat and Troy Hansen was in the ocean drowning and he'd called out for help, and since then I'd been throwing everything I had off the deck, trying to save the guy—life preservers, buckets, ropes, oars. Troy missed it all and was thrashing and twisting in the waves, sinking, staying under for longer and longer, growing weaker and weaker. There was nothing else left to do—I had to jump in.

I took a step back, raised my boot, and kicked in the Hansens' front door.

CHAPTER 66

THEY'D GONE BACK TO their breakfast. It was the cozy image of them sitting there at the little table with boiled eggs and buttered toast and a coffeepot between them that gave me the last bit of fuel I needed to really explode. Their only son was languishing in a prison cell, injured and terrified, and Barney Hansen had a forkful of eggs in front of his mouth and was about to take a bite.

I crossed the room in five fast steps and smacked the fork out of his hand.

"Jesus!" He tried to get up. I shoved him down.

"There was *so much* you could have done," I said, trying not to scream. My voice trembled. I had to clear my throat, it was so tight with anger. "So much."

"What are you talking about?" Barney snapped.

"You could have driven down to LA," I said, trying to keep it together. "You could have helped search for Daisy. You could have stood by your son while he was interviewed by the press. You could have waited for him after he was interrogated."

The Hansens stared at me.

"You could have spoken to reporters outside his house." My voice was rising. I couldn't stop it. "Told the world that your son was not a killer. You could have stayed at his house so Troy didn't have to rattle around in it alone, wondering what the hell was going to happen to him. There was so much you could have done to help your son through this ordeal. But instead, you chose to try to profit—*to profit*—from what's happening to him."

Barney's fists were clenched on the table. Reina's eyes were filled with tears.

"Woman," he said to me, his words as unsteady as mine, "you better get your fat ass back out that door you just broke or I swear to God, I'll pick you up and throw you through it."

"We'll talk," Reina blurted out. Barney and I looked at her.

"You shut your mouth." Barney pointed at his wife's face. "That's fifty-five grand you're danglin' over the edge of the goddamn toilet bowl right now, Reina. That kind of money can set us up for the rest of our lives. If we talk to this bitch, our deal with the TV people is worthless."

"I'm not here to get an exclusive!" I snarled. "I want to save your son!"

"He ain't worth saving!" Barney roared back at me. He stood up, and we were nose to nose. His breath was warm on my cheeks. "You don't get it, do you? We haven't told the world our son's not a killer because he *is* one, and we ain't goddamn liars!"

I had to step back, hold the door frame. My head swirled.

"Daisy weren't his first," Barney said. "Boy started young and just never stopped."

CHAPTER 67

I WAS THROWN OUT of the Hansens' house. It wasn't the first time I'd been kicked out of a place, but it was maybe the most dreadful I'd ever felt about it happening. Barney Hansen stood on his porch and fired a stream of abuse at me all the way to my car, but I hardly heard what he said. His words about his son in the family kitchen were ringing in my ears.

Daisy weren't his first.

It was maybe a twenty-minute drive to the nearest diner. The army-green truck wasn't present in my rearview, thankfully. I parked and settled on a stool at Rosie's and ordered the biggest thing on the menu without really looking at what it was. A guy in a greasy chef's apron poured me weak black coffee while I frantically checked back through the files on my phone, looking for Troy's previous arrests. My head thumped with humiliation at the idea that I could have missed mention of a violent crime in Troy's past. Then, when I discovered his record was clean, I felt stupid for entertaining the notion that both the police and I, not to mention the army of web sleuths, could've overlooked anything as obvious as that.

Even though I wasn't a practicing lawyer in California, I knew some back channels I could go through to check if there were any sealed or secret convictions attached to Troy's name. I sat tapping at my laptop. My confidence rose slightly when I discovered there were none.

So what was Barney Hansen talking about? If Troy had indeed killed before, he hadn't been charged. Had his parents covered for him? Was that the source of the misery and terror I'd seen in Reina Hansen's eyes when she peered out of the shadows behind her ferocious husband?

Briefly, I considered trying to gather the funds to find out. An offer of sixty thousand dollars might blow RealFeal Productions' fee out of the water and allow me to simply ask the Hansens whatever I wanted to know. I talked myself out of that idea pretty quickly. Something about Barney Hansen's hungry eyes and mean little smile told me he was the kind of guy who liked being listened to and that he'd get a real kick out of watching people bid fiercely for the privilege.

As the diner cook set my breakfast of sausages, eggs, toast, bacon, grits, and a side of pancakes in front of me, I got a text from Jamie about the army-green pickup just two minutes before the hundred-dollar deadline. His resources told him that the truck had been listed as stolen from a residence in Anaheim, near LA. It didn't comfort me to know the vehicle I'd spotted twice—that was possibly tailing me—was a stolen vehicle that had indeed come all the way from LA, but I filed it away to worry about later. I didn't have the bandwidth to focus on it now.

I checked my email and saw a file from Detective Will Brogan waiting for me. It was a scan of a sheet of paper with the Public Utilities Commission logo and a list of times, dates, and street addresses. Brogan's email told me it was a list of telephone-pole service calls assigned to Troy Hansen. I began to cross-check these against the last known locations of each of the ten missing people in the box.

My heart sank as I went down the list of addresses, comparing a map on my phone to one on my laptop screen. Troy had indeed serviced utility poles within a five-mile radius of each of the locations where the missing people were last seen and within two weeks of when they were last seen.

He had indeed been the Public Utilities Commission employee who replaced the box near the Muscle Beach homeless camp where Jarrod Maloof disappeared, and that replacement had occurred only eight days before Jarrod went missing.

In the case of Dennis Maynar, who was last seen walking to his car in the parking lot of his accounting firm in

Bell Park, Troy had been working on a pole two blocks down from that building on the very same day.

And Troy had repaired a Public Utilities Commission–owned telephone outlet at the ranger building at the edge of Franklin Canyon Park a mere month before Maria Sanchez disappeared on a hike.

There was no denying it anymore. What I was finding indicated that wherever Troy Hansen went, he left a trail of vanished people in his wake.

CHAPTER 68

I CLOSED MY EYES and tried to chase off the thoughts that were again darkening my mind. I'd spent days and nights and buckets of precious hope trying to save Troy Hansen, when it was becoming ever clearer that it was just his natural weirdness I'd sympathized with. I wondered at my failure to recognize Troy as a psychopath, since my track record for choosing truly misunderstood underdogs to root for had been near perfect. Maybe I was getting old. Maybe the move to California had rattled me.

Or had my vision been clouded by having Baby to care for as my sister and my business partner? I dejectedly typed in Dorothy Andrews-Smith's address, opened the Google Maps Street View, and looked at her house. It was a perky little white-stucco job with clay roof tiles and red bougainvillea crowding the front door. Dave Summerly's words floated back to me.

Dorothy Andrews-Smith was killed by a fucking gang, Rhonda. I know she was. And you will too.

I looked again at the glut of hits for Dorothy Andrews-Smith online. Her disappearance had tickled the interest of an *LA Times* journalist who seemed to believe Southern California was the West Coast hub of America's opioid crisis.

Dorothy, a deeply tanned grandmother who dripped with colorful jewelry in every online photograph, had been an outspoken opponent of the operation of a nightclub at Redondo Beach. She'd gone to the local papers and a number of online groups with accusations that the nightclub owners were selling fentanyl-laced cocaine to the young people who partied at the club. She had even submitted an application to the Redondo Beach mayor's office opposing the club's extension into a neighboring mechanic's workshop. A couple of overdoses in the area had given Dorothy's complaints traction, and the club's extension, which might have made the owners millions of dollars, was rejected. The *Times* stopped just short of suggesting that the club, the Update, was cartel-owned.

Then Dorothy had disappeared from her home, both her front and back doors left hanging open.

Perhaps feeding my misery, perhaps procrastinating to avoid beginning the eight-hour drive back to Los Angeles, I looked up the contact info for the *Times* journalist who'd written the article about Dorothy. Johnathan Brite. I was pleased when Brite took my call, but he sounded bored when I explained who I was and what I was seeking.

"The cartel killed her," he said. I heard a car horn blare. He was apparently spending his time the way most LA journalists did—stuck in traffic en route to or from a story. "She annoyed them by messing with their club expansion."

"Are you sure?" I asked Brite. "I mean, I've read the articles and I heard the same thing from a cop I know. But why is everyone so certain that that's what happened to Dorothy?"

"Because it makes sense."

"But—"

"They left the back and front doors open," Brite said. "The guy that owns the club? He's a high-ranking member of the local chapter of the Tormenta Thirteens. The open-doors thing is, like, that gang's calling card or whatever. It's supposed to represent a storm blowing through the house. *Tormenta* means 'storm' in Spanish, I think."

"Okay."

"They've rubbed out a bunch of people that way. Rival drug dealers. A couple of prostitutes who held back on their cartel pimps."

"So that's it? No other angles have been seriously investigated in Dorothy's disappearance?" I asked. "What if she ran off? Faked her own death? Or what if she fell victim to someone else?"

"You ever heard of Occam's razor?"

I sighed.

"Look, there's no angle here," Brite said. "I've written what I can about it. But they ain't ever gonna find that woman's body. They never do with these cartel guys."

"But if the cops and the locals are so sure that Dorothy was killed by a gang, why haven't there been any arrests?" I asked.

The journalist's laugh hammered my already battered ego.

"Sounds like a nice world you're livin' in, lady, where people commit crimes and the cops come around and do something about it," he said. "Be sure to let me know if a spot opens up for me there, will ya?"

I sighed again as Brite clicked off. The diner cook picked up one of my empty plates and gave a small, satisfied smile because I'd all but licked it clean. Then he stopped. Someone had dashed to my side.

I turned and felt a rush of adrenaline as I saw Reina Hansen lift her chin at the cook, her tiny hands spread wide on the counter beside me.

"Can I just get a quart of two percent, Hank, please?" she asked. Her jaw was tight and her eyes were firmly fixed on the cook. He set my plate back down and went to a section behind the counter where I assumed he kept grocery supplies for customers.

For a second, I thought Reina didn't realize that I was beside her. Which was unlikely—between the tattoos, the pink hair, and my outsize style, no one fails to notice Rhonda Bird. I looked down and saw that Reina held a couple of bills for the milk in her right hand, and in her left, the hand closer to me, she had a tiny roll of paper tucked between her index and middle finger, like a cigarette. She tapped the end of the rolled piece of paper on the counter to get my attention. I turned on my stool and saw Barney Hansen on the street, his head bent and a finger stabbing the air as he talked into a cell phone.

I took the piece of paper from Reina's fingers, grabbed my stuff, and moved swiftly to the restrooms before Barney could glance into the diner and see me. In the safety of the stall, I unrolled the paper and looked at the name written there in what I assumed was Reina's delicate, curly cursive.

Chelsea Hupp.

With trembling fingers, I got out my phone. The lock screen was covered with hundreds of notifications for news stories about the discovery of Daisy's body. I typed *Chelsea Hupp* into Google and sank onto the closed lid of the toilet seat. There were hundreds of Chelsea Hupps in the world. I added *Ukiah* and found a thirty-year-old news story:

"Police Stumped by Local Girl's Death."

CHAPTER 69

AS THE VETERINARY NURSE exited the emergency vet's examining room, she gave Baby the kind of disgusted look you give to something pulled out of a shower drain. Granted, Baby *felt* a little like something dragged through a pipe by a hook. She was tired, battered, and scared. They'd rushed Mouse to the emergency vet clinic, but it had been hours of waiting. The nurse directed the same look to Arthur as she peeled off her surgical gloves and tossed them into a bin behind the counter.

"That animal," she said coldly as she approached them, "has been used as a fighting dog. Is that correct?"

"I don't know," Baby said. "It's possible. We've had him only a few days. I noticed the scars on his belly and his throat." She tried to sound confident. "I assumed he got them either from dogfights or from beatings from his previous owner."

"Uh-huh." The nurse sighed through her nose. "And where did you obtain the dog, exactly?"

Baby thought of the ruse she'd pulled at the shelter. She licked her dry lips. "A friend gave him to us."

"Does this friend have a name?" the nurse asked. "Because we'd sure like to know about those beatings or dogfights."

"It wasn't my friend who, uh, who did them."

"Is the dog—"

"Mouse. His name is Mouse," Baby said.

"Is Mouse registered to you?"

"No... not yet."

The nurse sent her a look so icy, Baby felt the pang of frostbite in her fingertips.

"Look, we love that dog," Arthur said. "We didn't give those scars to him, and we don't know who did. How we got him isn't what counts here. What counts is that we've fed him and cared for him every second we've had him. If you choose to believe otherwise, I can't help ya. Just tell us what the hell's wrong with him and whether you can help him."

The nurse folded her arms and made them wait while she thought it over for a long, painful moment.

"Antifreeze," she said eventually. "Tastes sweet. Dogs love it. Just one lick can be enough to kill 'em, but not quick. Usually takes a couple of days. Shuts the kidneys down first, then goes through the body flicking lights off one at a time. Judging from his stomach contents, I'd say it was in the pork."

"We didn't give him any pork." Baby looked at Arthur. "He's been on wet and dry food but it's all chicken-based."

The vet nurse rolled her eyes. "I'll need you to fill out some forms. And I'll need a valid credit card to take a deposit for the treatment."

"Is Mouse going to be okay?" Baby said. "Can you at least tell us that?"

"I'll let the doctor decide what to tell you," the nurse said. "He's on the phone to the SPCA right now."

Baby went to the counter and tried to fill out the form she was given, but her hands were shaking too badly. She wiped sweat from her brow onto the shoulder of her T-shirt. Arthur was at her elbow, looking twenty years older than he had yesterday. The hard light of midmorning was tormenting them both, making his eyes water and hers sting. All she wanted to do was go to sleep, but back on Waterway Street, the air was thumping as loudly with stereo systems as it had been the previous night. She'd caught a small nap in the plastic chairs in the vet's waiting room as Mouse fought for his life somewhere in the bowels of the building. But it hadn't helped alleviate her guilt.

When Rhonda called, Baby let her thumb hover over the decline button for a long moment before picking up. "Yeah?"

"Listen to this," Rhonda said in greeting. "'A resident of Ukiah, six-year-old Chelsea Hupp, perished yesterday in a devastating forest fire that consumed acres of farmland on the east side of the county. Police said they are investigating how the large-scale ecological disaster began but won't say yet whether they suspect foul play.'"

"Well, that's horrifying," Baby said. "Is this your new side hustle? You call people and tell them awful news? How do I unsubscribe?"

"Baby," Rhonda said, "this is a story from thirty years ago. Troy's parents believe Chelsea Hupp was their son's first victim." She described the aggressive encounter at the Hansen house, Barney Hansen's assertion that his son had killed before, Reina Hansen delivering the covert note to Rhonda with Chelsea's name.

"So is the assumption that Troy lit the fire?" Baby said. "Even if Chelsea died in it, that doesn't mean Troy *wanted* to kill her. Maybe it was an accident. I mean, how old is Troy now?"

"I think thirty-seven?"

"So he would only have been seven years old when Chelsea died. Who starts killing at *seven*?"

"I need to know more. I'm coming home." Rhonda sounded like she was already driving. "Is everything okay there? Where are you?"

"I'm at the vet," Baby said. "Mouse, uh..." She thought about telling her sister that she was hopelessly, miserably stuck in a situation she saw little to no hope of resolving and then describing the myriad ways she might've destroyed Arthur's and Mouse's lives in her unwinnable fight against a murderous corporation. Baby thought about telling Rhonda that she was in over her head. That she'd been wrong.

She envisioned what would happen next: Rhonda would sweep in and clean everything up with the kind of calm certainty that comes only from experience. It was tempting. Baby chewed her lip and watched Arthur, who'd taken over filling out the veterinary forms.

"Mouse needed a checkup, that's all," Baby said.

There was a pause. Baby heard Rhonda's car rumbling. "I feel like there's more you want to say, Baby."

"There's not." Baby played with a pamphlet from a rack nearby. It was about intestinal worms. "When will you be back?"

"This afternoon." Rhonda gave a stressed sigh. "I had some trouble on the way up. Took me longer than I thought."

"What trouble?"

"Oh. It's nothing. I thought someone was following me but . . . I was wrong."

Baby felt the hairs on the back of her neck stand up. "I feel like there's more *you* want to say, Rhonda."

"There's not."

Baby nodded. The sisters were silent for a time.

"Travel safe, then," Baby said. "Keep me updated."

"You too."

As Baby hung up, an alert from the hidden camera on Arthur's porch appeared on her screen. She opened the app and saw two people standing at Arthur's front door: a man in blue coveralls with a clipboard under his arm—and Su Lim Marshall.

CHAPTER 70

THE MORE MILES I put between myself and Ukiah, the better I felt. There was no sign of the army-green pickup truck in my rearview, and the day was warm and bright. I drove and cleared the 2 Sisters Detective Agency voicemails of abusive phone messages and requests for me to speak about what Troy was really like on true-crime podcasts. Then I called Men's Central Jail in LA again and asked to speak with Troy. It took a few hours for the request to work its way through the system.

"Didn't seem like you were going to call me on your own," I said when Troy finally phoned back. My stomach was churning with competing emotions. "So I thought I'd give you a nudge."

"Oh, I've been trying," Troy said. "They gave me the form to say who I wanted on my approved-call list. I filled it out. They lost it. I filled it out again. Then I got a beatdown. By the time I was through the infirmary and back in my cell, the guards had lost the second form."

"Welcome to the American prison system," I said. "Their red-tape game is world class. I had a client who wanted a new pillow once. Took a year and a half for him to get it."

"Well, the one thing I have got going for me is a lawyer," Troy said. "Hired him this morning. And... and I don't know how to say this, Rhonda. But I'm going to need every dollar I have so I can pay him."

"So I'm still fired?" I laughed.

"You gave it everything you had."

"No, I didn't," I said. "I've got more to give. You'll have to do more than fire me to get me to drop this case, Troy. I need to know the truth. I need to know what happened to Daisy and to the people in that box. So I'm going to ask you a question now and I want you to tell me the truth no matter how you think it might affect your case."

"What?"

"Did you kill Chelsea Hupp?" I asked.

There was silence from Troy. The prison sounds rattled in the background of the call. Guards barking. Inmates hollering. Doors slamming.

"You were a kid," I offered. "You couldn't have known— "

"Who's Chelsea Hupp?"

I gripped the steering wheel hard and caught a flash of

my own fierce eyes in the rearview mirror. I looked fed up, and I was. The exhaustion was suddenly physical as well as mental, and I struggled to keep the car on the road. I saw a sign for a rest stop coming up and flicked my indicator on.

"You know what, Troy?" I said. "I'm getting damn tired of your naive-little-innocent-boy act."

"What?"

"You don't know who Chelsea Hupp is?" I asked. "You never heard that name before? You expect me to believe that? Because I've been asked to believe a whole lot of stuff about you in the past twenty-four hours, Troy. Like why your work route has followed the lives of those people in that box almost *exactly*. Do you have any explanation for that? For you being two blocks away from Dennis Maynar's workplace on the same night he disappeared?"

"I didn't know that I was."

"Oh, you didn't know that you were." I smiled. "How convenient."

I hung up and pulled into the rest stop. I desperately needed to use the bathroom after all the coffee at breakfast, and I had to stock up on energy drinks if I was going to stay awake all the way back to LA. I made certain to lock the Chevy before I went inside. When I got back to the car, it was still locked.

But a bloody handprint stood out against the white paintwork on the handle of the passenger-side door.

I stopped in my tracks, then put my energy drinks on the hood and went to look at the handprint. The knuckles were clearly defined in the concave handle well and a large thumbprint was perfectly impressed on the handle itself. I tried to tell myself the print was from some vagrant traversing the parking lot, trying his luck on every car, looking for any unlocked vehicle. But the parking lot and the surrounding areas were empty, and my car was the only one with a print on it.

I reached out and touched the blood. It was still wet.

CHAPTER 71

MARTIN ROSCO'S DARK FIGURE standing over me as I lay on the weight bench flashed before my eyes. His chest caving in like a wicker basket under my barbell. His blood on the wall outside Baby's bedroom. And now this new bloody handprint on the door of my car.

Dave Summerly picked up on the second ring. I tried to control my breathing.

"Someone is following me," I said.

"Huh?"

"Someone is—" I looked in my rearview mirror. I saw bright, sunlit highway. Random cars. A semitrailer. All the vehicles were keeping pace with me; no one was driving dangerously close or swerving to ride beside or ahead of me.

There was no army-green truck. Nothing visible to justify the terror fluttering in my chest.

"Someone is following me, Dave," I insisted. "And I'm scared." I told him about the incident at the gas station on the way to Mendocino County. "I've been able to push down what happened in my house," I said. "I've swallowed it and kept it inside all this time so I can work on the Troy Hansen thing. But I can't keep it down anymore. I'm scared that whoever hired Martin Rosco to come after me has hired someone else, and that person is coming for me now."

"Where are you?"

"I'm about three hours from home."

"Do you have your gun on you?" Summerly asked.

"Yeah."

"Well, you gotta establish whether you've got a tail," he said. "Get off the highway and go somewhere secluded. Forest or mountains. Park somewhere with only one way in and one way out. Then see if anyone comes along."

"And? What if someone does come along?"

"Shoot them in the leg and call the police, or get a photo of them and drive off. It's up to you, Rhonda."

"Something tells me you're not taking me seriously here, Dave."

"I'm not," he said. "For two reasons. First, because I'm just gearing up to speak to Dorothy Andrews-Smith's family and tell them that, yeah, their beloved grandmother was *probably* murdered by a gang, but maybe it's worse. Maybe she was murdered by a serial killer."

"And the second reason?" I asked.

"Because I feel like this stalker thing is bullshit, Rhonda," Summerly said. "I feel like you're just looking for an excuse to talk to me after we screamed at each other at your house. And 'I think I'm being stalked, please help me' is a pretty flimsy excuse, if you ask me."

"Oh, is it?" I said through my teeth.

"If you'd called and said, 'Dave, I want to apologize,' then, yeah, maybe I'd have more time for you right now. Or how about 'Dave, what I did was wrong.' Or maybe both!"

I hung up on Summerly, held the steering wheel tight, and tried to calm myself down. I thought about calling Baby and telling her what was happening, but I didn't want to drag her into any more danger. She was unpredictable enough, fiery enough, that she might take Arthur's station wagon and drive to meet me, and I did not want that. Whatever this was, I needed an experienced hand on it. So I dialed Detective Will Brogan and watched the rearview mirror for signs of the green truck.

"I need your help," I said, and I explained. He listened. Wherever he was, it was quiet.

"Okay," he said. "Send me your location on your phone. I'll get in my car now and meet you halfway. Whatever you do, don't stop driving. Keep calm and keep to the speed limit. We'll nail this fucker in a pincer movement."

"Thanks, Brogan," I said. "Thanks."

"I'll be right there," he said.

CHAPTER 72

BABY TOOK HER TIME getting Arthur set up in the veterinarian's waiting room—she bought him coffee from a local place, a newspaper to read while he waited for updates about the poisoned dog—and then went back to the house on Waterway Street. She parked his car a few blocks away from his house, away from the chaotic new landscape his street had become. Baby turned off the car, sat and breathed and took a moment for herself, then pulled some cucumber-scented wipes out of her handbag, adjusted the rearview mirror, cleaned and refreshed her face and neck, and fixed her hair and makeup.

Baby understood what Su Lim Marshall was trying to do. Marshall knew that Baby would see her on the hidden cameras. The corporate vampire wanted Baby to rush home, exhausted and brain-fried, mentally and physically a mess.

It was all mind games with these people. Strategy. Baby might not have read many of the books assigned in English class, but her father had made her read *The Art of War,* and one line had stayed with her: "The supreme art of war is to subdue the enemy without fighting." Baby was not beaten. She just hadn't had a chance to make a countermove yet. It was a struggle to stay straight-backed and confident. But she'd be damned if she'd let Marshall think the last move had penetrated her armor.

Baby restarted the car, drove over to the house, parked, unlocked the front door, and went inside. Everything seemed untouched. A few minutes later, there was a knock on the door. Baby greeted Marshall and the guy in the coveralls and was unsurprised to see a County of Los Angeles Public Health badge pinned to the man's chest.

"Hello, ma'am," the guy said. "My name is Richard Desmond. I'm from the public health department. I'm here to conduct an inspection on this dwelling in response to a complaint."

Baby held the door without inviting them inside. She looked at Marshall, noticed how her pin-striped skirt suit gripped her little body the way a surgeon's glove clings to skin.

"You know," Baby said to the woman, "calling in the health department is a cute move. But you spoiled it by coming along. You should have watched from the car, out of sight, or had one of these scumbags film it for you." She gestured to the corner boys, then to the junkies and pimps watching from distant porches. "You got no subtlety, Marshall. No sophistication. That's your problem."

"Ma'am," Richard the health department guy said, tapping his clipboard with a pen to draw Baby's focus back to him. "I'm going to ask you if you have knowledge of any of the following health hazards on your property: mosquito breeding zones, sewage discharge, insect or rodent infestations, damaged walls, floors, or ceilings. Do you have running water at this property? What about your electrical system? Are there any known faults?"

"Yes, the electricity." Marshall smiled. "That's what worries me most, as a concerned neighbor. The wiring on the side of the house looks old. Is it faulty? Because there was a fire in the area this morning. We'd hate to have another one."

Baby chewed the inside of her cheek.

"How about hazardous substances?" Marshall said. "We wouldn't want anybody to get sick."

Baby squeezed the edge of the door, tried to focus on the tendons in her wrist flexing so that she didn't lose control.

"Is this the way you really want to go?" Baby asked Marshall when she felt she could speak without growling. "Because there are laws against the furnishing of criminal activity within residential households in this county, Ms. Marshall. Just like there are with the health department. You might've sicced this spineless minion on me"—Baby gestured to Richard—"but what happens when it's discovered that Enorme is accommodating drug traffickers at a string of their properties?"

Marshall's hand flew to her chest as if she were shocked. "Drug traffickers?" She laughed, looked down the street. "Here? You're kidding. It's such a nice area."

Almost on cue, someone fired a gun a couple of houses down. The public health guy tapped the clipboard against his leg, looking increasingly nervous. His eyes locked on Marshall's for guidance. Baby felt for the man. He'd probably been offered a sizable envelope of cash to fudge the inspection and assumed he'd be walking into a run-of-the-mill neighborly dispute. He couldn't have known that this was an all-out David and Goliath battle.

"If you suspect criminal activity in any of these houses, Ms. Bird, you should call the police." Marshall gave an earnest shrug. "But I'm certain the men and women you see here have no violent or malignant intentions whatsoever. I'm sure they're simply homeless people taking shelter in these abandoned houses."

More gunshots. The health inspector tugged at his collar. "If you wouldn't mind, Ms. Bird?" Baby let him in. Richard was already slipping the bright orange UNSAFE TO OCCUPY notice to the front of the clipboard as he passed her.

"This doesn't solve your problem," Baby said to Marshall, who had been walking toward the street. Marshall stopped on the path and looked back as Baby continued. "So you get the house condemned and you kick Arthur out. Okay. Then what? He still owns the property."

"The increasingly *worthless* property." Marshall held up a finger. Shouting was coming from the house with the gunshots. "The property that will, in a few minutes, be written up for several municipal code violations that will incur fines in the tens of thousands of dollars if not seen to. You know, it's a real shame that Mr. Laurier didn't take my offer on the house when I made it, because even if he tries to fix the property to get it compliant again, I have a weird feeling that he'll have trouble getting builders in."

Baby felt like an elephant was standing on her chest. She kept her bearing only by focusing hard on her breathing and on the pain caused by her fingernails biting into the flesh of her palm as she squeezed her fist.

"Give up now," Marshall said, her ruse suddenly dropped. The tiny woman looked up at Baby from the cracked concrete path. "Or it'll get worse."

"No," Baby said.

"No?"

"Arthur is old. He's tired. You killed his wife," Baby said. Her voice was like black ink in the bright daylight. "I won't take that. I will never, ever let something like that slide. It's not who I am."

Marshall appraised her. Baby thought she saw a flicker of something in her eyes—annoyance and, hopefully, fear. But it was gone so fast, she might have imagined it. Marshall had been doing this a long time, and she was practiced at hiding her weaknesses. She smiled cheerfully at Baby and walked off as if she had somewhere better to be.

CHAPTER 73

I WATCHED THE MINUTES tick by on the clock in the dashboard, slowly calming as the numbers changed and the miles of desert and then forest flew by the windows. My panic simmered down to a quiet tension that stretched its limbs within mine. I was a smart, capable woman who could handle herself, yet conflicting emotions paraded through my mind: Guilt about keeping Baby in the dark about my current situation. Fury that Dave Summerly had dismissed my concerns so coldly. Embarrassment that I might be whipping the whole scenario into something more than it was and hysterically dragging a homicide detective in to back me up on a non-threat.

In the end, I didn't have any definitive proof that someone

was on my tail. I had only what I took to be evidence of their presence. I sighed and gripped the wheel and told myself that calling in backup had been the sensible thing to do. I would keep driving and not risk being attacked in a gas station or at a rest stop where innocent civilians could get in harm's way.

The traffic thinned. I started seeing billboards for big Los Angeles hotels and checked my phone. I was still streaming my location to Brogan. It calmed me further to see myself as a little blue bubble on the long beige highway, heading toward Los Angeles, my return home as yet uninterrupted by actual violence.

I'm gonna be okay, I told myself. *Brogan will call and tell me that he's nearby, and I will pull over, and he will reassure me, and we will convoy back to the city.*

The traffic dissolved. Mine was the only car on the highway when I felt a whump from under the car, and the sickening flapping sound that told me I'd blown a tire.

CHAPTER 74

AT ANY OTHER TIME in my life, the situation might have made me laugh. I'd always appreciated the simple beauty of the universe's little quirks, the unwritten laws that made sure five people texted or called the phone I'd left on the kitchen counter the very moment I slipped into a relaxing bath. The same laws ensured that if I chose to head to the supermarket makeup-less, disheveled, hung over, I would run into a client or an ex-boyfriend. Having car trouble in the middle of a post-apocalyptically unpopulated highway while I was worried about a stalker made sense within these laws. At least I didn't need help changing a tire.

I did need help staying alive.

I pulled over, got out, and swore loudly at the collapsing

back tire. I didn't go and inspect it, not yet ready to see evidence of a deliberate puncture, proof that I'd been set up to need assistance from a supposedly well-meaning stranger on a lonely stretch of road like so many murder victims before me. I waited, gripping my phone, staring hopelessly down the two-lane strip of blacktop on my side of a weed-infested island that stretched as far as I could see. Overhead, big dark birds circled, too high up for me to see what they were. I looked at my phone and noticed an error message in the location streaming app. **No service.** I looked for the reception bars. Nada. I was in a black zone.

Of course I was.

I pulled my shoulders back and went to the trunk of the Chevy, which opened with a wiry yowl from the squeaky hinges. I shoved aside my overnight bag and the other detritus of my life—gym gear, work files, a bottle of chlorine for the rooftop pool at home—and wrestled out the spare tire and the jack. A shiver passed through me as I worked. I dumped the spare tire on the ground and paused to watch the forest beyond the highway, imagining a figure standing behind one of the lonely trees, watching me.

There was no one. I held my ragged breath to listen for cars on the wind—there were none. I told myself that at least I'd broken down on a long stretch of flat road so I would see anyone coming from miles away. I'd have time to get my gun from the front seat. To hide. To call 911.

I didn't know what I would do if a carful of innocent people came along. Flagging them down might put them in danger, or there might be safety in numbers. It depended on how unhinged my follower was.

If there was a follower.

I got down on the blacktop and inspected the blown tire. My heart soared to see that the break in the rubber was from a roofing nail, not a knife slash. I jacked the car up, applied the tire iron, and loosened the lug nuts, keeping an eye on the road in both directions as I worked.

I wrenched the busted tire off the car, rolled it behind the trunk, and let it tip over and wobble to a stop on its side. I was rolling the new tire over to the axle when I heard a vehicle approach. An SUV appeared in the heat haze on the horizon. I straightened and took a couple of steps onto the road. When the car was within hailing distance, I saw a woman my age in the driver's seat and a teenage girl next to her. With a pit in my stomach, I let them go, not wanting to draw them into the potential danger.

The hammering of my own heart distorted the sounds around me. I told myself again that I was okay. But my breathing was the giveaway. I knew the thin wheeze didn't come from changing the tire. I was in better shape than that. I kept working, trying to watch the road as I sweated in the late-afternoon sun.

I heard the rumble of another car approaching and looked up to see a blue pickup. I tried to calm my breathing as I watched it approach. Before it was close enough for me to get a good look at the driver, it veered off the road.

It disappeared into the trees. After a few seconds, it

reappeared, taking a dirt road I hadn't noticed. I tracked the vehicle as it rumbled through the forest, parallel to the highway. It was level with me when it passed the army-green pickup, parked in the shade.

The tire iron fell from my grasp and clanged loudly on the blacktop. As I bent unsteadily to pick it up, my instincts telling me to arm myself and hide behind the rear of my car, I heard a voice.

"Don't *fucking* move, Rhonda Bird," a man said.

CHAPTER 75

BABY HAD A NEW plan of attack.

She had never been to Jamie's apartment before, and seeing it now, Baby thought it was probably dirt cheap, being only a few inches of concrete away from one of Skid Row's busiest nightspots. It had taken some work to get the surly bartender to put down his paperwork and give her access to the place. She crossed the empty nightclub, her boots crunching on shards of fluorescent-colored plastic shot glasses and making tacky sounds on years of spilled liquor. She went up a dark flight of musty carpeted stairs, found a door, and banged on it. Then she banged again.

When Jamie opened it, she saw that his Afro was crushed

on one side and there was drool shining on the cheek on the same side.

"What in the World of Warcraft is this? It's a home visit, that's what. I'm here for an in-person consult," Baby announced before Jamie could say anything. "I need help and it's more than I care to put in a text message or say over the phone." She nudged the door with her boot. "Let me in."

"Wait, wait, wait, wait." Jamie held his head. "There *ain't* no in-person consults. That's not a service I provide. To anyone. Ever."

"Things change," she said, and she slapped three thousand dollars cash against his chest as she barged in. It was from her personal savings. "Get some caffeine, get on the computer, and do your thing."

Five minutes later, her personal hacker was seated in his elaborate gaming rig in his dark, cluttered den of an apartment while Baby perched nearby, sipping the energy drink he'd offered her and marveling at the perfect half-moon shape of his hair. Jamie tapped and dragged and clicked, doing things on a bunch of screens, grumbling about it being the middle of the night in his universe.

Baby looked around. The apartment was nice under the sea of garbage, but Jamie had decorated it like a teenage boy's bedroom, not the space of a guy in his mid-twenties. There were heaps of clothes in the corners, an unmade bed, nudie pictures of manga women on the walls. Baby needed to use the bathroom but didn't dare.

"Why are all hackers such clichés?" she asked, wiping

unidentified stickiness from her palms onto her jeans. "Aren't there any online weirdos with nice, neat houses and families and dogs running around the yard?"

"Your creative space is supposed to be a physical representation of your mind," Jamie said. "Welcome to my nightmare. I hope you get out alive."

"Ugh."

"So you want me to hollow out these Enorme creeps." He sighed, bringing up a blank screen. "Tell me what to look for and I'll find it faster. You think they're into corporate fraud? Money laundering? Have they got shady investors?"

"Probably all of the above," Baby said. "But I don't want you to target the whole company. I want you to look into one woman specifically. Her name is Su Lim Marshall."

"Ah." Jamie smiled. "It's personal."

"It's strategic," Baby said. "Enorme is a global corporation, okay? It's everywhere. Even if I bring what Marshall is doing to the executives' attention or dangle some of their own illegal practices in front of them, they're big enough to claim they had no idea it was happening, and they'll just move her to the other side of the country, where she'll do what she's doing now to someone else. If I go to the media, the best I can hope for is an exposé in the *Times* that fifty people will read. And that's assuming the *Times* is even brave enough to face the lawsuits."

"If you say so." Jamie slurped his energy drink.

"The only way to stop Marshall is to attack Marshall," Baby said. "Tell me who she is. Get me some juice.

Everybody's got a deep, dark secret, and finding deep, dark stuff seems to be your talent."

Jamie tapped. White text that meant nothing to Baby skittered across the dark screen. Her phone rang, and she frowned when she saw it was Dave Summerly but answered anyway.

"If you're calling to ask me what kind of flowers Rhonda likes," Baby said, "she doesn't like flowers. You want to make up with that woman, you gotta get her a case of beer and a pepperoni pizza."

"It's . . ." Summerly began. "It's not that, exactly. Where are you?"

"Skid Row."

"Can I get an exact address? I'm not that far away. I need to run something by you."

She hung up and sent him a pin. Jamie had filled two screens with ones and zeros and weirdness.

"That better not be a cop you just invited here," he said.

"Why not?"

Jamie's elaborate gaming chair creaked and hummed as he swiveled to face her. "I'm a hacker, Baby. I make my living breaking into virtual lockboxes. I'm like those guys from that old movie *Heat,* only it's firewalls I'm blasting through, not bank vaults."

"If you say so." Baby hid a tiny smile.

"Everything you see here?" He spread his arms wide, indicating the machines that covered the desks around him. "This is all hot. You can't even *get* this kind of stuff in the States. Not legally."

"Dave Summerly is an old-school police officer," Baby said. "Until last year he used a flip phone. He can't tell a router from a toaster."

Jamie huffed but went back to his tapping.

Ten minutes later, Summerly arrived. It was a challenge for him to squeeze his bulky body into the tiny room crammed with devices, crates of wires, and humming, bleeping, whirring boxes making a city skyline in the dark.

"Here's the thing," he said when he had found a crate to sit on. "I might have failed to take Rhonda seriously on something that was maybe . . . uh . . . serious. I think she might be in trouble, and I've let her down."

CHAPTER 76

"WHAT ARE YOU TALKING about?" Baby studied Dave Summerly's face in the dim blue light from Jamie's machines.

"You know about the trophy box, right?" he said.

Baby nodded.

"Well, I just came from Dorothy Andrews-Smith's daughter's place," Summerly said. "The daughter looked at Dorothy's bag—the missing-person article, the little oil-painting kit. Then she said she just couldn't understand it. I said, 'You can't understand what?' She said, 'That oil-painting kit wasn't my mom's.'"

"What do you mean?"

"The little oil-painting kit belonged to Dorothy's daughter, not to Dorothy. And it wasn't even anything, ah"—

he waved his hand—"*special.* It wasn't a treasured personal item. She said she'd been at her mother's place one afternoon and wanted to do something crafty. She bought it but never used it."

Baby stared at him. Jamie's clicking and tapping was like a soundtrack to her thoughts turning and ticking around.

"Why would a serial killer take an item from a victim that didn't even belong to that victim?" Summerly asked.

"Maybe, you know, he just assumed..." Baby struggled. She was speaking her thoughts as they came to her, the urgency making her talk faster and faster. "Maybe he stalked Dorothy, went in, killed her, and grabbed whatever was nearby as a memento. Just because the kit meant nothing to Dorothy doesn't mean it meant nothing to the killer. That's why they take things, isn't it? So they can, like, go back and relive the moment?"

Summerly and Baby fell into their own thoughts. Jamie slurped his energy drink and ignored them both.

"See, there's more to it." Summerly shifted. "When I started unpicking the Dorothy-painting-kit threads, I found I could also unpick other threads about the other items in the box. I called Jarrod Maloof's parents. Jarrod, the crazy homeless kid from down on Venice Beach?"

"Yeah. I know who you mean."

"Jarrod did have a special football jersey for his team, the Torrance Titans. It was a beloved personal item, the kind of thing you'd expect a serial killer, hunting and stalking and choosing his victim, would take as a trophy. But you know what?"

"What?"

"The Maloofs still have it."

Baby stared at him. The hairs on her arms were standing up. "What?"

"Jarrod had *two* jerseys," Summerly said. "The one he wore during games and a newer, cleaner one he wore for team photos and stuff. The kid was superstitious. He always wore the same jersey for the actual game. It was stained and torn in places. He kept the nice one at home in a drawer and pulled it out only for photographs or videos or whatever."

Baby's throat felt tight.

"If you were going to *fake* a serial killer's trophy box," Baby said slowly, "and you saw the article in the paper about Jarrod Maloof being missing... what item would you guess best represented him?"

"The football jersey," Summerly said. "Football star—football jersey."

Baby felt her thoughts ticking faster and faster.

"It's the same with Dorothy," Summerly said. "She was an eccentric. The muumuus she wore, the jewelry. Her house had all kinds of dingle-dangles and wind chimes and stuff. If you didn't really know her but wanted to grab something of hers that you thought she loved, the oil-painting kit would be a good guess."

"The hairbrush," Baby said, her thoughts racing. "From Maria Sanchez. It was in all of her Instagram tutorials."

Summerly and Baby stared at each other.

"The box is fake," Summerly said.

"But who faked it? Why?"

"I don't know."

"Who would have had access to all those places connected to the missing people in the box?" Baby asked. "To their houses, their bedrooms, their drawers?"

CHAPTER 77

A MAN I DIDN'T recognize was pointing a gun at me. He was tall and had bony shoulders that made his T-shirt look like it was on a coat hanger. He had close-cropped dark hair, and his skinny arms were covered in track marks. My instincts rammed into each other, causing a skidding, screeching pileup of vastly different inclinations.

Something told me that I had seen this man before. Still, he seemed so dark and dangerous, it was like he had stepped out of another world, a shadow dweller arrived to end me. I had the stomach-churning sense that whoever had hired him to come after me had dug deep into the well of hatred and pulled out an unhinged man with nothing to lose. I knew I was about to be shot dead right there on the deserted highway. The man's eyes told me so.

"Get in the car," he said.

"Hell no," I replied.

The man with the bony shoulders lowered the gun and shot me in the leg.

There was no hesitation. No warning look. He was sending me a message—he would tell me what to do once and once only, and if I didn't comply, there would be pain.

The bullet had smashed into my shin, slipped past the bone, and left through the back of my calf. My leg was knocked out from under me. I didn't have the breath or the time to scream before he marched over and grabbed a fistful of my hair.

"I know why you're following me," he growled. "And it ain't happening. You should know that by now. You've been listening in on me for months. Years, probably. Through the Wi-Fi. Through the phones. I know everything. I know what you people *do*. And I'm not going to come home and join you. Mom and Dad and Uncle Ollie, they can all throw their lot in with the CIA if they want. But I'm not coming ba—"

I'd raked the tire iron up from the asphalt with the tips of my fingers and now I swung it upward as hard as I could into the man's crotch.

His words died on his lips. He collapsed inward like a folding chair and flopped to the ground. He dropped the gun. We both fumbled for it, sending it skidding across the loose gravel at the edge of the road and beneath my car. I saw in a flash that I would have to seriously incapacitate my attacker to buy enough time to get the gun from under the car or to get my own weapon from inside my car. Trouble was, he had a similar thought. I swung the tire iron again but missed, and I caught an elbow in the nose for my efforts.

I'd been hit in the nose by a man once before. A teenage client's father had wanted to smack his son for getting arrested but smacked me instead when I stepped in to protect him. I felt then as I did now—like a giant wasp had wrapped its legs around my skull, jammed its massive stinger into the center of my face, and skewered my brain with its upcurved barb. I was momentarily blinded. I heard my attacker drop to his belly and slide under my car. When the explosions of color cleared and the road stopped spinning, I looked up and saw him staring down at me with the pistol pointed right at my face.

A big, dead tree made a halo around his head as he stood there. The dying leaves looked like dark curls. That's the only reason it finally clicked and I recognized him.

My mouth fell open as shock consumed the terror inside me.

"Are you Jarrod?" I asked. *"Jarrod Maloof?"*

The tired, world-weary, and emaciated version of Jarrod Maloof cocked his head, his jaw tight and mean. I recognized the shell of the bright-faced boy I'd seen in the article in the box Troy had given me. It was hard to believe that this skeletal and crazy-eyed man gripping the gun was the same teenage boy.

Jarrod bared his yellowed teeth at me.

"You know who I am, Rhonda Bird," he said. "Don't play dumb. You're part of the organization."

"What organization?"

"Well, guess what, bitch?" He wasn't even listening now. "*You're* going back. You're going back in a body bag. That's what happens when they send agents after me."

"Jarrod." I put my hand out. It was covered in blood from my nose or my calf, I didn't know which. "You're unwell. You're not thinking straight. I can explain everything."

There was a noise, and his eyes lifted away from me. He flinched sharply. I thought it was a reaction to what I had said. Then my mind registered the blood on his shirt, dark purple and then red as it soaked through the fabric from a gunshot wound to his heart.

He fell against my car, then dropped, unmoving, onto the asphalt.

I looked up and saw Detective Will Brogan on the other side of the road. He holstered his gun and came running over. My breath caught in my throat as he helped me to my feet.

"Jesus," I said. The shock was hitting me now, wrapping its warm, numbing arms around me. "Jesus, Jesus, Jesus."

"Come on, Rhonda," Brogan said. "It's okay. Let's get you in my car."

He helped me limp across the island and the north-traveling lanes to his vehicle. I got into the passenger seat, watching Brogan go back across the empty highway to retrieve my phone and gun from my car, then jog over and climb into the driver's seat beside me.

But even as I sat and breathed, the rational part of my brain was telling me that this wasn't right. That you didn't shoot a man and leave him for dead in the middle of the highway without trying to render aid. Without even checking his pulse. Without even moving his body out of the middle of the road.

As Brogan tucked my phone and gun under his seat, my brain screamed that he was doing that because he didn't want me to be able to reach them. And as he started the engine, I knew, with every piece of me, that he couldn't have been in Los Angeles when I called him for help. He'd arrived at the scene of my attack far too quickly. Most likely, he'd been on his way to Ukiah to find me.

But I couldn't react to any of that, not then. My body was frozen. I'd just seen a man murdered, coldly and brutally, in the bright light of the afternoon.

And I knew that was what I was going to have to do to Brogan if I was going to get out of this car alive.

CHAPTER 78

DAVE SUMMERLY LEANED ON the horn. When the minivan driver in front of them flipped them the bird, Baby moved over and hammered on the horn herself.

Los Angeles late-afternoon traffic was only slightly worse than Los Angeles traffic in general, which meant they'd struggled their way out of Skid Row as though driving through molasses. Summerly took the detachable emergency light from under his seat, reached out of his window, and smacked it onto the roof of the car. He rolled up his window and flicked it on. The wailing siren meant they both had to raise their voices on the separate phone calls they were making.

"I'm trying to find out the *name* of the *last police officer* or *detective* who came to your house to speak to you about your missing husband," Summerly said, enunciating his words in order to be heard over the muffled wail of the siren. "If you can just... oh, you don't? Do you have a—a badge number or did he leave a business card? Even just a description of the guy... yes. Yes. If you could ask her what she remembers and call me back..."

Baby was drumming her fingernails on the dashboard, fighting the crazy impulse to get out of the car and run through the traffic to the highway.

"I want to speak to Troy Hansen," she growled into her phone. "Now. It's a matter of life and death... No, I don't know his inmate number. You know who he is! The man has been all over the internet for the past week and a half!"

She threw the phone into her footwell at the same time Summerly threw his, and the two devices banged into each other on the floor.

"Fuck!"

"God*damn* it!"

They watched the traffic lazily clearing ahead of them, the cars making a gap wide enough for a person with a shopping cart to weave through and not much else.

"Where did Rhonda say she was?"

"About three hours from home." Summerly sighed. "That was around three o'clock."

Baby looked at the map app on her phone. "If she kept driving at the speed limit, that would put her"—she pointed—"about here."

The gap ahead widened. Summerly and Baby rocked

back and forth in their seats as he surged and braked, surged and braked. "If we can get through this mess I can make it in an hour. Jesus." He held his head.

"What?"

"I don't know." He shook his head. "Maybe there's a chance. What if it's someone from one of those missing-person volunteer groups? The families agree to see them. They have a meeting in the home, look at the victim's room, nab an item to put in the box. Maybe we're looking at someone from a church group? What about a journalist? Maybe a reporter visited every single family— "

"Dave." Baby put a hand on his leg. "Your desperate hope that the world isn't stuffed full of evil cops is seriously cute, but it's wrong. It had to be a cop who snuck into Troy's house and placed the note saying where Daisy's body was. Only a cop would know they didn't have the back of the house covered. And only a cop could have taken it from him at the crime scene."

"I just can't get my head around the fact that it's a cop who's done this," he said. "This is . . . it always makes me sick, this stuff. Don't look at me like that. I'm not an idiot. I've been through a lot of corruption sweeps in my time. Guys I have known and trusted were picked up. I just never get used to it. Feels worse to me when it's a cop."

"It's the only thing that makes sense," Baby said. Her phone rang. Men's Central Jail. She picked both phones up and handed Summerly his.

"Troy." Baby drew in a deep breath. "I've got a lot of things to run by you."

"Before you start, I have something that might help," Troy Hansen said. Baby put a finger in her ear to block the sound of Summerly making another call beside her. "I spoke to Rhonda earlier. She asked me about a girl named Chelsea Hupp. Asked me if I killed her."

"Right?"

"I've never heard of Chelsea Hupp," Troy said. Somewhere in the background, a prison door buzzed and slammed. "I've been racking my brain about it. I'm certain that I've never heard that name before. But Rhonda said the girl died when I was a kid."

"Okay?"

Troy struggled. His voice came out thin, shaken. "I did something when I was seven or eight. My parents told me that nobody got hurt, but... but maybe they were just trying to protect me. Or themselves."

CHAPTER 79

"HEAR ME OUT," Will Brogan said.

"Hear you out?" I snapped. My senses were returning; the numbness was fading. I was coming to the knife-edge of jittery, uncontrollable fury now, my flight reflex subsiding and my fight reflex taking over. My instincts were telling me to punch Brogan in the side of the skull. I could see myself doing it. But I tamped the urge down. We were going eighty miles an hour down the highway, and he had his gun in the cup holder by his left knee, out of my reach. I already had a bullet hole in my calf that was slowly filling my right shoe with blood. I didn't need another one in the stomach or the chest.

"Imagine my life back then," he said. The urge to punch

him sizzled in me again. "I've been demoted at the precinct and we're struggling for money. My wife tells me she's leaving me. My second wife. Not the one I told you about before. I'd literally just walked out of our last marriage-counseling session in Burbank. She paid for a bunch of sessions and wanted to use them all, even though our marriage was in the toilet. The last one was supposed to be about us figuring out a way to stay friends. But she decided at the end that she didn't want to do that."

"Brogan," I said, seething. "Are you really trying to tell me about your fucking divor— "

"Shut up," he said. He spoke the words calmly. Quietly. With a deadly finality. The eyes that cut toward me were hollow.

"She said that what had happened to me when I was a kid had killed all the feeling between us. And it was systematically destroying everything I touched," Brogan said. "According to her, until I dealt with it, I was just going to continue on in one job after another, one marriage after another, one friendship after another. On and on and on, never finding an escape from the anger."

I said nothing. The car slowed. Brogan turned off the highway onto a dirt road.

"I left the therapy session with that idea on my mind," he said. *"Deal with what happened, or you'll keep destroying everything."*

"What happened?"

"Troy Hansen happened," Brogan said.

Now we were climbing through rocky forest, the car kicking up dust. I could hear cicadas in the trees and the distant wail of emergency vehicle sirens. Someone must have called in the scene on the highway: Jarrod's body on the road. My car standing there with the door open and the wheel off.

"I was five," Brogan said. "Chelsea was six. She was a Hupp, and so was her mother. Me and my dad were Brogans. Both my mom and Chelsea's dad had died, and our parents met when the two of us were just toddlers. They never got married. Not officially. But Chelsea was my sister, you know? I thought of her that way. We were just smitten with each other. We did everything together. I couldn't remember my life before Chelsea and my stepmother. We lived in a farmhouse outside Ukiah. Same town as Troy. We were happy."

A rabbit was startled out of the forest, froze in the middle of the dirt road. Brogan didn't slow. I winced, waiting for the wet thump. It didn't come. I turned in my seat and saw the rabbit rise from the huddled shape it had frozen into and skitter away.

I also spied the clothes in the back of the car, the leather belt lying coiled on the seat like a snake.

CHAPTER 80

"I LIT A FIRE," Troy said.

Baby gripped the phone, listening. The traffic had cleared and Summerly was talking on his phone and driving one-handed, sailing past cars on the freeway like they were standing still.

"It was so stupid," Troy said. "I was a stupid little boy playing with matches. That was all. Nothing, you know, *calculated*. My parents left me at home alone while they went to the store, and I took matches out to the yard and started lighting them and flicking them into the grass. The grass caught. Of course it did. It was the middle of summer. I don't know what I was thinking."

Baby held on to her seat belt as they zipped between two massive semitrailers.

"I guess I wasn't thinking anything. I was a kid."

"How big was the fire?" Baby asked.

"Sixty acres."

"Jesus."

"It took out three farms, a bunch of the forest, and a grain silo. The town didn't have power for two weeks," Troy said. "My father beat the shit out of me. He said I'd taken a life. I thought he meant a horse. I knew some horses had gotten trapped in their stables. I never learned much about the fire. We moved away for a few years after that, to get away from it. The shadow of it. By the time we came back, it was a non-topic in my household."

"You think Chelsea Hupp died in the fire?" Baby said.

"Maybe she did. Maybe Mom and Dad just figured I was so young, there was no sense in me knowing I'd done a thing like that. Killing changes a person, right?"

CHAPTER 81

"THE FIRE CAME UP on us suddenly," Brogan said. "It blocked off the only road out of the farm. My father told us to climb into the water tank. We all got in. Chelsea didn't get out."

We were climbing still, the rocky mountain road narrowing. Water-starved eucalyptus trees reached for the hard blue sky. I brought my good leg onto the seat with difficulty and started unlacing my shoe. Brogan glanced over.

"So here I am, thirty years later, leaving my goddamn therapy session, heading to a bar to try to drink the night away," he continued. "I stop in a corner store to get some cigarettes. This beautiful woman is at the counter checking her lottery ticket in the little machine. Blond. Perfect body. Yoga pants. Her skinny, douchey husband is in the aisles trying to decide on what crackers to get. I'm waiting at the counter to buy my smokes and the blonde suddenly starts screaming. Everybody in the store stops to watch. The husband rushes over. She tells everyone they've just won the lottery."

Brogan was wringing the steering wheel. I pulled my shoe off.

"Everybody is clapping, and the two of them are dancing around and hugging," Brogan said. "And I'm hating on these lucky assholes. But what can I do? I wish them the best, I congratulate them, I ask their names. That's when I find out—it's him. It's Troy fucking Hansen. This is the guy who obliterated my family. Who killed my sister. Who drove my father to the bottle and my stepmother to pills. I hadn't seen him since his family split town. My own family also moved to get away from the memories. But now here he is, right in front of me, with his beautiful wife, jumping up and down celebrating his fucking *lottery win*? Are you kidding me? And, oh, of course. I can see it all as I look at him—his blessed, *blessed* life. His parents probably never told him about what happened in the fire. Maybe nobody in town did. I mean, everybody knew, but it just became a thing nobody talked about. Maybe people figured why burden him with that?"

I peeled my sock off, rolled it into a tight little ball half the size of my fist.

"I followed Troy and Daisy home," Brogan said, watching me idly, caught up in his own memories. "And the more I learned about Troy, the easier the weight of my own life became. The trouble I was having at work didn't matter. The ex-wives and their bullshit were just background noise. I watched Daisy. Learned her habits. I followed Troy on his route around the telephone poles. It was always in my mind to *deal with it,* like my ex-wife said. Like the therapist said. *Deal* with my anger. I knew I could do that if I really fucked up Troy's life. Made things even."

"You're not the meditation-and-forgiveness-and-affirmations type, huh," I said.

"There were opportunities," he said, ignoring me. "I learned about Daisy's affair and thought about revealing it to him. I thought about matching his telephone-repair route to a bunch of burglaries. I even paid some techie asshole to show me how to copy Troy's work log and alter it so I could make it look like he'd been at certain locations on certain days."

I'd fallen for that one.

Brogan wiped at his eyes. I looked over. He'd lost interest in what I was doing and was gripping the steering wheel, staring ahead, tears brimming in his eyes.

"I was looking at the girlfriend, the psychologist. That's how deep I was into Troy and Daisy and their lives. I'd signed up for Daisy's nutrition program, and I'd bought Alex Brindle's fucking books. I read her dissertation on serial killers. Then I thought, *What if it isn't burglaries that Troy's route matches?*" he said. "*What if it's murders? I* knew Troy Hansen was a murderer. I wanted the world to see him that way."

I shook my head. Brogan didn't notice.

"So I dug around at work and found a bunch of open assignments. No-hoper cases," he said. "I took my time.

Looked at each case carefully. Made *sure* it was a no-hoper. I chose cases where it was pretty damn clear the victims would never be found. Where they'd obviously jumped off a bridge or gotten lost in the wilderness and been eaten by coyotes or whatever the fuck." He gave a sad smirk. "Jarrod Maloof back there? Jesus. I had *no idea* he was still alive. All the signs pointed to suicide. He'd been talking wacked-out conspiracy theories for months. Saying he was going to jump off Santa Monica Pier and let the tide take him out. I was sure that's what he'd done."

"How did you get their personal items?"

"I visited the families. Conducted more interviews. Took an item each time."

"You assembled the box," I said, alternately watching the road ahead of us and watching Brogan's speed on the speedometer. Waiting for my opportunity. "Then you went to plant it at Troy's house while he was out. But Daisy came home unexpectedly."

He nodded, sucking in a long, deep breath.

"She found you in her home," I said.

"She broke her routine," Brogan said. "I turned around and she was just...there. In the kitchen. I'd been washing my hands after burying the box. She was staring at me. I hadn't even heard her come in."

"So you killed her," I said.

"She came at me first." Brogan's eyes were now dry. "She was a strong woman. Vicious. Athletic. All I was trying to do was subdue her."

"Martin Rosco," I said. "Did you send him after me to try to get me to drop the case?"

"That was a stupid move." Brogan shook his head. "Rosco had always been unreliable. But Troy hiring a PI was a complication I didn't need."

"I'd just love to know why you're bothering to tell me all this," I said. "Is it because you're hoping I'm going to come over to your side, help you plead out to manslaughter for what you did to Daisy?"

He didn't answer.

"Or is it because you're trying to make yourself feel better about what you're about to do?" I looked at the scrubland around us. "Because I gotta tell you, Brogan, your heartfelt explanation of what you did? It's got a little less coldness to it than some of the murder confessions I've heard in my time."

He looked at me.

"But," I went on, "if you think all that is gonna stop me from killing you to save my own life . . . you're dead wrong."

I put my rolled-up sock in my mouth. The sour taste of my own foot sweat made me wince. I tugged my seat belt tight and bit down hard on the sock.

"What the hell are you doing?" Brogan asked.

I reached over, grabbed the steering wheel, and yanked it toward me. The car swerved. Brogan did exactly what I'd expected him to—he slammed on the brakes. The tires bit into the road and the vehicle flipped.

CHAPTER 82

BABY WATCHED THE ROAD ahead as Dave Summerly drove. The cars had thinned out, and steep, rocky mountains in sunset orange crowded the highway on either side of them. She dialed Jamie, her hand sweating as it held the phone.

"Leave me alone," the hacker said. "I'm deep in the weeds with this Su Lim Marshall chick. Are you offering bonuses for any gold-plated, diamond-encrusted skeletons I manage to scare out of her closet? Because if so— "

"I don't have time for that now," Baby said. "I want you to look up something else."

"Are you serious?"

"This one should just be a simple record search," Baby said. "Chelsea Hupp. Little girl, died about thirty years ago."

She heard tapping. Summerly talked quietly on his cell phone, his big shoulder touching hers across the car's center console.

"Okay, I got her."

"Known relatives?"

"None living," Jamie said. "Dad predeceased her. Died of a heart attack. Mom died of a drug overdose. Looks like Mom never remarried. No known siblings."

"Come on. Dig deeper."

"What am I digging for?"

"Someone in her family circle is a cop or a journalist or a goddamn... missing-persons volunteer."

"What?"

"The answer is here, Jamie! It's right here! I just need you to find it!" Baby screamed. Summerly reached over and put a hand on her arm. She shoved him off.

"Jesus." Jamie's voice was small. "My fee triples when you lose your shit at me."

"I'm sorry." Baby held her throbbing head. "I'm sorry."

"I, uh—" Jamie tapped and clicked. "I'm tracing Melanie Hupp's estate. That's the mother."

Baby waited. Precious seconds passed.

"Looks like the guy she left all her shit to was a cop. Does that help?"

"Yes." Baby sat bolt upright. "What's his name?"

For a moment, Baby listened so hard that every sound in the car became amplified: The wind rushing by the windows. The tires thrumming on the blacktop. Summerly talking on the phone beside her.

"Do you remember the officer's name?" Summerly asked.

"William Brogan," Jamie told Baby.

"William *Brogan*?" Summerly took his phone away from his ear for a second and stared at it like it had become a snake in his hand. He looked at Baby and put it back to his ear. "Did I hear that right?"

CHAPTER 83

TIME PASSED; I COULD only guess how much. I was upside down, looking at the airbag. My seat belt cut across my sternum and ribs, crushing my breaths to thin, raspy puffs. I spit out my sock. My teeth felt loose in my skull, but they were all still there and intact, thanks to my makeshift mouth guard. The unconscious detective beside me was also hanging from a seat belt, but his airbag hadn't deployed; blood poured from his chin.

I unclipped my seat belt and fell onto the ceiling of the car amid the detritus of crushed cigarette packs, takeout containers, articles of clothing. I had to fight my airbag to get upright. There was no telling where either of our weapons were now. I grabbed the belt I'd spied earlier on the back seat, now coiled against my window, and went searching for my phone. Brogan groaned and unclipped himself too. He shoved open his door and tried to get out. I didn't know where he thought he was going—maybe toward a weapon or into some dream landscape induced by his face-plant on the steering wheel. But it wasn't going to happen. Not on my watch. I looped the belt through itself and threw it like a lasso over his head.

"Don't even *think* about it," I snarled in his ear as I yanked it tight around his neck.

I shoved him out of the driver's side, followed him, and pinned him against the dirt beside the vehicle, the belt pulled taut, my knee in his spine. Fuel and coolant spilled from the car onto the scrubby earth. My thoughts were ticking slowly as I pieced together a plan. I told myself the first step was to neutralize the current threat. *Bind Brogan's hands. Find a phone inside the car or around the crash site. Call 911.* Assistance would likely come quickly—we hadn't driven far from the shoot-out on the freeway.

I adjusted my grip. As I reached for a T-shirt inside the car to wrap around Brogan's wrists, I heard a scraping sound. I looked down and saw that one of his hands was by his jeans pocket. He was flicking the drum on a cigarette lighter. I had time to gasp, but that was all—the spilled fuel lit and the ignition pressure wave *whump*ed and blew me away from the car.

CHAPTER 84

RED AND BLUE SHEETS of light cut through the deep purple of the forest shadows, making the trees that lined the highway look weirdly festive. Dave Summerly pulled the car to a stop two hundred yards or so from the incident and parked at the end of a long queue of vehicles. Baby could see the pink mist of road flares in the distance. She was unsteady on her feet as she stepped out.

It was the reflective tip of a mini-pop-up camping marquee that made the yelp escape her throat. She knew what those foldout marquees were for—patrol cops erected them over bodies in the road to shield lookie-loos from the carnage.

"Oh God, Rhonda! Oh God!"

Baby took off running. Vehicles idled on either side of her.

Ordinary families and single travelers checking their phones, trying to see ahead, adjusting their radios. Separated from her nightmare by mere glass. She could feel Summerly at her heels, but he wasn't yelling for her to stop. The marquee came into view, surrounded by squad cars and uniformed officers. Baby spotted the nose of Rhonda's white '58 Chevy Impala through the chaos. The classic car was pulled over onto the shoulder. A tire was off. The door was hanging open.

Baby didn't even see the officer waiting to catch her until he cut expertly into her path, secured her waist in a bear hug, and spun her to a stop.

"Hold it, ma'am. Hold it. Hold it."

"That's my sister!" Baby screamed. "I've got to get to her!"

"No one can access the site at this moment. Absolutely no one. I'm gonna have to ask you to—"

"I'm Officer Dave Summerly." Baby looked up. Summerly had his badge out. "You gotta tell me who's on that scene," he said.

"I ain't gotta tell you shit, sir!" The officer puffed his chest at Summerly, his hand out, palm up. "This is a closed cordon! I've got my orders."

Baby didn't make the decision to kneel; the ground just seemed to rush up at her, welcoming her with its sun-warmed steadiness. She pressed her hands against the asphalt and tried not to be sick. She was aware that Summerly was barking orders and cursing and there was shoving going on above her, but all she could do was look at the little black bits of tar on the surface of the highway under her fingers.

And then a string of words hooked her and dragged her up like she was a fish on a line.

"Look, buddy, all I can tell you is it ain't anybody's damn sister under that tent."

Baby grabbed Summerly's jeans and climbed up him. His arm wrapped around her like a great, solid life buoy.

"It's a dude." The cop yanked off his hat, raked a hand through his hair, and turned to check the whereabouts of his boss. "Okay? *Okay?* The victim's a male. Now go back to your goddamn vehicle, will ya?"

Baby and Summerly walked back along the line of cars, the curious faces of drivers following them, and tried to regroup.

"Is it Brogan?"

"I don't know," Summerly said. His eyes searched the asphalt.

"If it's not him, who is it?"

"I don't know."

"Why is her car here?" Baby roared. "Where is she?"

"Baby," Summerly said. "I know exactly as much as you do right now."

They held each other. With her chin on his shoulder, Baby looked down the highway and saw a thin smoke tendril rising from the distant forest.

"What's that?" she asked.

She turned him around, pointed. The smoke was drifting diagonally with the evening breeze.

CHAPTER 85

WILL BROGAN HAD HOPE. That was the terrifying part. After the explosion, I sat against the base of a tree and watched the car burning and thought about Brogan's hope.

All he'd been doing since he killed Daisy Hansen was trying to clean up his mess, and there was still a chance he could do that. He'd burned Daisy's car and her body, removing all traces of himself. He'd lured Troy to the scene and then disappeared the note he'd used to do so. I'd conveniently brought the box buried in Troy's crawl space to the police's attention for him. If Brogan could pin Jarrod Maloof's murder on me, another loose end would be neatly tied up. He was probably hoping that he could kill me now and pass it off as self-defense.

A killer with hope, even struggling, flickering, fading hope, is unspeakably dangerous. The door was closing on Brogan's escape. He had one final problem to solve before he could slip through and be free.

And yes, I was tired. I was wounded, and shaken, and probably concussed. I'd lost blood. I was unarmed.

But I had one advantage—I had more to lose than Brogan. My kid sister was right behind me on the trail of discovering who had set up Troy Hansen, and Baby would never believe that Brogan had killed me in self-defense. Brogan would have to take her out too.

And my love for Baby would trump a killer's hope any day of the week.

In the aftermath of the blast, I'd glimpsed Brogan crawling into the trees, but I didn't know if he'd grabbed a weapon from the wreckage before he went. Slowly, carefully, I eased onto my hands and knees and started to crawl back toward the car.

A shot smacked into a tree above my head, showering splinters. I flattened myself against the earth. Smoke was pouring through the forest, coiling upward, black and choking. I looked up from the dirt and inspected the vehicle. Brogan's cigarette lighter had detonated the fuel in the tank at the rear of the car, but the flames hadn't reached the engine yet. I knew a second explosion was coming. I waited and gripped the ground and hoped the roaring noise of the fire wasn't masking the sound of Brogan repositioning to get a better angle on me.

Then Brogan stepped out of the forest and said, "Get up." I saw that his front teeth were chipped from the accident. His left arm was tucked into his shirt; that shoulder was either broken or dislocated. He raised the gun and pointed it at me. I kept flat, knowing a shot in the back wouldn't fit his tale about killing me to defend himself.

"Get up," he ordered again.

I shook my head.

"Get up!"

The windows of the car burst out, showering me with glass. The radiant heat from the vehicle seared my skin, even from ten yards away.

"I said get up!"

I locked my eyes on him and was about to fire off a bunch of obscenities when I noticed movement in the trees behind him.

I thought it was a hallucination at first. Strange details about the image reached me through the heat and fog. There was no way that could be my kid sister. I didn't recognize the gun she held, a standard-issue police Glock. She gripped it with both hands, shaking, wild-eyed, and pointed the barrel at Brogan from twelve feet away. Seeing Baby holding a gun at all seemed absurd. Watching her aim it at a man's head with deadly resolve made me sick.

Three things happened in one awful second:

Baby stepped on a dry branch, snapping it.

Brogan turned at the sound.

Baby froze.

Her finger was on the trigger, her aim was true, and her teeth were gritted as she braced for the kickback. But the mental absence that you need to take someone's life wasn't in Baby's eyes. She was so full to the brim with feeling all the time that firing the gun at Brogan in that moment would be akin to firing it at me.

And that was her strength. But it was going to get her killed.

Brogan raised the gun—but a shot took him from the side, spinning him, and he fired off two wild shots as he fell.

I ran to my sister just before a second explosion from the vehicle knocked me and Baby together. We fell against a tree, gripping each other, and watched Brogan take his final breaths on the forest floor. The dying man half buried in the scrub, the burning car behind him, and the smoke haze made me feel like I had suddenly found myself trapped in some hellish war movie.

Then the surrealness of it all was swept away coldly, quickly, as if a director had called, "Cut!" Without a word, Baby let go of me and rushed off into the forest. I followed. So many questions I'd been deliberately ignoring were all answered at once.

And none of the answers were ones I was ready for or wanted.

I knew Baby wouldn't have come after me alone. I knew who she'd choose to bring. I knew who the second shooter in the forest had to be. And I knew, in my heart of hearts, that the two wild shots Brogan had fired as he went down had hit that person.

I just felt it.

I arrived in the small clearing.

Dave Summerly was lying on the ground behind a big log.

There were two bullet holes in his chest.

As I reached Baby, she was shaking him and crying and stroking back his stiff, sandy hair to look into his cold gray eyes.

But I could tell that Dave, my Dave, was gone.

CHAPTER 86

TWO DAYS LATER, BABY stepped out of the Uber and onto the freshly swept concrete of the Enorme building's ring driveway. She thought the security guards at the front were actively ignoring her this time, as if they knew she was a problem and they were working on their plausible deniability. The receptionist must have had the same plan because just as Baby entered the echoing foyer, she disappeared through a black glass door, leaving the room empty. Baby took the elevator to the third floor with no one's approval but her own.

She pushed open the door to Su Lim Marshall's office and wondered at the deep sense of calm that filled her. She didn't feel any more trepidation than she would have felt if she were visiting a friend's house to deliver some uncomfortable news. *This is what it feels like to bring a gun to a knife fight*, she thought. To whack a mosquito with a sledgehammer.

She sat before Marshall, who was waiting for her with her hands clasped on the ridiculously large desk, the black glass top of which perfectly reflected her image.

"Tell me you're here to accept the money for the house," Marshall said. "Mr. Laurier's rat-riddled, insect-infested, structurally unsound house. Show me how smart you are, Ms. Bird. Because we all know Mr. Laurier's property is a death trap. I'm offering half of what I did earlier, but that's still far more than it's worth."

Baby smiled at the slow and deliberate way Marshall said *death trap;* she was obviously trying to ensure that her implications were perfectly clear. Like Baby wasn't quick enough to grasp that Marshall would just keep making Arthur's home a literal trap to cause his death, one way or another, unless Baby ended the war now. Baby had grown to enjoy being underestimated. Not only did she have a metaphorical big gun in her pocket, but Marshall clearly thought it was a water pistol. Baby couldn't wait to pull it out and show the older woman what a big bang it made.

"How *smart* I am?" Baby said. She crossed one of her long, lean legs over the other. "You know what I think is smart? Finding a system and sticking with it. I think that's the kind of intelligent life philosophy you'd admire, right, Marshall? When you're representing a company like Enorme?"

She gestured around the huge room. Marshall didn't move.

"'Business-expansion solutions that harness nature-taught growth,'" Baby quoted. "'I thrive with Enorme!'"

"What are you trying to say?" Marshall asked.

"Nature," Baby said. "Plants. Seeds. Growth. Find a system and stick with it. A plant figures out how to spread its seeds and it just does it, the same exact way, for the next billion years. Doesn't try to upgrade or shake things up or get risky. It just does the same thing over and over and over."

Marshall twitched in her seat.

"I thought I knew what I was going to find when I looked into your background, Marshall," Baby continued. "I figured there'd be a string of people like Arthur and Carol Laurier, people who had been bullied and harassed and even killed for not doing what you wanted them to do. A system. A pattern you'd found and stuck to. Because you were so *good* at what you were doing to Arthur. You were practiced. But it turns out it wasn't because you'd been doing it for Enorme."

Marshall glared at her.

"You've been doing it at home," Baby said.

Marshall stood. Her hands were splayed on the glass top, her head bowed. She and her reflection stared at each other, their fingertips touching. Narcissus reaching for himself in the pool.

"I had your entire work history combed over. Nothing. Clean." Baby leaned back in her seat. "Then someone suggested I look at your personal life. I didn't think it was relevant, where you'd grown up. Where you went to school. Who you were married to. Until suddenly... it was."

Marshall's lip curled into a mean sneer.

"Because *that's* where all the bodies are," Baby said.

CHAPTER 87

BABY COULD SEE IT all flashing in Su Lim Marshall's eyes.

The high-school ex-boyfriend in South Korea, arrested when his computer was found stuffed with forged exam results, all mysteriously downloaded in a single day. That same ex-boyfriend who, stricken with shame, had committed suicide by stabbing himself in the heart.

The landlord in Los Angeles who had raised the rents in the building where Marshall lived and who died after falling down the stairs of that same building.

Then there were the two former husbands. The first one went out fishing one night and never came home; the second one had been killed in a drive-by shooting at three a.m. in a neighborhood he shouldn't have been near.

Marshall had to be wondering which of her past sins Baby was about to expose, which ones she had uncovered and locked onto.

Because surely Baby hadn't found them all.

But Baby had.

Together, Baby and Jamie had traversed the labyrinth of false names, accounts, addresses, and identities Marshall had used to hide who she really was. Jamie, on the keys, followed links, and Baby—while also trying to clean and organize his den of disgustingness—chimed in with suggestions about what avenue to explore next.

Baby watched Su Lim Marshall go to the huge windows and look out at Los Angeles. She saw Marshall make the decision to kill her right then and there. It came over her like a stiffness. Living rigor mortis. Baby guessed you had to be like that to kill as efficiently as Marshall had over the course of her life. You had to be so completely and utterly disconnected from the act that your body lost itself in the task, like the automatic motions of a Roomba doing its slow waltz across the floors.

Marshall didn't even say she needed a water or a notepad or to call the receptionist, didn't make some petty excuse to reassure Baby as she crossed to the cabinet at the side of the room because the stupid big black glass desk didn't have anything as practical as drawers in it. Baby didn't mind that Marshall thought so little of her, that she wouldn't even pretend she wasn't going to kill her. Because, Baby supposed, in the end the woman *wanted* her to figure it out, to get up and rush toward her. It would make Marshall's claim of a sudden attack and a struggle during which she had to defend herself all the more believable.

But Baby didn't do that. She didn't even look at the woman. She just sat quietly and listened. She'd been doing a lot of that the past couple of days, listening rather than talking. She'd been listening to Rhonda crying in her room at the beachside mansion at night. She'd been listening to Arthur and Mouse puttering around the big kitchen in Manhattan Beach, adjusting to life in the huge house with Baby and Rhonda after the Waterway Street house had been declared uninhabitable. Now Baby listened as Su Lim Marshall opened a thin, sleek drawer in the cabinet and placed her hand on what was likely a thin, sleek gun. She heard the door to the office fly open. She heard Marshall gasp and heard Mouse's low, hellish growl. She heard the big dog's nails on the hardwood as he and Rhonda stepped into the room.

Baby finally looked over. Her sister held the chain connected to Mouse's collar with both hands, and her boots were planted on the floor, and still Rhonda had to lean all of her two hundred and sixty pounds back to stop the animal from getting to Marshall. It was as though the dog knew exactly who'd poisoned him.

Marshall froze with her hand in the drawer, and Mouse let out a series of eardrum-shattering barks that bounced and echoed around the huge room so it sounded like an army of devil hounds had arrived.

"You let go of what you're holding and put your hands in the air right now, Marshall," Rhonda said, gripping the chain with all her strength, "or I will."

CHAPTER 88

I KNEW BABY WANTED to be at the front of the crowd outside the Men's Central Jail release gate, ahead of the jostling media and internet people waiting for Troy's release. She wanted to be where the action was.

My baby sister had been a ball of fiery excitable energy since the brief of evidence she'd submitted to the Los Angeles chief of homicide had been accepted and charges had been laid against Su Lim Marshall in relation to three mysterious deaths on US soil. That had happened two days earlier, and a swirl of activity had followed—Arthur Laurier's property had been released back to him with the condemnation reversed, and the nefarious new neighbors had vanished from Waterway Street, both of which only added to Baby's vibrancy.

She twitched and paced beside me as we waited for the gates to open, but she stuck by my side, because I wasn't a front-of-the-crowd person, and because she had been worried about me since Dave Summerly died in the forest.

I was worried about me too. About how I was ever going to forgive myself for not telling the guy how I really felt, for not taking a moment to stop what I was doing with the agency and Baby to work out whether he and I should be together. He'd died saving my life, and now I would have to wonder for the rest of that life what "we" had been to him in his last seconds. What we could have been. Or should have been. Baby had dealt with her grief the same way she dealt with most things. She'd hidden from it in the hurricane of activity she had generated for herself. But I hadn't yet figured out what I was going to do. I was keeping it together for my sister's sake, presenting a strong front out of habit.

Troy Hansen was led out of the automatic doors beyond the release gate, and he came to the front of the scrum with that small, uncertain, weird smile on his face. It widened slightly when he saw me and Baby, and widened further when George Crawley stepped out of the throng and hugged him. The two men rocked back and forth in the big bear hug. People in the crowd were clapping. I felt a little sick.

"*Casey's Crime Channel* has always believed in Troy Hansen's innocence," a young woman nearby said, filming the hug and the scrum and herself with a phone on an extendable selfie stick. "It's a glorious day for Troy Hansen supporters here at Men's Central. We're so excited to see him walking free today. Like and follow for more or DM me on how to subscribe to the podcast."

Troy and George tried to get to a car in the lot, but the crowd followed them, so the man of the hour bent his head and spoke into someone's mic, probably hoping a quick statement would make the crowd back off.

What he said made Baby squeal.

It made me roll my eyes.

"I wouldn't be free today without the Two Sisters Detective Agency." Troy waved at us. "Rhonda and Baby Bird. If you need help, call the Birds!"

Before the crowd could come after us, Baby and I hightailed it to my Chevy Impala, which police had released back to me a few days earlier, Baby grinning all the way. The afternoon sun had warmed the leather seats, and as we left the lot, Baby drummed the dashboard so hard and fast, it was like a hum.

"Did you hear that?" She cackled, gave her drumroll a big smacking finish. "Man. That was great. 'If you need help, call the Birds!' What better endorsement is there? The guy was *walking out of prison* because of us."

"That little endorsement is the last thing we need," I told Baby. "It's just going to double the size of the mess that's already waiting for us."

"What are you talking about?"

"Listen to that," I said. I cupped an ear. Baby listened. Over the thrum of the engine and the rumble of the traffic was the sound of a phone vibrating, a constant rhythmic buzz coming from the glove compartment. She opened the compartment, took out my phone, and looked at the number flashing on the screen.

"That's the agency line," I told her. "I haven't answered in days because it just keeps ringing. We've got about two hundred voicemails from people who want us to take their cases and triple that in email inquiries. We've got to figure out how the hell we categorize all this new business. There's everything from murder to mail fraud in there, and I don't want someone who really needs our help to get lost in the chaos."

As Baby held the phone, it stopped ringing, then promptly started again. She smiled at me, and I sent a brave smile back. My kid sister slumped in the seat, flipped her sunglasses up, and started scrolling through the messages.

"I guess we'll just have to hire some staff." She shrugged. "That's what happens when you get a whole lotta cred all dumped on you at once."

I thought about that. More staff. Bigger offices. Our pick of cases. It was too early to know if that's what I really wanted, if that's what was good for me and Baby.

We stopped at a traffic light, and a couple of Hollywood-agent types crossed in front of us, both talking on their little earpieces and carrying cups of coffee. A city bus roared by, and I followed Baby's gaze to a telephone pole just outside of her open window. On it was a sign with the word MISSING above a photo of a fluffy beige poodle curled up on a tasseled silk pillow. Baby looked at me, and I had to laugh, because her big, brown, dog-loving eyes were wide with desire.

"We shouldn't forget our roots, I suppose," I said, and nodded at the poster. "No matter what happens. No case is too big, no case is too small, right?"

Baby grinned, leaned out, and ripped down the poster. Behind it was an older one, dimpled and yellowed by rain. It was another poster with the word MISSING and a photo, this one of a man and a woman at the rail of what looked like a yacht. They were arm in arm, and something about their happy smiles suddenly drained all the warmth out of the car. I looked at my sister and knew that she felt exactly what I was feeling. The sense that the people in the picture, whoever they were, needed the Birds.

"Grab that poster too," I told her.

photo: David Burnett
JAMES PATTERSON
THE WORLD'S #1 BESTSELLING WRITER

ABOUT THE AUTHORS

JAMES PATTERSON is the most popular storyteller of our time. He is the creator of unforgettable characters and series, including Alex Cross, the Women's Murder Club, Jane Smith, and Maximum Ride, and of breathtaking true stories about the Kennedys, John Lennon, and Tiger Woods, as well as our military heroes, police officers, and ER nurses. Patterson has coauthored #1 bestselling novels with Bill Clinton and Dolly Parton, and collaborated most recently with Michael Crichton on the blockbuster *Eruption*. He has told the story of his own life in *James Patterson by James Patterson* and received an Edgar Award, ten Emmy Awards, the Literarian Award from the National Book Foundation, and the National Humanities Medal.

CANDICE FOX is the coauthor of the *New York Times* and *Sunday Times* number one bestseller *Never Never*, the first novel in the Detective Harriet Blue series, which was followed by *Fifty Fifty*. She won back-to-back Ned Kelly Awards for her first two novels, *Hades* and *Eden,* and is the author of the critically acclaimed *Fall, Crimson Lake,* and *Redemption Point*. She lives in Sydney, Australia.

JAMES PATTERSON *RECOMMENDS*

From the Creator of the #1 Bestselling Women's Murder Club

JAMES PATTERSON

2 SISTERS DETECTIVE AGENCY

FIRST TIME IN PRINT

& CANDICE FOX

2 SISTERS DETECTIVE AGENCY

Discovering secrets about your own family has a way of changing your life...for better or for worse. Attorney Rhonda Bird learns that her estranged father had stopped being an accountant and opened up a private detective agency—and that she has a teenage half-sister named Baby.

When Baby brings in a client to the detective agency, the two sisters become entangled in a dangerous case involving a group of young adults who break laws for fun, their psychopath ringleader, and an ex-assassin who decides to hunt them down for revenge.

1st Time in Print

JAMES PATTERSON

A DOC SAVAGE THRILLER

THE PERFECT ASSASSIN

AND BRIAN SITTS

THE PERFECT ASSASSIN

Dr. Brandt Savage is on sabbatical from the University of Chicago. Instead of doing solo fieldwork in anthropology, the gawky, bespectacled PhD finds himself enrolled in a school where he is the sole pupil. His professor, "Meed," is demanding. She's also his captor.

Savage emerges from their intensive training sessions physically and mentally transformed, but with no idea why he's been chosen and how he'll use his fearsome abilities. Then his first mission with Meed takes them back to her own training ground, where Savage learns how deeply entwined their two lives have been. To prevent a new class of killers from escaping this harsh place where their ancestors first fought to make a better world, they must pledge anew: Do right to all, and wrong to no one.

JAMES PATTERSON

AND BRIAN SITTS

THE NEW YORK TIMES BESTSELLER

CRIME HAS A NEW ENEMY.

THE SHADOW

A THRILLER

THE SHADOW

Only two people know that 1930s society man Lamont Cranston has a secret identity as the Shadow, a crusader for justice—well, make that three if you include me, and it is my great honor to reimagine his story. But the other two are his greatest love, Margo Lane, and his fiercest enemy, Shiwan Khan. When Khan ambushes the couple, they must risk everything for the slimmest chance of survival . . . in the future.

A century and a half later, Lamont awakens in a world both unknown and disturbingly familiar. Most disturbing, Khan's power continues to be felt over the city and its people. No one in this new world understands the dangers of stopping him better than Lamont Cranston. And only the Shadow knows that he's the one person who might succeed before more innocent lives are lost.

JAMES PATTERSON

J.D. BARKER

ONE KISS
AND YOU'RE DEAD

1ST TIME
IN PRINT

DEATH OF THE
BLACK WIDOW

DEATH OF THE BLACK WIDOW

A twenty-year-old woman murders her kidnapper with a competence so impeccable that Detroit PD officer Walter O'Brien is taken aback. It's pretty rare for my detectives to be this shocked. But what Officer O'Brien doesn't know is that this young woman has a knack for ending the lives of her lovers—and getting away with it.

Time after time, she navigates her way out of police custody. Soon Walter becomes fixated on uncovering the truth. And when he discovers that he's not alone in his search, one thing is certain: This deadly string of secrets didn't begin in his home city…but he's going to make sure it ends there.

For a complete list of books by

JAMES PATTERSON

VISIT

JamesPatterson.com

Follow James Patterson on Facebook
JamesPatterson

Follow James Patterson on X
@JP_Books

Follow James Patterson on Instagram
@jamespattersonbooks

Scan here to visit JamesPatterson.com and learn about giveaways, sneak peeks, new releases, and more.